SAM FISHER

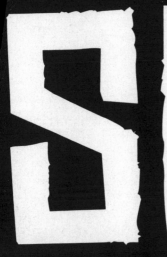

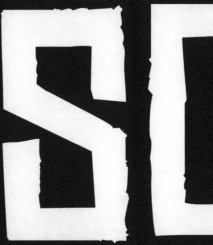

REAPER

THE MIDNIGHT DOOR

SCHOLASTIC PRESS / NEW YORK

Library of Congress Cataloging-in-Publication Data available

ISBN 978-0-545-52163-5

10 9 8 7 6 5 4 3 2 1   15 16 17 18 19

Printed in the U.S.A.   23
First edition, April 2015

Book design by Phil Falco

For my mother, who taught me
the importance of never growing up

CHAPTER 1

THE NIGHT WATCH

Morton stared up at the emotionless faces of the Zombie Twins. Their eyes were almost invisible in the deep shadows cast by their heavy hoods. It was difficult to imagine that those same eyes had once glowed red like fiercely hot coals and that their bleached bone faces had made his heart pound in uncontrolled terror. It was nearly impossible to believe that just a few short days ago these same molded foam toys had been as real and alive as he was. The normal routine had resumed so quickly that everything that had happened was already starting to feel like a half-forgotten dream. Reality had simply taken root again, just as James had said it would, and the Zombie Twin toys stood lifeless on his shelf, exactly where he had placed them. There was no doubt that at long last Morton's trouble with magic was all over.

So why was he still awake?

Every night had been the same. He'd lie there, his eyes wide open, his senses on full alert, his nerves tingling with repressed dread, and yet nothing had happened. That is, not until now. This time, as Morton lay awake, he heard a noise that sent a quiver of fear running down his spine. He heard what sounded like the sagging screen door to the kitchen

1

creaking open with a rusty moan. Of course the noise itself was not particularly scary, but for Morton that sound, coming as it did in the middle of the night, reminded him of one thing and one thing alone:

James.

That's how it had all begun. When Morton's brother first started his horrifying transformation into a Wargle Snarf, he'd developed a habit of creeping out at night to go scavenging for rotting food. And things quickly got worse from there. Soon he began to grow spines along his back and arms, and his eyes turned a sickly shade of purple and he started belching out great clouds of acrid yellow smoke and . . .

Morton took several deep breaths. He was getting carried away again. It was all over, he reminded himself. James was back to his old, reliable self. He wasn't out prowling the shadowy streets of Dimvale eating maggoty meat. He didn't need to chew coal to settle the brimstone in his stomach, and he wasn't about to change into a nine-foot-long centipede-like creature with multiple rows of razor-sharp teeth.

Morton was probably just imagining the noise anyway. It could have been a creaking branch on one of the many trees that surrounded the house, or the aging Victorian plumbing. Whatever it was, he told himself it was nothing to worry about. He told himself he should just roll over and go to sleep.

But of course he didn't. He slipped quietly out of bed, pulled on his tartan robe, and peered down the empty hallway toward James's room. His door was open a crack but no light spilled out. In fact, it was almost the opposite. A dense blackness seemed to reach from within and soak up what little light was in the hallway like a dark sponge.

Fortunately Morton wasn't afraid of the dark, and he continued down the hall to James's room, treading extra softly as he passed by Melissa's bedroom door.

Morton knew he was being irrational, but now that the idea of James creeping out into the night had lodged itself in his brain, there would be no getting rid of it until he was sure his brother was still safely sleeping in his bed. When he arrived at James's door he pushed it open and was instantly relieved to see James sprawled flat on his back amid a tangle of bedding, breathing in a haphazard rhythm that was completely typical for him. Until a few months before, when they'd moved to Dimvale, Morton had always shared a room with James, and one thing he knew was that James never slept calmly. He rolled and fidgeted and mumbled and sometimes got so knotted up in his bedsheets that by morning he looked like a disheveled Harry Houdini about to perform an impossible escape. In fact, Morton remembered one time when Mum had had to cut him loose from his bedding with a pair of scissors.

"Wimble dump bother!" James mumbled, flopping over onto his side like a giant sleeping fish.

Morton smiled and pulled the door closed. Nothing could be more normal, he thought, and headed back to bed.

Unfortunately he didn't even make it three steps before he heard another noise, and this time there was no doubt about it. There was someone moving around downstairs, and by the sound of it they'd just tripped over the ash bucket by the fireplace. Morton stepped back toward James's room and pushed himself into what he hoped was the darkest corner of the hallway. He strained his ears and listened, focusing all his concentration on the sound below. The slow, intermittent shuffling of feet resumed, as if someone were taking a step, feeling their way around in the dark, then taking another step. Morton pushed his back even harder against the wall. He couldn't begin to imagine who could be down there. Dad was working at the observatory as usual and wouldn't be home until sunrise. And anyway, it didn't sound at all like Dad. Whoever — or whatever — was moving downstairs seemed to be fumbling slowly about, almost like a blind person. . . .

Morton tried to block the image from his mind before it could form, but of course it was too late. He knew only too well that this house had once belonged to the legendary John King, an eccentric and possibly insane comic book author and illustrator who went blind shortly before he died.

Morton had seen impossible things, like creatures conjured from other dimensions and a closet that went on forever, and unlikely though it seemed, for all he knew it was entirely possible that the ghost of the sightless John King was taking a midnight prowl through the house where he had spent so much of his life. The house where he had died.

The shuffling stopped momentarily as the thing fumbled its way to the staircase. Morton heard the first step creak and then the next, as something plodded toward him. He held his breath, determined not to make a sound, until a softly lit, pale blue figure slowly emerged on the stairs. Morton bit his tongue and forced himself not to look away. If he'd learned one thing in recent weeks, it was that you never take your eyes from potential foes. The figure drifted on up until it reached the landing. Morton could barely see anything in the intense darkness, only a vague, shimmering, silky blue form, but as his eyes adjusted, he could make out a person with a long gown of some kind, its pale ghostly hands stretched out in front of it and its slender fingers tipped with bright pink nail polish and . . . small fuzzy blue slippers on its feet?

"Melissa!" Morton hissed, stepping suddenly out of the shadows, waves of relief and confusion washing over him at the same time. "What are you doing?"

Melissa didn't respond at all the way he expected. She whipped her head around, took one look at Morton, and screamed so loud that the lamp shades on the sconces began to rattle. At that same moment James's door burst open with a snap and James sprang out, a baseball bat clutched in his hands and his hair wobbling wildly above his head. Unfortunately for James, one of his bedsheets was still tangled around his left ankle and no sooner had he emerged from his room than he tripped and landed flat on his face. The baseball bat flew out of his hands and bounced off the banister, heading directly for Melissa's head. Melissa ducked just in time, and the bat hit the wall and then rebounded down the stairs, making a horrific clatter as it went.

The three siblings looked at one another in shocked silence for a moment before erupting into a tirade of accusations.

"What are you doing out of bed?" Melissa demanded.

"Me?" Morton said. "You're the one groping through the house like Helen Keller."

"Was not!" Melissa snapped.

"Well, what were you doing out here?"

"I — I . . ." Melissa stopped and looked confused for a moment. "I was hungry. Thought I'd get a snack."

This didn't sound right at all. "Don't try to tell me you had a craving for one of Dad's pickled eggs," Morton said, making it very clear from his tone that he didn't for one minute believe her.

"Okay, fine, I was checking the yard to make sure there were no, you know, monsters," Melissa confessed.

"Monsters!" Morton exclaimed. "Why were you looking for monsters?"

"I don't know! Why were you prowling on the landing?" Melissa shot back in a defensive tone.

James, who had by now pulled himself back to his feet and disentangled himself from his bedsheet, started waving his hands in a calming gesture. "Look, it's obvious what's going on here," he croaked loudly, "and there's no point getting upset at each other. We're all too wound up. We still don't believe it, that it's over, but it really is. We need to relax and start to live our normal lives again."

"You can talk, sleeping with a baseball bat beside your bed," Melissa mumbled while biting on her nails.

"I said *we*, didn't I?" James replied. "I'm guilty too. Every night I check under my bed, make sure the windows are bolted, and, I'll admit, I even sneak into Dad's office to make sure the hatch to King's secret attic is still closed. But it's time to move on, and we can only do it if we stick together."

"So we're all just supposed to think happy thoughts?" Melissa quipped.

"We could try!" James exclaimed.

Melissa fell silent and looked guiltily at her fuzzy blue slippers.

"We're sorry," Morton said. "I should have stayed in bed, but I thought I heard a noise and I just wanted to be sure that you weren't —" Morton stopped himself, but it was too late. A look of hurt disappointment clouded James's face.

"Oh. I see. Wanted to make sure I wasn't wandering the streets eating small children," he said.

"No, it's not like that!" Morton protested.

"What do I have to do to convince you guys that I'm human?" James exclaimed. "Here, you can inspect my arms for spines if it makes you feel any better."

"That won't be necessary," Melissa said, staring harshly at Morton. "We're all going back to bed now."

Morton suddenly felt as if an old sock were lodged in his throat, and even though he wanted to say sorry, he was unable to make any sounds, so instead he shuffled back to his room in silence.

James and Melissa also retreated to their rooms, and a few minutes later Morton found himself lying exactly as he had before, staring up at the Zombie Twin toys on his shelf, only now feeling a lot worse. He decided that James was absolutely right. They really did have to try harder to settle down to a normal life, and so Morton forced himself to stop thinking nervous thoughts and eventually he managed to drift into a shallow, restless sleep full of sharp teeth and savage claws. . . .

CHAPTER 2

A STRANGE ENCOUNTER

The next morning Morton awoke with an odd nervous sensation in his stomach. It was the same feeling he got before going to the dentist or when standing in line for a particularly scary roller coaster. But he wasn't going to do either of those things today. With a twinge of regret Morton realized that he was feeling nervous because today was Halloween.

Morton had once thought of Halloween as the most thrilling day of the year, better than birthdays, better even than Christmas. For him Halloween had always felt, quite literally, like a magical time. But unfortunately his feelings about magic had changed. Magic, he'd learned from experience, was a bit like the Kamikaze Cobra. You had to treat it very, very carefully or it might blow up in your face.

Morton pulled himself out of bed and tried to push his nervous feelings aside. This was going to be a fun Halloween, he told himself, *without* magic, just like every Halloween that had gone before. And besides, his friend Robbie had found him a truly awesome Zombie Twin costume that was too good to go to waste. It had a long gray cape made of real leather, with authentic brass rings hanging from the hood and a mask that looked and felt like real bone. Despite everything that had happened, when Morton opened his closet and saw it hanging there on the hook, it brought a smile to his face.

When he arrived at the breakfast table a few minutes later with the long cloak over his clothes, he was surprised to find Melissa sitting glumly, wearing a plain white shirt and black pants.

"Where's your costume?" he asked.

Melissa sighed and grabbed a ragged pair of bunny ears from the table and stuck them on her head.

"That's it?" Morton said incredulously. Melissa might not have loved Halloween in the same way he did, but to his knowledge she had never missed a chance to wear an outrageous outfit.

"I'm just not in the mood," she said. "And frankly, I'm a bit shocked that you decided to wear that ghastly costume. Don't you feel like you might be tempting fate?"

"Tempting fate?" Morton echoed. "I thought we'd agreed we were going to get back to normal. That it was all over."

"I suppose we did," Melissa said, sighing again.

"Then why don't you wear a proper costume?"

Melissa shrugged. "Now that my closet's gone I just don't see the point," she said wistfully. "Honestly, if there was one day of the year when an infinite closet would be useful, it would be Halloween. I just wish —"

"No more wishes!" James blurted, suddenly appearing in the doorway.

Morton turned to see James wearing round plastic glasses, a fake beard, and a dark wool suit and holding a phony plastic pipe in his left hand. This was also a surprise, since

James had confided in Morton that he didn't really want to wear a costume this year.

"I thought you weren't going to dress up," Morton said.

"I didn't want to be a killjoy," James replied, shrugging. "And I decided that so long as I'm dressed as a human, it's fine."

"Wait, who exactly are you supposed to be?" Melissa asked.

"I am Sigmund Freud of course," James said, putting on a German accent.

"Freud smoked a cigar, not a pipe," Melissa retorted flatly.

James looked at the pipe and frowned but continued in character, sitting beside Melissa and staring right into her eyes. "Ah, I see, Herr fräulein, somesing seems to be troubling you. Tell me, vat are your deepest fears?"

"Well, as it turns out we all share the same deepest fears, and you're about to come face-to-face with them."

James leaned back, surprised by the answer.

"Dad says he's serving fresh-baked scones for breakfast," Melissa explained.

"Oh no," Morton and James groaned in unison.

Scones had always been a Clay family favorite when Mum baked them, and Dad had tried his best to re-create her recipe on several occasions, but the results had always been disastrous. Once, Morton had stomach cramps for a week, another time Melissa's tongue swelled up, and on yet another occasion James broke a filling trying to bite into one.

"What are we going to do?" James said, a tinge of panic in his voice.

"Stuff them in our pockets when Dad's not looking," Melissa said.

"I don't think I have pockets," Morton said, glancing down at his costume, and he was about to suggest hiding them in the fireplace when Dad bustled in from the kitchen with a tray of scones and a proud gleam in his eyes.

"Morton," he said cheerily. "You're just in time."

Morton gave a wooden smile and sat nervously at the table.

"I thought I'd try and get some decent food in you before you cram yourselves full of candy tonight," Dad went on.

"Mmm. Great idea," Melissa said, and then whispered under her breath, "but where are we going to get decent food?" James elbowed her in the ribs and she let out a yelp.

Dad didn't seem to notice this exchange and put jam, butter, and the ever-present large pot of tea on the table and helped himself.

Nobody else moved.

"Tuck in," Dad said, "before they get cold."

James and Melissa each dutifully took a scone, and Morton hesitantly followed suit, but the moment his hands touched one of the small round pastries he knew something wasn't quite right. Instead of being a heavy, leaden lump of over-baked dough, the scone felt light and fluffy. And when he cut into it he didn't have to hack at it like a lumberjack splitting a log. It was as soft as a pillow.

"I can't believe it," Melissa said, taking a bite. "These are totally delicious!"

Morton cautiously bit into the scone in his own hand and was amazed to discover that Melissa was absolutely right.

They *were* delicious. He took another, larger bite, and then, as usually happened on the rare occasions when good food was put on the table, the kids began eating in dedicated silence until every last morsel was gone.

At last Melissa flopped back in her chair and put her hand on her stomach while Morton licked the crumbs off his plate.

"Not so bad, eh?" Dad said with a satisfied grin.

"Awesome," James said.

"They were almost as good as Mum's," Morton said, trying not to sound incredulous.

"Yeah, they were," Melissa agreed, her expression suddenly shifting to suspicion. "Wait a minute. Did you just buy them from the bakery?"

"No, I did not!" Dad said with a tone of mock offense. "They're homemade."

"So *you* made them, all by yourself?"

Dad scratched his ear the way he always did when he wasn't being exactly truthful. "Well, actually, no. I didn't do that either."

"Aha!" Melissa said. "I knew it!"

"But if you didn't make them, who did?" James asked, still chewing his last mouthful.

"Mrs. Smedley very kindly brought them over early this morning."

"Mrs. Smedley?" Melissa said. "The old lady from across the street? I'm surprised she could manage to walk this far. I saw her shuffling down her driveway with her walker last week, and she was moving so slowly I thought she'd keel over and die before she got to her door."

"Melissa!" Dad said. "Don't be rude. Mrs. Smedley is a very energetic and generous woman. You be sure to thank her next time you see her. Now, it's time for school. Off you go. Put something useful in your heads."

Morton jumped up and grabbed his schoolbag and Zombie Twin mask, and a few minutes later the three kids tramped out the door. Melissa's classmate Wendy was waiting for them at the bottom of the winding driveway, wearing a tight-fitting panther costume.

"Great costumes," she called as they approached. "You must be young Albert Einstein," she added, smiling encouragingly at James, who for some reason had dropped his pipe.

He picked it up quickly and gave Wendy a disappointed look. "I'm Sigmund Freud," he said.

"Oh, really?" Wendy replied with a confused expression. "I was sure he smoked a cigar."

"He did?" James said, scratching nervously at his beard. "Well, anyway, your, uh, costume looks really good."

"Thanks!" Wendy said. "And I'll tell you something: It's a lot more comfortable than that duck costume I wore last year."

Melissa frowned disapprovingly. "You wore a duck costume? Don't you know the rule? Mice, bunnies, carnivores, or princesses. Anything else is bad taste on a girl."

"Oh, at least I got the carnivore thing right, then," Wendy said. "And I can do the growl too."

"No need to get carried away!" Melissa said, glaring. "In fact, we all have to remember not to get carried away. Especially today. Don't even think about magic!"

At that moment an old yellow car stopped right in front of their driveway. Morton saw a nervous-looking teenage boy in a cowboy hat sitting in the driver's seat. He wore a brass sheriff's star on his striped red-and-gray shirt.

"Oh, I forgot," Melissa said. "That Jim boy is giving us a ride this morning."

"Actually, his name is Jake," Wendy corrected.

"Jake, Jim, Jack-in-the-box. He's the boy with the car is all I remember," Melissa said, waving her hand dismissively.

"Why do you need a ride?" James said. "Your school is even closer than ours. It's like five blocks away."

"Yes, and I'd like to see you walk even one of those blocks with these shoes on," Melissa said, pointing at her white pumps.

James screwed his nose up, and Morton was fairly sure that he and Melissa were about to start bickering about the merits of sensible shoes, which was a favorite disagreement they had, but fortunately the teenager driving the car got out and waved eagerly even though he was only a few feet away.

"Hi, Melissa. Hi, Wendy," he said, and then turned to James and Morton. "Hi, I'm Jake. You must be James and Morton. I've heard lots about you."

"You have?" James said with a look of complete surprise on his face.

"Sure," Jake said. "Melissa says you're both really cool and —"

Melissa suddenly stepped in front of Jake and pulled the car door open.

"Yes, well, I don't think we have time to stand around

and chat," she said, glaring at Jake. "I mean, we all have school to get to, right?"

For some reason Jake blushed slightly as he nodded. "Uh, yeah, well, nice to meet you both," he said, and climbed back in the car.

Wendy got in the backseat and Melissa gave the boys another warning glance. "Remember, don't even think about you-know-what," she said, and then jumped in after Wendy.

Jake struggled with the gears, waved to James and Morton one more time, and then lurched off down the road.

"Don't you think Melissa's overreacting to this whole Halloween thing?" James asked as he and Morton turned to head in the other direction.

Morton didn't know how to respond to this. On the one hand, he had to agree with James that they were *all* overreacting a little. But on the other hand, he wasn't sure it was true to say Halloween was just an ordinary day. One of the things he used to love about Halloween was the fact that it was one of the oldest practiced traditions in the world. It was older than Christmas, dating back to pagan times and quite probably older even than that, and try as he might, he just couldn't shake the idea that if it had been around for that long, there had to be something to it.

"I don't know," Morton said, deciding not to share his concerns. "Nothing's ever happened to us before on Halloween, so I don't suppose there's any reason for something to happen now."

"Hm!" James said. "You don't sound very optimistic. What does it say in *Scare Scape* about Halloween anyway? I only ever remember that one funny story about all the pump-kins coming to life at midnight."

Morton remembered that story, but he also remembered lots of others, and they all had one thing in common: On Halloween night, the magical realm has a habit of spilling over into the normal world.

"I'm sure it's going to be fine," Morton said, but even as he was saying this he had a pang of doubt.

At that moment Robbie came bounding up behind them, looking just about as cheerful and excited as Morton had ever seen him. He was wearing a very authentic pirate costume, minus the cutlass, because Principal Finch had made it very clear that there were to be no swords or guns as part of the costumes.

"The cape looks great," Robbie said. He then looked more closely at James's outfit and smiled. "You must be that painter guy, what's his name? Salvador Dalí."

James frowned. "Sigmund Freud actually."

Robbie cocked his head curiously. "Really? Didn't he smoke a —"

"Look, does it matter?" James cut in crossly. "I mean, it's just a costume."

"Uh, sorry," Robbie said, clearly puzzled by James's tone. "Listen, I can't stop. I have to go and meet with Nolan about his new band."

Morton was completely surprised by this statement. "New band?" he said. "I thought you weren't interested in joining his band."

"Yeah, I know, but he kept asking me and I figured it

might be fun. The only bad news is that the first rehearsal is tonight."

"On Halloween?" Morton exclaimed.

"I know, I'm sorry to miss trick-or-treating. But Nolan's already got a concert scheduled for next week, so he says we need to start practicing right away."

Morton didn't quite know what to say. He'd been so looking forward to having Robbie join them that it was difficult to hide his disappointment.

"Oh well, at least your teeth will be happy that you're missing out on Halloween," James said in his usual optimistic tone. "What kind of music are you playing?"

Robbie smiled. "It's punk rock. Very loud, very cutting edge. It's going to be pretty cool. And I can get you guys into the shows for free!"

"Oh, uh, wow!" Morton stammered, wondering why Robbie thought he'd have any interest in going to a punk rock concert.

"You will come to the shows, right?" Robbie said.

"Yes, of course!" Morton replied, trying to sound enthusiastic.

"Great! It'll be fun, you'll see. Anyway, gotta run." And with that Robbie started sprinting on ahead.

"See you at recess," Morton called.

Robbie slowed down momentarily. "Oh, I might be meeting with the other band members then," he said over his shoulder. "I'll let you know!"

Morton sighed. "I can't believe he's joining that stupid band."

"I don't know," James said, shrugging his shoulders. "It might be cool. That Nolan kid seems pretty smart."

"I guess so," Morton replied, but he couldn't help feeling that this was a bad start to Halloween.

When they arrived at school Morton was pleasantly surprised to find that there were a lot more *Scare Scape*–inspired costumes than he had seen in his previous school, where he'd been practically the only fan. Barry Flynn wore a Gristle Grunt costume, one girl who Morton didn't recognize wore a silky blue Toxic Vapor Worm outfit, and, not surprisingly, Timothy Clarke was also dressed as a Zombie Twin, although Timmy's cape wasn't nearly as authentic as the one Robbie had found for Morton.

Aside from that, everything looked and felt just like any other Halloween he'd experienced. Most of the costumes were of cats, ghosts, and grim reapers, and everyone was just a little more excited and mischievous than usual, which of course led to the usual spate of minor accidents and pranks. Oliver Jones tripped and sprained his wrist while trying to play soccer in his clown feet, Nelly Stark broke out in a rash because her fluffy pink cloud costume was made of fiberglass insulation, and Karen Blandford got tangled in her cloak and stumbled into Mrs. Wallis's fossil table, sending the collection flying across the floor. Fortunately neither fossils nor bones were broken.

When morning recess arrived, Robbie was nowhere to be found, and Morton stood around looking at costumes and wondering just how many meetings a punk band really needed. From what he understood, they mostly just made noise.

As he stood there, a boy approached him wearing an expensive-looking silver space suit with a plastic bubble helmet.

"Hey, Morton!" the boy said. "I hear your dad's from England?"

Morton stared at the boy, wondering who he was, and only when he got much closer did Morton spot the slicked-back, perfectly combed hair and realize it was Derek Howell, a boy his age. Derek usually wore fancy clothing consisting of pleated pants, a buttoned-up collared shirt, and formal shoes, so he was barely recognizable in his space suit.

"Uh, pardon?" Morton said, confused not only by the comment but also by the fact that Derek was talking to him at all. On several occasions Morton had tried to strike up conversations with him, but Derek had always either ignored him completely or answered curtly and walked away.

"Your dad, he's from England, right?" Derek repeated, now standing face-to-face with Morton.

"Uh, yeah, I guess so," Morton said warily. "Why do you ask?"

"Oh, no reason. I just think England's a fascinating country."

"Fascinating?" Morton echoed.

"Yes. And cricket is my favorite game. I suppose it's yours too?"

"Um, not really," Morton said, realizing this was a vast understatement. He'd never even played cricket, although Dad had bought James a cricket bat once, long ago.

"Oh!" For a moment Derek looked so appalled that Morton was sure he was about to do his usual trick of just turning away and walking off, but for some reason he didn't and the expression quickly passed and he put on a faint smile. "Do you want to see the rest of my costume?" he said. "It's in my locker."

"Sure, that would be fun," Morton said, happy that Derek seemed to have come out of his shell and wondering if he might have found a new friend.

Derek led Morton to his locker, which was tucked away at the end of a long empty corridor on the top floor.

"Since you're a *Scare Scape* fan I thought you might like this," Derek said, opening his locker and pulling out a large, futuristic-looking toy rifle. Morton recognized it at once. He'd seen it advertised in the back pages of *Scare Scape* many times, but it was one of the more expensive collectibles and it had never really appealed to him as much as the monster toys. According to the advertisement, it was an Antigravity Laser Cannon. Morton remembered that the ad showed a kid sitting on a floating chair in a classroom while the teacher and all the other kids looked on in shocked amazement. Of course, Morton knew the descriptions in those ads were always hugely exaggerated.

Derek handed the rifle to Morton proudly. "I'm keeping it in my locker until I go home because of Principal Finch's stupid ban on toy guns, but it's part of my costume."

Morton held the laser. "How does it work?" he asked.

"Pull the trigger. Try it out," Derek said in a gloating tone.

Morton pointed it down the hall and pulled the trigger. A faint green bulb flickered in the barrel of the gun and a tinny electronic sound emitted from a small speaker in the handle. It was far from impressive.

"Oh, uh, that's pretty cool," Morton said, trying to sound enthusiastic, but Derek seemed put off by his reaction.

"Well, *I* think it's cool," Derek said, sounding offended, and he reached to take the laser back, but before Morton could hand it over, a voice that froze his heart reverberated in the hall behind him.

"Morton Clay, why am I not surprised to find you flouting school rules?"

Morton turned, the laser cannon still firmly clutched in his hands, to see Principal Finch pacing toward them with angry, bulbous eyes.

"Sir, I . . . It's not . . . ," Morton stammered, but Derek cut in before he could say anything coherent.

"He made me show it to him, sir. I told him it wasn't allowed, but he made me."

Morton turned and stared at Derek, his jaw dropping in disbelief.

Finch stopped just a few feet from Morton. "Hand it over."

"But, sir, it's mine," Derek said desperately. "I was keeping it in my locker until after school when —"

"It's not in your locker now though, is it?" Finch shot back. "Hand it over, Morton. I'll keep it in my office. You can collect it after school tomorrow."

Derek's face went deathly white. "But, sir, it's part of my costume. I need it tonight."

"Don't care. You're lucky you're not getting detention."

Morton handed over the toy. Finch took it and stared down at him as if about to say something. He cleared his throat, but then an odd expression flashed across his face. To Morton's confusion, it looked like fear. But the expression vanished as quickly as it had come, and Finch paced off without another word. A moment later Morton and Derek were alone again.

"Now what am I going to do?" Derek snapped bitterly. "That was part of my costume."

"I'm sorry," Morton said, still pondering the odd expression on Finch's face, "but I didn't *make* you do anything."

"Well, Finch *never* comes up here," Derek said with a scowl. "You know what I think: It's true what everyone says about you. You and your whole family, you're jinxed." And with that he slammed his locker shut and ran off down the stairs.

Morton stood there for a minute in stunned silence, not sure whether he was more shocked by Derek's ridiculous behavior or the outlandish accusation he'd just made. Surely the other kids believed no such thing.

But Morton thought again of the expression on Finch's face, and about how the principal had come out of nowhere, as if he'd been lurking in the wings, just waiting for Morton to step out of line. He realized with despair that Derek was probably right. Even though nobody could know for certain about Morton's role in recent strange events, that wouldn't stop them from having suspicions. And it was just beginning to dawn on Morton that people would probably imagine all kinds of odd things — things that might even be a lot worse than the truth.

For the first time he realized that even without the cloud of runaway magic hanging over their heads, settling into a normal life in Dimvale was going to be a long and difficult road.

CHAPTER 3

ALL HALLOWS' EVE

Any lingering concerns Morton had about his family's reputation in Dimvale were pushed to the back of his mind as the sun went down and preparations for trick-or-treating began in earnest. It turned out that Wendy had convinced Melissa to find a better costume, and she appeared just before dark dressed as an Arabian princess. James quickly made a paper cigar, and Morton put new batteries in his mask to make the eyes glow as brightly as possible.

At six o'clock the doorbell rang and Wendy arrived in a very excited, bubbly mood.

"Ready to roar?" she said, making a soft but convincing growl, which seemed to have an odd effect on James.

"As ready as we'll ever be," Melissa said.

"I suppose I'll have to stay here and hand out candy," Dad said, donning the same silly hat and rubber nose that he'd worn each year for as long as Morton could remember. "Which means you'll be on your own, so stick together."

"We will," James promised.

"And don't stay out too late. You still have school tomorrow, remember."

"Like we could forget," Melissa groaned, and the four of them ventured out into the night.

Wendy led them directly to the nearest side street, which she promised was a hot spot for candy, and Morton was surprised to find it already crowded with kids and parents dressed in all manner of creepy and whimsical costumes. It was also extravagantly decorated. There were softly glowing pumpkins at every door, fake cobwebs stretching in the branches overhead, and dozens of ghosts, spiders, and plastic bats hanging from porches and draped over fences. Not only that, but a soft mist had settled over everything, illuminated by the few sparsely placed streetlights. The scene couldn't have been more perfect if John King himself had illustrated it. In fact, Morton suddenly realized, John King *had* drawn this street, or at least a few of the houses on it, in various issues of *Scare Scape*. The house closest to them was an old shingled building with a twisted bell tower that Morton remembered from a story about a man whose house became infested with Smother Fish, and just beside that was a square house with a widow's walk on the roof that had been featured in a story about a woman who turned into a giant moth every month.

It was while he was looking up at the widow's walk that he saw three dark shapes flitting about against the silvery sky.

"Uh, that's weird!" Morton said. "You see those bats up there?"

The others all stopped and looked up in the direction Morton was pointing.

"Oh, yeah, cool," James said. "What could be more perfect? Bats at Halloween. We never saw bats in the city."

"Mm! Actually you never normally see them here at Halloween," Wendy said, squinting up at the tiny black shapes.

"That's because they're supposed to be hibernating this time of year," Morton said, feeling a strange twinge of anxiety.

Melissa looked down quizzically at Morton. "Are you trying to tell us something?" she asked.

Morton paused before answering. He wasn't really sure what he was thinking. But there was something about the shape of these bats that didn't look right. Their heads seemed a little too large for their bodies, and Morton couldn't help but think of the mythical Bat Eyes, creatures that looked almost identical to bats but had one singular large eye instead of a face.

"Well?" Melissa prodded.

Morton still didn't respond. He peered up at the hovering bats, trying to make out their exact shape, but the tiny black creatures swooped away and vanished from sight, lost in the darkening sky.

"Morton's getting wound up again," James said. "We're just having unusually warm weather and the bats are hibernating late. Isn't that right, Morton?"

Morton looked at Melissa's concerned face and realized that James was probably right.

"Uh, yeah," he said. "It's nothing."

"Exactly. It's nothing," James reiterated. "This is going to be a normal night, remember? Come on. Let's have some fun."

Melissa stared at Morton for a moment longer and then sighed and put on a brave smile. "Okay, but for once let's do what Dad suggests and stick together, all right?" she said.

"Sure. I think that would be sensible," James replied, and he pulled Morton's arm and led him off down the street. Almost instantly, Morton found himself jostled along with the crowds of other kids running up and down driveways, visiting house after house and rapidly filling their bags with candy.

To Morton's surprise, Melissa seemed determined to collect more candy than anyone else, and she seemed determined to eat more of it than anyone else too.

"I thought you hated Halloween candy," James said as she stuffed an entire bag of blood-colored marshmallows in her mouth.

"I phoo," she spluttered back. "But ith thtill better than Dad'th cooking."

James looked at her aghast for a moment and then burst out into hysterical laughter. Melissa pushed her hand to her face, fighting off a chuckle, but a moment later she exploded with laughter herself, spitting the entire gooey contents of her mouth over a nearby lawn.

"Oops!" James said, looking at the half-chewed globs. "I hope you weren't enjoying those."

"No, they were completely disgusting," Melissa said, and they all burst into laughter again and ran off to the next house.

For the rest of the evening everyone seemed to be in high spirits, and James and Melissa didn't bicker or argue once. That, combined with the fact that Dimvale really was the perfect Halloween town, should have made Morton feel completely happy, but no matter how hard he tried, he simply couldn't relax. And it wasn't just because of the bat sighting. He couldn't help feeling that somehow everything was out of joint, like a reflection in a cracked mirror that looked almost right, except the picture didn't quite line up.

Despite this, Morton did his best to appear to be having fun. He smiled at all of the homeowners and he laughed at all of James's and Melissa's jokes until after about two hours they finally wandered along a narrow, deserted street and Melissa dropped her heavy bag of candy on the sidewalk.

"That's it," she announced. "I can't take another step — or eat another thing, for that matter."

"Me neither," Wendy said. "I don't know what's hurting me the most: my stomach or my feet."

"Definitely my stomach," James said.

"Definitely my feet," Melissa countered. "What about you, Morton?"

Morton was about to answer when he heard a faint noise, almost like a distant sea pounding against the shore, coming from down the street. He turned his head sharply and looked in the direction of the sound.

Melissa seemed to notice the shift in his mood instantly.

"What is it?" she said. "More bats?"

"Shhh!" Morton said. "Don't you hear it?"

Everybody listened intently. After a moment James shrugged. "It's just the wind in the trees," he said.

Morton shook his head. "You can't have wind and fog at the same time. And look at the trees — they're dead still."

The smile dropped from James's face. Melissa, who was already looking tense, stepped closer to Wendy and glanced around nervously. "If it's not the wind, then what is it?" she said.

"There isn't an ocean nearby, is there?" James said, trying unsuccessfully to restore the light mood that had so rapidly vanished. They were a hundred miles from the nearest ocean, and they all knew it.

Morton peered into the fog, and as he watched, a shape emerged from the swirling shadows down the road. It looked like a dragon, loping along on hind legs, its head flopping from side to side like a giant green rubber metronome.

James jumped closer to the girls.

A moment later the dragon's head fell right off, revealing the sweaty and frightened face of a boy beneath. But the boy didn't stop to pick up his lost head. In fact, if anything he started running faster.

"Run!" he screeched breathlessly as he tore past Morton and the others without so much as a backward glance.

Morton pulled off his mask and gazed into the darkness. At first he could see nothing in the thickening fog, but then he noticed what looked like a dark shadow creeping across the ground and moving rapidly toward them.

He heard Wendy gasp and felt Melissa's hands clutching at his elbow in the same instant that his fears were confirmed. The dark, flowing shadow was a swarm of rats — but not just any rats. They were Two-Headed Mutant Rodents, vile vermin from the pages of *Scare Scape*, and there were so many of them so densely packed that they moved as one solid amorphous mass.

A sick, heavy feeling oozed up from Morton's toes and overtook his whole body, and it had nothing to do with Halloween candy.

Melissa tugged hard on his arm. "Run, you idiot!" she said, and suddenly he and the others were racing down the street. But Morton realized very quickly that it was almost impossible to run in his long leather cloak.

"Wait, I can't . . . ," he called out. But the others weren't looking back, and even Melissa, who didn't seem to be having any trouble running in her long dress, was already out of earshot.

Morton slowed to a stop and struggled with the cloak's bone-shaped buttons. He tried not to look at the broiling pool of yellow teeth and brown fur that was rushing toward him, but he couldn't shut out the sound. The sound was the worst of all: a screeching, scampering, wet writhing sound that seemed to convey the force of a small cyclone. Struggling wildly, he managed to release three of the buttons, but the final one just wouldn't come loose, and suddenly a two-headed rat leaped onto his arm and sank its teeth into the thick leather of his cloak. He let out a shout and swung his arm, throwing it off, but by now the rest of the swarm had reached his feet and a dozen more clambered up his cape, gripping effortlessly with their sharp claws. The fetid smell of sewage and filth hit his nostrils, and the high-pitched screeching became unbearable. Before he had time to react, his entire cloak was covered in rats, so many that he felt the weight of them dragging him down, and for a second he was sure his knees were going to buckle beneath him.

Morton flung his sizable bag of candy over his shoulder and then tugged with all his strength at the remaining button. This time it popped free, and he tore off his cloak and hurled it into the swarm. Suddenly he was running again, and now he had no trouble outpacing the oncoming mass and soon caught up to James, Melissa, and Wendy, who were waiting at the corner. Morton stopped a moment to catch his breath. He noticed that the rats were slowing down to eat the candy that had showered the sidewalks like confetti, and he realized that the others had also dropped all their candy in the panic.

"We need to keep moving," Wendy said. "Come on, I know a shortcut back to Hemlock Hill." And with that Wendy took off with such speed that it was everything the other three could do to keep up with her. At first she continued straight along the street, as if heading away from home, but then she made a sharp turn into an overgrown yard and led them around the back of a run-down, boarded-up old house. She strode purposefully to the wooden fence at the end of the yard and lifted up a loose board. "This was the old Grippen mansion," she said, slipping through the narrow opening. "It's been abandoned since I was little. We always used to cut through here."

Morton clambered through after Wendy and the others, and he was surprised to find himself in the parking lot of the funeral home that he knew was only a few blocks from their house.

Wendy started running again and didn't slow down until they turned at last onto Hemlock Hill, where Morton was relieved to see parents and kids meandering along the streets as if everything were completely normal. They all slowed to a walking pace but nonetheless kept moving toward home.

"I think we'll be safe here," James said, still gasping for air. "I don't imagine even two-headed rats like crowds that much."

"Let's hope not," Melissa said.

"But where did they come from?" Wendy said, scanning the streets anxiously. "Those things were from *Scare Scape*. I thought we unwished them all."

"We did!" Melissa exclaimed.

Morton cleared his throat. "We might not have," he said, remembering now how he and James had seen a stray Mutant Rodent darting down a drain after they had undone their wishes. "I mean, we don't really understand how any of this magic stuff works."

"Well, whatever the reason, fortunately it's only a few dozen rats. We should be able to get rid of them without too much trouble, right?" Melissa said, looking at Morton with a hopeful expression.

Morton looked at his feet, feeling uncomfortable under Melissa's gaze. "I'm not so sure," he said. "The problem is they hide in the sewers and breed really fast. There could be twice as many tomorrow."

"So, you're saying we'll need a lot of traps?" James said.

Morton shook his head. "They're too smart for traps, and they're immune to all known poisons."

Melissa and the others stopped walking and suddenly all eyes were on Morton. "Just what are you trying to tell us?" she said.

"I think . . . I think we might need to use magic again," Morton said.

"What! Are you crazy?" Melissa screeched, losing her calm completely. "We're not getting involved in more magic."

"We might not have a choice," Morton said. "I mean, you saw them. There are already hundreds of them. By next week there will be thousands, and by the end of the month, who knows?"

"I've killed plenty of monsters without magic," Melissa said. "All you need is a good, sharp sword."

Morton rubbed at his legs, which felt shaky and sore. Melissa really didn't seem to be grasping just how deadly the Two-Headed Mutant Rodents could be. "You'd need a thousand swords," he said, "and a thousand Melissas to go with them."

"Now that's a scary thought," James said.

Melissa scowled at James but then quickly turned her attention back to Morton.

"Let's presume for one minute you're right and that we do need to use magic," she said. "We don't know anything about magic, other than that it's really dangerous. Where would we even begin?"

At that moment a group of kids and parents dressed as giant insects passed them on the sidewalk, glancing curiously in their direction.

"I think we'd better keep walking," James suggested, "and maybe keep our voices down a bit."

They all did so and Morton reluctantly told them what he was really thinking. "Look, I know you're not going to like it," he said, "but I think we might have to get The Book of Portals out of the attic and see if it has any spells in it that can help us."

Melissa, James, and Wendy all began screeching and yelling at the same time.

"No way!"

"We can't!"

"That book is dangerous. We swore never to look at it again."

"I know. I know all that," Morton said in a calming voice. "But that was when we thought it was all over."

"It is all over," James said. "We just have a few stray rats to deal with."

"A few!" Morton exclaimed. "I almost got eaten alive."

"Either way, for once I agree with Melissa. We don't need magic."

By now they had arrived at Wendy's house and they all came to a stop at the small white fence that ran around her front yard.

"What do you think?" Melissa said to Wendy. "You're the rational one."

"Well, Morton has a habit of being right," she said reluctantly. "And we definitely have to do something. But we also made a promise to one another to never look at that book again, and Robbie was in on that promise, so I say we can't make any decisions without him being here. I think we need to have a meeting with Robbie to talk about it."

Everyone agreed that this was a good idea, and Wendy darted off along the paved path and vanished into her house. As soon as she was gone, James, Morton, and Melissa shuffled wearily across the road to their own house and stepped through the side door into the brightly lit warmth of the kitchen.

Dad, who was now busily ironing shirts, looked up to greet them with a soft smile. "Ah, the pilgrims return," he said. "How was it?"

"The same as every other Halloween," Melissa said with a dismissive sigh. "Boring."

CHAPTER 4

A WEIGHTY MATTER

The next morning Morton was pleasantly surprised to find the view from his balcony window completely normal. Before going to sleep the previous night he'd reread the original *Scare Scape* story about the Two-Headed Mutant Rodents and it had been even more terrifying than he remembered. In the comic, the rats had been created by a genetic engineer to breed and multiply faster than any natural creature ever could. They'd also been engineered to be immune to most poisons and smart enough to avoid traps, making them a formidable foe capable of laying waste to a city in a matter of weeks. Morton had half expected to wake up to a post-apocalyptic, rat-infested Dimvale. Fortunately no such scene awaited him, although this did little to calm his nerves. If the story was right about the Two-Headed Mutant Rodents — and the stories in *Scare Scape* had been right on many occasions — then he needed to convince James and Melissa just how dangerous the situation might be.

He hastily got dressed and grabbed the comic and headed down to breakfast.

When he arrived in the dining room and found Melissa drumming her fingers nervously and James poking absently at his toast with the tip of the butter knife, he realized that he wasn't the only one who'd been worried. Melissa glanced up at Morton with heavy eyelids and immediately spotted the comic in his hand.

"Please don't tell me you're still reading that thing!" she growled.

"Oh, I was, uh, I wanted to show you something that, uh . . ."

"Don't mind her," Dad said, peering up from behind his newspaper. "She's in a miserable mood this morning."

Melissa stopped drumming her fingers and glared at Dad. "I am not in a miserable mood," she protested.

"Normally I'd blame the weather, but it's a beautiful day out there," Dad went on, completely ignoring Melissa's futile attempt at denial.

"I'm just tired of living with boys," Melissa said, putting on her best scowl.

James, who also looked unusually miserable, shot Melissa an angry glance. "What's that supposed to mean?" he said.

"Oh, you know," Melissa said scornfully.

"No, I don't know," James persisted, which was obviously the wrong response, because Melissa jumped suddenly to her feet and started ranting in an angry, tremulous voice.

"Yes, you do! Of course you do. It's all monster comics, monster toys, monster collector cards, and . . . Just monsters, everywhere!"

"I don't collect monster cards anymore!" James protested. "And I don't even read the comic."

"It's not just that!" Melissa went on. "I'm tired of living

with boys. Stinky socks and . . . and . . ." Melissa paused, as if trying to think of something else. "And nobody ever puts the toilet seat down!"

James turned his nose up in disbelief. "What's the toilet seat got to do with anything?"

"It's bad manners. I mean, I don't go into your bedroom and open all the drawers and leave them open, do I?"

"That is not even vaguely the same," James said.

"Yes, it is," Melissa screeched, now completely losing her cool. "Only you don't get it because you're a boy and boys don't understand anything!"

"Okay, that's enough," Dad said, putting his newspaper down and raising his hands. "No need to shout."

Melissa opened her mouth and for a moment looked like she was about to bark at Dad, but then she flopped into her chair and stared at the untouched food on her plate.

"You're just as bad," she mumbled. "You should try being the only girl sometime."

Dad frowned sympathetically. "You know, Melissa has a good point," he said. "It can't be easy, and just to show you how much we care, we're all going to make more effort to keep the house tidier and to put the seat down from now on. Right, boys?"

James obviously wanted to protest, but Dad shot him a warning glance.

"Uh, yeah, okay," he said.

"And you too, Morton?"

Morton nodded, even though this whole issue of seats up or down had never actually made any sense to him, and he couldn't figure out why girls were never asked to put the seat back up.

"There you go. That settles it, then," Dad said, but Melissa didn't look happy, and nobody spoke for the rest of the meal. It felt to Morton as though a giant black thundercloud were hanging right over the table, which of course had nothing at all to do with toilet seats.

On the walk to school James continued to be sullen and Morton kept trying to bring the conversation around to the problem of getting rid of the rats.

"I have that Mutant Rodent issue if you want to look at it," he said, holding the comic up in front of James's face.

James shook his head and turned away, almost as if the very sight of the comic made him feel ill. "I don't need to see it," he said. "You've already told us all about it."

"Yes, but I think it might be even worse than I remembered."

"Worse than the whole town getting eaten alive?"

"Well, no, but it might happen a lot faster than I thought."

James made a frustrated sigh, which Morton found a little out of character. "Look," he said, "Melissa and I were talking last night and —"

"Last night?" Morton cut in, surprised. "When last night?"

"Uh, after you went to bed," James replied, trying unsuccessfully to sound casual. James was probably the worst liar Morton had ever met, and he wondered just why he and Melissa had been talking behind his back.

"You were asleep," James went on, "and we didn't want to wake you. We were talking about the rats and we agreed that they're probably not as bad as you think."

"Not as bad as I think!" Morton exclaimed, pushing the comic up at James again. "You need to read this."

James pushed the comic away and shook his head. "In the end they're just rats, right? They can't do mind control or any weird magic stuff, so we think that we should just stay out of it and let the authorities deal with them in a normal way."

Morton felt a rising sense of panic. "But you can't deal with them in a normal way," he protested. "We've been over this. Try killing a million of them. We're going to need —"

"We're not using magic again!" James snapped, cutting Morton off abruptly.

Morton was shocked by the outburst, and the two of them lapsed into silence for a moment as they continued walking along the leafy sidewalk. Morton could feel himself starting to lose his temper. He didn't want to use magic either. He'd been as determined as anyone to leave the whole incident with the gargoyle behind them. But obviously that wasn't going to be as easy as they'd hoped, and it wasn't going to do anyone any good to just pretend everything was back to normal.

"We've got to do something," Morton said in the calmest voice he could manage.

"We already did," James said. "We made an anonymous call to the police last night and told them about the rats. Turns out we weren't the only ones who called, and they've already got pest control experts on it, so there's nothing to worry about."

"But you can't really believe that!" Morton exclaimed.

"Morton, they're just rats with two heads. They're easy to deal with. I squashed one with a baseball bat, remember?"

"Yes, but —"

"Let the adults handle this one," James said. "We should focus on being kids again. You know, get on with that normal life we promised ourselves."

Morton was about to respond when they spotted a large white van in the middle of the road up ahead with two police cars parked on either side of it to block traffic. The van had the words *Dimvale Pest Control* written along its length, and a man in white overalls was kneeling beside it, right over an open manhole. Several police officers were standing around him, looking curiously into the open sewer.

"You see," James said with a smile. "They're already on it."

Morton and James walked past the pest control van. Morton couldn't be sure, but he got the impression that nothing constructive was happening. It seemed to him to be just a huddle of people all standing around a hole and scratching their heads.

"I can't believe you called the police," Morton said when they finally rounded the corner onto the next street. "Now Inspector Sharpe is going to be all over this, and she won't have forgotten about the two-headed rat carcass they found in school."

Inspector Sharpe was one of the few people who genuinely scared Morton. She had come closer than anyone to figuring out that he and his siblings were largely responsible for the magical mayhem of the last few weeks, and she'd also come perilously close to figuring out that James was suffering from a self-inflicted magical curse. Despite this, since the "disappearance" of Mr. Brown, she hadn't so much as shown her face, which Morton found very suspicious. In fact, Sharpe's seeming lack of interest in them gave Morton the uncomfortable feeling that somehow they were part of a clever game of cat and mouse, in which they, of course, were the mice.

"She was going to find out sooner or later," James said. "Not much we could do about that, given that they were swarming down the middle of the street last night. And I'd say in this case, sooner is better than later."

Morton at least had to agree with that, and although he still had serious doubts about getting rid of the rats in any non-magical way, he decided to let the subject drop for now.

A few minutes later they arrived at school and Robbie broke away from a group of kids and ran over to them. Morton immediately saw that the expression on his face was one of panicked anxiety.

"You're okay," Robbie said, with a tone of surprise and relief. "I was worried that, uh . . ." He trailed off, eyes darting to James.

"I guess you heard about the rats, then?" Morton said.

Robbie shook his head. "Rats?" he said. "I didn't hear anything about rats."

Morton and James quickly recounted the events of the night before.

Robbie didn't respond at once but scratched his head in confusion.

"So the Mutant Rodents are back," he said. "But this time they're not your toys come to life."

"Right," Morton said. "The ones I have left are still sitting on my shelf."

"And Melissa's closet didn't get bigger again?"

"No."

"And what about . . ." Robbie looked at James but didn't manage to finish his sentence before James threw his arms up and let out an exasperated groan.

"Why does everyone expect me to turn into a Wargle Snarf? I'm fine, okay?" He pulled up his sleeves. "No spines, no yellow smoke. What do I have to do to convince you guys?"

"Sorry, I didn't mean —" Robbie began, but James was already upset.

"I'm going to the library," he said, turning to leave.

"The library?" Morton said. "Why would you go to the library at this time in the morning?"

"Why do you think? To eat the librarian, of course!"

Morton and Robbie watched James walk away in silence.

"I'm really sorry," Robbie said after James had gone.

"It's not your fault," Morton replied. "He's been really sensitive about it. Anyway, you still haven't told me what you were so worried about."

"Oh, yeah," Robbie said, rubbing his chin. "The thing is, last night I thought . . ." Robbie paused and seemed to struggle over what to say next. "Honestly, I don't know, but I thought I maybe saw a Snarf."

An icy chill ran down Morton's spine. "A Snarf?" he said.

Robbie took a deep breath. "Well, yeah. That's what I thought anyway. But now I'm thinking maybe I was imagining things."

"How do you imagine a Snarf?" Morton said, his stomach tightening. "I mean, it's not like you're going to mistake somebody's pet poodle for one."

Robbie didn't laugh, just continued to look puzzled. "Well, you know how the band was supposed to meet last night?"

Morton nodded.

"Well, the thing is, Nolan didn't show up."

"What!" Morton exclaimed. "But you missed Halloween because of that rehearsal!"

"Yeah, I know. Believe me, we were all pretty annoyed. We waited at the rehearsal space for like an hour and finally decided to go trick-or-treating together, just so we didn't feel like we'd wasted the whole night. So we went around to a few houses and then went back to Julie Bashford's to hang out and, you know, eat candy and stuff. It was getting really late when I finally headed home, and I was just crossing Mill Road when out of the blue I had this sudden sense of panic. It was really weird, like my heart just started going crazy for no reason."

"That *is* weird," Morton said.

"Yeah, and then I heard this bizarre noise that sounded kind of like an angry whale that had just swallowed an even angrier elephant. And then I saw this large shape in the distance. I mean, I couldn't really make it out. The street was really dark. But for some reason I was convinced it was a Snarf. You know, they do that thing with the fear pheromone,

43

which would explain why I felt that weird panicked feeling, right?"

Morton nodded thoughtfully. "Maybe. But you didn't actually see a Snarf?"

Robbie rubbed his face nervously, and Morton could tell he was still holding something back.

"What is it?" he prodded.

"I didn't see a Snarf. I saw a shape, which ran off in the opposite direction, and then I went to get a closer look and . . ." Robbie paused again and pulled his bag from his back and delved inside. "I found this," he said, producing something wrapped in a loose paper bundle.

Morton took the bundle and unwrapped it carefully to reveal what appeared to be an oversize porcupine quill soaked in purple dye.

Morton suppressed a gasp. He had to admit this did look a lot like the spines that had grown from James's skin during his transformation.

"So am I imagining things?" Robbie asked.

Morton wrapped the spine carefully back up in the bundle and handed it back to Robbie. "I don't know," he said, "but I think you should get rid of that as soon as you can. Throw it in the fire or something, and whatever you do, don't touch the tip."

Robbie took the bundle back and replaced it in his bag. "I was kind of hoping you'd say I was letting my imagination get the better of me. I mean, James is obviously perfectly normal now and there's no way he could have turned back into a human if he was a Snarf last night, is there?"

"I don't know," Morton said, mulling over all of the bizarre things he'd already witnessed. "Anything is possible when it comes to magic."

Robbie rubbed his chin thoughtfully and opened his mouth to speak, but just then the morning bell rang and all the kids began moving toward the main entrance.

"Come on," Morton said, relieved to have a reason to change the subject. "We've got Punjab this morning. She hates it when we're late."

It turned out that the morning's class was on fractions, and Morton tried his best to push all thoughts of Wargle Snarfs and Mutant Rodents aside and listen closely to the lesson. Unfortunately he wasn't very successful. Despite his determination to dismiss any suggestion that James might be turning into a Snarf again, he couldn't ignore the familiar sensation of a knot tightening in his stomach. Could Robbie have really seen a Snarf? And what would they do if James did start to turn again? Morton was fairly certain he couldn't handle it a second time, watching his brother's skin turn silvery gray, and his eyes turn mint green, and his pupils swell to an immense size, and . . .

Morton suddenly realized that he'd broken into a cold sweat. He raised his hand to go to the bathroom, hoping that splashing cold water on the back of his neck might calm his nerves.

"It's almost break time, Morton," Mrs. Punjab said with an air of irritation. "Can't you wait?"

"Uh, no, miss, I drank too much tea at breakfast," he replied, knowing this would cause a few titters, but also knowing that Mrs. Punjab wouldn't make him wait. As expected, she sighed and waved her hand toward the door. Morton jumped to his feet, grabbed the large cardboard hall pass in the shape of a plus sign, and hastened out of the classroom as quickly as he could.

Morton made his way to the top-floor restrooms, even though they were up two flights of stairs, because nobody ever went there and he needed a few minutes alone.

He pushed open the heavy swinging door, filled one of the large porcelain sinks up to the top with cool water, and was about to splash it over his face when somebody spoke.

"Morton, is that you?"

Morton practically jumped out of his sneakers. He'd been sure he was alone but realized he hadn't checked. He whipped his head around quickly to see . . . no one. He was alone, unless . . .

He walked around the corner to where the stalls were. "Hello!" he called nervously. But the stall doors were all open and the stalls were empty.

"I'm not in there," the voice came again. This time Morton didn't jump, but he felt the hairs on his arms stand on end.

"Uh, then where are you?" he asked tremulously.

"You promise you won't tell anybody about this?"

Morton looked around feverishly. The voice seemed to be echoing around him, coming from all directions at once, and it sounded frail and afraid. But what was it talking about?

"If you mean am I going to tell anybody about a disembodied voice in the top-floor boy's washroom, then no,

I'm definitely not," Morton said, beginning to feel a little braver.

"But you have to help. You have to promise to help without telling anybody. I won't ever speak to you again if you don't promise to help."

Morton didn't think this was a good strategy on the part of the voice. He quite liked the idea of it never speaking to him again on account of the fact his life was plenty complicated enough without disembodied voices. But in spite of himself, Morton knew he had to promise. Dealing with mysterious spooky problems seemed to be his lot in life.

"Okay, whatever you are. I don't know if I can help, but I can promise to keep a secret."

The voice sniffled to itself for a moment and then cleared its throat. "I'm up here," it said. "On the ceiling."

Morton tilted his head back very slowly, trying not to imagine the worst. The bathroom was L-shaped and the ceilings were very high, so at first he didn't see anything other than the fluorescent lights and the sprinkler pipes, but as he leaned to one side, at last he saw who he'd been speaking to. There, lying flat on the ceiling as if he'd been pasted up like a sheet of wallpaper, was Derek Howell, with a look of misery and terror on his face.

"I'm scared of heights," he said. "But I can't get down."

Morton did a double take and shook his head to make sure he was seeing things properly. The sight of Derek splayed to the ceiling like a starfish gave him an odd sense of vertigo.

"Uh, why, I mean how . . . ?" Morton had so many questions that he couldn't seem to get any of them out.

"It's that stupid Antigravity Laser!" Derek spat bitterly, pointing to one of the stalls. Morton saw then that the toy gun was lodged behind the toilet, presumably dropped from above.

He looked back up at Derek quizzically. "But how —?"

"Isn't it obvious? I pointed it at the mirror. The next thing I knew I was on the ceiling."

"You mean, it works?" Morton said, feeling unusually dense.

"Of course it works, you idiot! How else do you think I got stuck up here? It's like my gravity is upside down. Look!"

Derek wriggled clumsily around onto his haunches and attempted to leap back down to the floor, but he only got a few feet before he fell back up again and hit the concrete ceiling with an audible slap.

"But it didn't work yesterday," Morton said.

" 'But it didn't work yesterday,' " Derek mimicked rudely. "Are you just going to stand there and say stupid things or are you going to help me? It works today obviously. And I'm supposed to be in Miss Francis's class right now and I'm her favorite student, so she's sure to be worried about me."

Morton, who was finding it very uncomfortable looking straight up at Derek, was beginning to get a whole new appreciation for the phrase *pain in the neck*.

"What makes you think I can help?" he said, with half a mind to just leave him to his fate.

Derek looked around shiftily. "I know you're mad at me because of what I said to Finch yesterday, but this is going too far. You'll get into real trouble if you don't get me down."

If Morton's mouth hadn't already been wide open from gaping at the ceiling, his jaw would have dropped.

"You think I have something to do with this?"

"Of course you do," Derek sniveled. "Everybody knows you're behind all this crazy stuff. You made Timmy's toys come to life. Practically the whole school saw it. I don't know how you're doing it, and I don't want to know. If you get me down, I promise I won't say another word about you or Robbie or that weird brother of yours."

Morton became suddenly angry. "Look, firstly, my brother is not weird, and secondly, I don't know why you're stuck up there any more than you do, and thirdly, I definitely don't know how to get you down, and fourthly, even if I did, the way you're behaving, I don't think I'd bother."

Morton headed promptly for the door and pushed it open. He stopped when he heard Derek start sobbing. He turned back to see a tiny drizzle of tears dripping from his nose. "Please help," he said. "I'll give you all my Halloween candy."

Morton clutched his temples in frustration.

"I don't want your candy," Morton snapped. "Just . . . just be quiet and let me think."

As soon as Morton said this, the bell rang for recess and it was immediately followed by the sound of classroom doors bursting open and the hustle and bustle of kids filling the halls. Morton was thankful that they were in the least-used restroom in the school, but still, he had to face the fact that somebody could come barging in at any moment.

"Okay, I'll go get Robbie," he said. "He'll have some ideas. Stay still and don't attract any attention."

Morton bounded out of the restroom and down the stairs only to find that Robbie had already left the classroom and was nowhere to be seen. He quickly returned the hall pass and grabbed his things, and after what felt like hours (but was really only a couple of minutes), Morton found Robbie with the rest of the band. He was standing beside Julie Bashford and the blond twins, Rachel and Rachelle, and they were all facing Nolan Shaw. Nolan looked tired and worried, which was unusual for him. He usually had a bright, bouncy look in his eyes.

Morton, who had been dashing around the school like a confused lemming, tried to compose himself and sauntered over to the group, making every effort to appear casual.

"Oh, uh, hi, guys. Hi, Nolan," he said.

"Oh, hi, uh, Melvin, isn't it?" Nolan grunted.

"Morton," Morton said, surprised that Nolan didn't remember his name. "Robbie tells me you didn't make it to rehearsal last night," he went on. "Hope everything is all right."

Nolan shrugged. "It's my grandmother," he said. "She hasn't been very well and she had to go into the hospital last night, so I ended up spending most of the night there with my parents."

"Oh, I'm sorry to hear that," Morton said, and then, not wanting to sound rude, he turned to Robbie and said, "Uh, do you have a minute?"

"We're kind of in a meeting," Julie Bashford said in her croaky voice.

Julie was a thin girl with pale skin and silver hair that she'd dyed with purple streaks. Morton didn't really know her well, but he had noticed that no matter what the situation, she always seemed supremely confident and vaguely annoyed.

"Yes, I know," Morton said. "But this is important. Something, uh, well, something's *up*."

"So we're *not* important?" Julie chimed in, stepping menacingly up to Morton, her drumsticks tucked under one arm. Morton stepped back, feeling intimidated, even though she was no taller than he was.

"I . . . I didn't say that," he said.

"No, you just implied it," she said gruffly, stepping even closer. Morton found himself staring directly at her face and he couldn't help noticing that even though she behaved like a tough kid, she actually had very soft features, with rosy cheeks, a delicately shaped nose, and the palest blue eyes he'd ever seen.

Morton's neck tensed up and he felt strangely off balance. He couldn't figure out if he was afraid of Julie, or just in a general panic. Either way the feeling was unfamiliar to him. "I think the band is important," he said, trying to stay calm. "But this — *thing* — is important *and* it's urgent. So unless this *important* meeting is also *urgent* maybe I could just borrow Robbie for one minute."

Nolan glanced sideways at Morton and gave him a penetrating stare, and Morton remembered what Derek had said about his reputation. The last thing he wanted to do was make anybody even more suspicious of him.

"We'll only be another five minutes," Nolan said, and he led Robbie and the blond twins off in the opposite direction.

"I'll find you later," Robbie said, looking over his shoulder with an apologetic shrug.

For some reason Julie lingered behind a moment, and Morton stood motionless, watching the others go, wondering what to do.

"Look, it's none of my business," Julie said, "but it's probably a good idea for you to spend some time doing stuff without Robbie."

"Huh?" Morton said. "What's that supposed to mean?"

Julie rolled her eyes in a way that somehow made Morton feel like a complete idiot.

"Well, it's hardly a secret that you've been stuck to Robbie like a leech since the day you started this school."

"I haven't been stuck on him — we're friends!" Morton exclaimed.

Julie scoffed. "Maybe you were. But lead singers get new friends. Friends who aren't obsessed with stupid kids' comics."

"What?" Morton felt as if he'd just been slapped. "Did Robbie say something?"

Julie shook her head and leaned in to whisper in Morton's ear. "It's not what they say," she said, "it's how they act." And then she turned and jogged down the hall to catch up with the others.

Morton stood for a moment longer, not really sure how he was supposed to feel, but then remembered that Derek was still stuck on the ceiling and realized that he really was going to have to figure it out on his own.

He headed back up the stairs, but before he reached the top landing, a horrible high-pitched shriek reverberated along the hall. Morton bolted the rest of the way and burst into the bathroom.

At first he didn't understand what had happened. There, with a slightly guilty look on his face, was Phillip "Frizz" Ferguson, a small boy with a tower of curly hair on his head. He was holding the Antigravity Laser Cannon. The screaming, however, was coming from Derek, who was now lying on the floor, no longer stuck to the ceiling.

"Sorry," Frizz said. "I was only trying to help."

"What do you mean?" Morton said, still puzzling out the scene before him.

"Derek said his gun got him stuck on the ceiling, and I found a reverse switch on the handle," Frizz answered. "And so, well, yeah, I just, you know, thought, no harm in trying, but yeah, I guess it's a long way down."

"He broke my leg!" Derek screamed, writhing on the hard tile floor. "Frizz broke my leg!"

Morton felt panic rising in his chest and didn't have a clue what to do. He really wished that Robbie were with him, and he really wished that Frizz Ferguson had not stumbled in on the scene.

"Maybe I should get the principal," Frizz suggested.

"No!" Morton snapped, the mention of Finch bringing him back to his senses. "I'll deal with this."

He then looked back down at Derek and realized that Derek was wriggling and writhing a lot. Too much, he thought, for someone with a broken leg.

He went over and crouched down by his side. "Which leg is it?" he asked.

"Both of them!" Derek whimpered. "And my arms!"

Morton was hardly surprised by the answer and began prodding Derek in various places. Derek stopped whimpering and looked on in silence as Morton prodded. After a moment, Morton pronounced his verdict. "I don't think you've broken anything," he said. "Except the world record for the loudest scream."

"What? Really?" Derek said, suddenly sitting up and touching his own legs gingerly. "But it hurts."

"Yeah, believe it or not, you can feel pain without breaking any bones," Morton said, feeling irritated by Derek's melodramatic display. "Here, see if you can stand up."

Sure enough Derek was able to stand without any real trouble, which seemed to be more of a relief to Frizz than anybody.

"Sorry," Frizz said again. "Seemed like a good idea at the time."

"Well, it was a stupid idea!" Derek snapped, wiping the last of his tears from his face. "You should mind your own business!"

"But you asked me to help," Frizz said, looking genuinely hurt.

"Just give me my laser cannon back." Derek reached out to snatch the gun from Frizz's hands, but Morton bounded between them before he even realized what he was doing.

"I don't think that's a good idea," he said.

Derek stopped, surprised, and looked down at Morton as if he'd just stepped in something very unpleasant. "It's mine," he said.

"But it's dangerous," Morton said. "What if you'd floated

out the window? Who knows what could have happened to you."

"Well, obviously I'm not going to make the same mistake twice, am I?" Derek said in his usual mocking tone. "In any case, it's none of your business. My father paid for that gun and he'd be very upset if somebody *stole* it from me. He might even call Inspector Sharpe."

Morton froze, wondering how Derek knew that he was afraid of Sharpe. Derek smirked and pushed Morton aside, reaching again for the Antigravity Laser Cannon. Frizz glanced questioningly at Morton, then handed the cannon over quietly. But Derek had barely taken it from Frizz when something snapped in Morton and he shot forward and snatched the toy away from Derek. Surprising even himself, he jammed the long barrel of the gun between two sinks and yanked back, snapping it cleanly in two. A pulse of energy burst out from the innards of the shattered toy, and a strobe of iridescent light momentarily blinded them.

Morton was only mildly surprised by this strange pulse of light, and dropped the pieces to the floor. "There," he said, looking back at Derek. "Tell Sharpe some bad boys broke your toy, why don't you?"

Derek swallowed hard and stared back, his mouth twitching in anger. At last he spoke. "You're going to regret that," he said, and he spun on his heels and paced directly out the door.

Frizz remained standing like a statue, staring at the shattered remnants of the toy. "Uh, do you know what's going on here?" he said.

Morton puffed his cheeks and leaned heavily on one of the sinks. The truth was, he had absolutely no idea what was going on, but how would he convince Frizz of that? And more important, how would he stop Frizz from telling the whole school?

CHAPTER 5

A FLOCK OF SHADOWS

Morton spent the rest of recess pacing around in the school yard waiting tensely for Robbie so he could tell him all about Derek's misadventures on the ceiling and ask him if he thought Frizz Ferguson was a trustworthy kid. Before leaving the restroom he'd tried to convince Frizz that he must never tell anyone about what had happened because Derek would get into trouble. Frizz had promised, but Morton had no idea if he was being honest or just telling him what he wanted to hear.

Unfortunately Robbie didn't show up until nearly the end of recess, and even then he was still with Julie. The two of them appeared on the steps in front of the main entrance and stood talking. Normally Morton would have dashed over to him the instant he appeared, but the sight of Julie held him back. Her comments from earlier were very much at the front of his brain, and he wondered just how true they might be. There was no doubt that he'd been with Robbie practically every minute of every day since he started school, but surely it was a mutual friendship. Even as Morton was thinking this, he realized that he hadn't exactly made Robbie's life pleasant. Since meeting Morton, Robbie had been accused of stealing half the town's cat population, attacked by monsters, and almost killed by an evil history teacher. Perhaps joining a band and making a new group of friends was just what Robbie needed right now.

As Morton was mulling this over, the bell rang and Julie and Robbie headed directly back into the building. Morton sighed and shuffled off to class alone. As he sauntered along the hallway, he was so deep in thought that he walked straight into a tall, older student.

"Sorry," Morton said, stepping aside to go around the heavyset boy whose stomach had just collided with his face, but as he did so, the boy also stepped aside, this time blocking his way intentionally. It was only then that Morton looked up to see the large, round, puggish features of none other than Brad Evans.

Brad was probably Morton's least favorite person in school. He used to be the lead singer in Nolan's band until Nolan threw him out for bullying Robbie, which only made Brad more of a bully, and he'd later tried to beat up James. Fortunately James had sort of won that fight, mostly because he was turning into a Wargle Snarf, and Brad had left them alone for a time. But Morton had wondered how long that would last.

"If you don't mind, I'm trying to get to class," Morton said, hoping he sounded braver than he felt, and he tried again to brush past Brad. This time, Brad reached out his hand and grabbed Morton's arm, pinning him to the spot. Morton gritted his teeth and glared up at Brad, determined not to let him see any fear, which was not easy because Brad was by far the most fearsome kid in school. In fact, looking up at him now, Morton thought he seemed even larger than he remembered. Or maybe it was just his clothes. Brad usually wore a T-shirt, probably because he liked to show off his muscular arms, but now he was wearing a hooded sweatshirt with a loose-fitting trench coat over the top.

Morton continued to look Brad in the eye, telling himself that even Brad wouldn't be stupid enough to try and beat him up right in the middle of the school hallway — although he wasn't certain of this because as far as he could tell there wasn't really a limit to Brad's stupidity.

"Where's your brother?" Brad croaked.

"How should I know?" Morton said. "You think I always know where he is just because he's my brother?"

Brad glanced all around him, twitching with a nervous energy that made Morton think that he might lash out at any moment. Fortunately he didn't.

"Well, you can tell him I'm looking for him," he said, and then he pushed Morton roughly aside and lumbered off.

It wasn't until Brad was out of sight that Morton started to tremble, and he couldn't figure out if he was trembling because he was afraid or angry or confused. Not that it mattered. Either way, Brad had obviously decided it was time to get back at James, which was hardly good news, especially in light of everything else that was going on.

Morton hurried on to history class and was the last one to arrive. Miss Francis, who was the substitute teacher for Mr. Brown, was already handing out workbooks. On the way to his desk, Morton passed by Robbie's desk and Robbie beckoned him over.

"Sorry about earlier," he said. "What was it you wanted to talk about?"

"It's complicated," Morton replied in a hushed tone. "Let's meet up after school and I'll tell you then."

"Oh, I can't," Robbie said apologetically. "I have to go to the dentist right after class. I'm getting a filling."

"Oh, well, maybe you could come over to our house later tonight?"

Robbie swayed his head doubtfully. "Uh, I'm not sure. I'm supposed to learn my lyrics tonight. Can it wait until tomorrow?"

Morton wanted to screech at Robbie that, no, it couldn't wait until tomorrow, but stopped himself. Maybe it was selfish of him to drag Robbie into this mess. For all James's and Melissa's talk of living normal lives, Robbie was the one who seemed to have actually accomplished it. The last thing Morton wanted to do was take that away from him.

"No, it's fine. It can wait until tomorrow," Morton said, and went to sit at his desk at the front of the class.

At the end of the day, Morton met up with James, who was waiting beside the large cast-iron gates just outside the school grounds as usual.

"Come on, Squirto," he said, starting to walk as Morton approached. "I've got tennis with Wendy, remember. I don't want to be late."

Morton ran to catch up with him, feeling flustered and confused by the day's events. He was also surprised to find James so preoccupied with something as mundane as tennis practice when only yesterday they'd been attacked by a swarm of Mutant Rodents. It almost seemed as though he was intentionally trying to ignore the whole situation, and Morton felt a prickle of irritation.

"I have some bad news," he said, strutting rapidly along to keep pace with James, who was walking much faster than usual.

James's pace faltered for a moment, and he cast Morton a quick sideways glance, but then he continued walking. "Oh?" he said in an airy, overly casual tone, which caused Morton's irritation to ratchet up another notch.

"No, seriously, I think we might have a real problem on our hands."

"Is this about the rats again?" James asked with a sigh.

"No!" Morton exclaimed. "It's about Derek's Antigravity Laser Cannon." And then he quickly described the incident with Derek, leaving out the part about how he'd tried — unsuccessfully — to get Robbie to come and help him.

"So, is this left over from your wish too?" James asked. "I mean, do you think you made the gun real when you touched it, like what happened to Timmy's toys?"

James was alluding to the time several weeks earlier when Timmy Clarke had rushed up to Morton in the school hall with a bag full of his newly purchased *Scare Scape* monster toys, which had somehow come to life the moment Morton laid hands on them. The incident might well have been fatal had it not been for the sudden appearance of the Zombie Twins, who had whisked them away like a pair of spooky Pied Pipers.

"It can't be that," Morton said. "I've handled all kinds of toys since we reversed the wishes, and none of them has come to life, and that includes my Zombie Twins, a Gristle

Grunt, and the King-Crab Spiders that are still sitting on my shelf."

James started rubbing his forehead in exactly the same way that Dad did when he was feeling overwhelmed. "That is a bit strange," he said.

"A bit strange!" Morton shrieked, the tension of the day's events finally catching up with him. "That's like saying Mr. Brown was a bit unkind! It's more than strange — it's bizarre! And it means that we were completely wrong about being rid of all the magic."

"Look, don't panic," James said, waving his hands in a calming gesture. "It's still too early to jump to any conclusions. It might not be all that serious."

"I'm not panicking!" Morton shot back. "I just don't see how you can be so calm about it all."

"Well, I've been thinking," James said, "and I'm wondering if this might be sort of like an echo."

"Huh?" Morton said.

"Well, you know, we expected the magic to stop all at once, but maybe that's not how it works. I mean we definitely reversed the wishes, but maybe there will still be a bit of magic floating around for a while, kind of like an echo. And like an echo it will sort of just die down naturally over time."

Morton could hardly believe his ears. "You think it's just going to go away on its own?"

"It might," James responded with a hint of impatience. "Either way we don't want to do anything rash."

Morton thought about Robbie's possible Snarf sighting and wanted to ask James if that was part of his "magical echo" but thought better of it, mostly because by now they were walking along Hemlock Hill and Morton spotted Wendy leaning against the fence at the top of her yard. Wendy saw them approaching and waved anxiously, pointing to an imaginary watch on her wrist.

"Look, we're going to have to discuss this later," James said.

"But this is urgent," Morton persisted.

"What's urgent?" Wendy asked, now within earshot.

James and Morton came to a stop beside Wendy, and James made a big sigh. "If I explain it now, we'll definitely miss practice," he said.

"Does it have to do with the rats?" Wendy said.

"It's a lot more than that," Morton cut in before James had a chance to speak. "It's something completely new, and we need to discuss it right away."

Wendy gave James a questioning look, and James rubbed his forehead again. "It *might* be something new," he finally admitted. "In any case, it can wait another hour. Wendy can come for supper and we can talk about it after Dad leaves for work, okay?"

Morton was forced to agree that this sounded reasonable, and James and Wendy continued along Hemlock Hill toward the tennis courts.

Just over an hour later, Morton was sitting at the table doing his history homework when, as promised, Wendy and James returned, and James asked if Wendy could stay for dinner. Dad, who was busily stirring pots and chopping up ingredients, of course agreed, proudly announcing that he was making one of his favorite dishes. The dish involved rice, lumpy cheese sauce, and sweet corn. He called it his

"Globular Cluster," and while this described it perfectly, Dad seemed incapable of understanding why the name was no more appetizing than the meal. Despite this, Wendy very politely ate everything on her plate and even offered to wash the dishes, which Morton helped her with because he knew from experience that Globular Cluster was very difficult to clean up, especially the pans, which usually had a thick rubbery coating on the inside that needed to be scraped off with a knife.

By the time Dad left, the sun had already gone down and a cold chill crept through the house, reminding Morton that winter was rapidly approaching. Melissa, who had been unusually quiet throughout dinner, decided to start a fire in the large fireplace in the living room. Morton whipped up some hot chocolate for them to drink, which was not only comfortingly warm but also helped wash away the peculiar aftertaste of supper.

Morton then told Wendy and Melissa about the inexplicable incident with Derek and his toy laser.

As soon as he had finished his tale, Melissa let out a dramatic sigh. "Well, if that's not magic, then Dad's a master chef."

"I couldn't agree more," Wendy said. "But where's Robbie? Shouldn't he be here for this?"

"Oh, he's kind of busy with the band," Morton said.

"Not that stupid punk band?" Melissa exclaimed. "I can't believe he'd rather be out damaging his eardrums than hanging out with us."

"Look, Robbie's business is his own," Morton said, surprised at just how annoyed the subject made him feel.

"The important thing here is that magic is obviously still happening and we have to do something about it."

"And by 'do something,' I presume you mean start messing with magic from Brown's horrible book of spells," Melissa said, glancing at James in a way that made Morton feel, not for the first time, as though they'd been talking about him behind his back.

"I'm not suggesting we 'mess' with anything," Morton replied calmly, "but I think we obviously need to learn more about magic, and right now the only way I can think of to learn more is by taking a closer look at The Book of Portals."

"And I still say it's too soon," James cut in. "And anyway, what do you expect to do with The Book of Portals? Conjure another Galosh and get it to eat all the rats?"

"Hey, that's not such a bad idea," Melissa said.

"Yes, it is a bad idea," James said, gritting his teeth and glaring at Melissa. "Magic is dangerous, remember?"

Morton clutched his head in frustration. "Look, at least read the story before making a decision," he said, and rushed to grab the Mutant Rodent issue from his schoolbag and place it open to the final page of the story.

Melissa, James, and Wendy stared for a long time at the image of a million rats swarming over the last survivors of the small town, who were attempting unsuccessfully to find refuge in a church.

"Don't you ever get tired of the 'and they were all eaten unhappily ever after' endings?" Melissa said at last.

"I don't write the stories," Morton said. "But I'm telling you, if there's any truth to this, then we're going to need more than a few bags of rat pellets to get Dimvale back to normal."

For the first time all evening, Morton thought he saw a shift in Melissa's mood. "I guess that is pretty terrifying," she said in a serious tone.

"But it's just a drawing," James said, directing his comments at Melissa. "Who says that's what's going to happen here?"

"I think James is right," Wendy said. "It's too soon to start messing with magic again."

Morton was hardly surprised that Wendy was siding with James, but he turned hopefully to Melissa, who was still staring at the open comic on the table.

Melissa chewed on her lip for a long time, until James cleared his throat loudly. Melissa then glanced up at James, gave him a strange look, and said, "James is right. It's too dangerous."

James clapped his hands almost gleefully. "That settles it, then. It's three against one, so let's not hear any more talk of doing magic."

Morton opened his mouth to protest, but James cut him off immediately. "Morton, we've made a decision. Now let's not ruin the rest of the evening by arguing about it."

"Ruin the evening?" Morton echoed, jumping to his feet. "You want to just sit here and make small talk as if everything is normal?"

"Well, it would make a nice change," James said, in a tone that made it clear that was exactly what he wanted to do.

Morton felt his whole face flush with heat. Part of him could understand why nobody wanted to venture back into

King's attic and relive the horrifying memories of the time when Brown conjured a Galosh. But to blithely announce that their whole strategy for dealing with the ongoing outbreaks of magic was to intentionally ignore it was nothing short of suicidal.

"In that case, I'm going to bed," Morton spluttered, and he stomped across the room, snatching his comic as he went. "And I'll take this," he added, "so that you guys don't have to think any unpleasant thoughts while I'm gone."

Morton had barely made it to his room when he started to feel embarrassed. It wasn't at all like him to lose his temper and he wasn't quite sure why he'd gotten so upset. There was something about the way James and Melissa had been behaving since the appearance of the rats that gave him the feeling that they were conspiring against him.

Morton changed wearily into his pajamas and clambered into bed, thinking again about the purple spine Robbie had found. Might it be possible James was turning into a Snarf at night and then somehow transforming back into a human in the day? Might that somehow explain James's behavior? Could Melissa possibly be in on it? Morton lay there for a long time, pondering this over and listening to the hushed voices of the others downstairs.

At some point he must have fallen into a deep sleep, because the next thing he knew the moon had vanished from his window and the voices had stopped. Something had awoken him, however. His senses were on full alert. He sat up and looked into the dense shadows around him. Dark blotches swam across his vision, which at first he took as a sign that his eyes were adjusting to the lack of light. But then he realized the truth: Something was moving. Something was in the room with him.

A strange shape seemed to hover before him, shifting and oozing in the air like a pool of oil and accompanied by a rhythmical flapping sound. He couldn't make any sense of it. He felt his whole body tense and coil like a spring.

Suddenly the shape lurched toward him, and before he could react, his head was plunged into a moving sea of shadows. Something cold and fleshy brushed against his face, and a sharp claw settled on his shoulder.

Morton threw up his arms and lashed wildly at his attacker, then leaped for the light switch beside the door. His room burst into a blaze of brightness, and he saw at once that the dark shape was not in fact one creature, but half a dozen Bat Eyes, fluttering around in a tight swirl of leathery wings. Morton felt a wave of relief wash over him — Bat Eyes were not usually dangerous. But at the same time he was puzzled. What were they doing here?

Without warning, the Bat Eyes swooped into motion. At first Morton thought they were about to swarm his head again, but in fact they whooshed right past him and fluttered with one mind out through his bedroom door and down the landing.

Morton turned to watch them go and immediately spotted that the small door to the main attic was ajar. The Bat Eyes were headed right for it in an orderly single-file line. Morton remembered that there were several small broken windows in the attic and he realized that this was probably how they had gotten into the house. He also realized that they were probably now racing to escape.

In a flash Morton snatched a sheet from his bed and bounded down the hall in pursuit. In some deep part of his brain he realized that if he could catch one of these Bat Eyes alive, it might be the evidence he needed to convince James that recent events were more than just some harmless magical echo.

He skidded to a halt at the base of the attic stairs just in time to catch sight of the winged creatures slipping through the door at the top. He leaped after them, taking two steps at a time, and he opened the sheet like a net in front of him and lunged into the attic, intending to fling the sheet over the flock and bring at least one of them down to the ground. But as he dashed forward his left foot smashed into something hard and heavy, and the next thing he knew he was falling flat on his face. A plume of dust billowed up his nose, causing him to sneeze, and by the time he managed to pull himself into a sitting position the last of the Bat Eyes was flitting away through one of the small, broken dormer windows.

Morton cursed his luck and clambered back to his feet, taking care not to put too much weight on his injured toe. Aside from being very annoyed at having completely failed to capture a Bat Eye, he was now also perplexed as to what exactly had collided with his foot. In the faint glow spilling up the stairs from his bedroom, he could just make out the shape of a small wooden chest with heavy metal straps running around the lid. Morton had only ventured into this attic once before, on the very first day they'd arrived in the house, and even though it had been crammed with all manner of discarded artifacts, he was quite certain there had not been a wooden trunk lying in the very center of the entrance.

Despite the lateness of the hour and the cold air seeping in from the broken windows, Morton's curiosity got the better of him, and he crouched back down beside the box and lifted the lid.

Morton wasn't really surprised to find that the box contained nothing more exciting than a few dusty old documents, and he was about to close it again when he spotted a stack of yellowing photographs right at the bottom of the pile. He pulled the photos out and leaned over into the shaft of light to get a closer look at them.

Morton was fascinated to see that they were all photos of John King at various stages in his life. At the top of the pile was a relatively recent photo of him with his wild, straggly gray hair and dark glasses. This photo, Morton knew, would likely have been taken shortly before he died, but as he moved through the pile, the photos became increasingly older and John King became increasingly younger. There were several photos of him receiving awards at various comic conventions, and at each one the gray in his hair diminished until Morton reached a photo of a very handsome young man with jet-black hair, a sharp and delicate nose, and piercing dark eyes. The next photo showed the same youthful King, arm in arm with a smiling young woman with frizzy curls and pale blue eyes. This image was the most surprising of all. He'd always presumed that King had been a somber, brooding hermit his whole life, and yet here he was, seemingly happy and carefree, and quite possibly in love.

There was only one more photo, and this one was definitely the oldest. It was black-and-white, and scarred with creases as if it had been carried in a wallet for many years, and it showed two teenage boys standing in front of a storefront. The dark-haired boy, who was obviously King, had a big smile on his face and was standing on a ladder with a paintbrush in hand. It looked like he had just finished painting the ornamental letters on the sign above the door, which read *Crooks Collectible Books*. The other boy was much lighter in coloring, with a round freckled face, and he was standing at the base of the ladder.

Morton flipped the photo over. On the back were written the words *My brother Syd and me, age 14*. This came as a complete surprise to Morton. He knew for a fact that King had always claimed to be an only child in numerous articles and interviews, and he even remembered one article that insisted he'd been a homeless orphan. Yet this photo contradicted all of that. Was it possible that everything he'd read was entirely false? He knew that his publishers had spread false rumors about him to make him appear more sinister than he really was, but surely some of what he'd read had to be true.

Morton placed the photos carefully back in the bottom of the box and scanned through the other documents, wondering if he might learn more about the enigmatic man who had once owned their home. There were a few old passports, postcards from various seaside resorts, and a fiftieth birthday card from someone named Beatrice. In short, nothing that seemed too important.

Morton yawned and started rubbing his eyes. Realizing that he really did need to get to bed, he pushed the trunk off to the side so that whoever ventured up here next didn't trip on it as he had done. He then padded softly down the stairs, thinking about King's past and the big smile on his face in the photograph. To his surprise, even though the man was a stranger to him, Morton felt a comforting glow inside at the thought that King might have enjoyed a happy childhood despite the stories his publishers had spun. Unfortunately the feeling didn't last more than a few seconds.

Just as he was about to turn and head back to his bedroom, he saw a flash of light coming from inside Dad's office. The flickering was unmistakably that of a flashlight beam dancing across the windows and walls. But who would be snooping through the house at this time of night with a flashlight?

Morton knew only too well that The Book of Portals was hidden in the secret attic above Dad's study, and a jolt of panic shot up his spine. Was it possible that somebody was trying to steal it? That would certainly explain why the Bat Eyes had been snooping around.

Morton dashed back into his bedroom and retrieved a baseball bat from inside his closet. The night's terrifying adventures, it seemed, were far from over.

CHAPTER 6

EYE SPY

Morton shuffled silently back onto the landing, hardening his nerves for whoever, or whatever, was prowling in Dad's office. He decided the best thing to do would be to awaken Melissa first, remembering that she still had swords hidden under her bed that she'd found deep inside her once infinitely large closet, yet as he approached her room, he saw that her door was open and her bed was empty. He then spotted something else that made no sense to him. From where he was standing, he could see right into Dad's office, and there in the center of the room was the jagged outline of a stepladder — and at its base was a bright pink toolbox.

He recognized the toolbox immediately because it had once been his mother's. Morton himself had painted his father's red toolbox pink one day and given it to her as a joke, since she'd proven far better with tools than Dad.

But what kind of burglar didn't bring his own tools? Morton had a feeling he knew the answer.

He crept quietly into Dad's study. Looking up, he saw that the dark wooden hatch in the ceiling was wide open. The face on its garish brass handle stared down at him, and despite himself he shivered at the sight of it. Nonetheless he forced himself to climb the ladder.

When he reached the top, he peered over the jamb of the hatch, and the smell of dust and wax and burned parchment hit his nostrils and triggered a rapid series of memories to flash through his head. Suddenly he was back. Back on that horrible night when Mr. Brown had conjured a Galosh and tried to kill them. Back on the night when James had almost fully transformed into a Snarf, the night when somehow, from beyond the grave, John King had wreaked his vengeance on Brown and saved them from certain death.

Morton had a moment of dizziness so intense he had to grasp at the opening to steady himself, but as he did so, his feet shifted and the ladder twisted beneath him, toppling over with a loud crash. Morton dropped the baseball bat and suddenly found himself hanging by his fingertips like a chimpanzee. In the same instant he looked up to see a pale face glaring down at him from within the attic. Before he had time to react, a pair of equally pale arms dropped down out of the impenetrable dark and hoisted him up.

"Morton! What the heck do you think you're doing?"

Morton found himself standing on the rough planked floor of King's secret attic staring into the bemused face of Melissa.

"What am I doing? What are you doing?" he said, finally getting his bearings and glancing around the room. Everything was just as he remembered it. The five stone candle holders. The five desiccated animal carcasses and the painted spiral leading to the ornately carved stone font at the center. The only thing that was not exactly as they'd left it was The Book of Portals, which they'd hidden under a loose floorboard, but that now lay on the floor just beside Melissa's purple leather school satchel.

Melissa noticed that Morton had seen the book and her cross expression shifted to one of guilt. "It's not what you think," she said.

"No? What is it, then?" Morton said, feeling both betrayed and angry.

"Well, the truth is, I don't think James is right about this magical echo thing. Something else happened today that —" Melissa stopped suddenly and gave Morton a tortured look. "I can't . . . I can't talk about it."

"Why not?" Morton demanded with a mounting sense of outrage.

Melissa pressed her lips together and seemed to be having some kind of internal struggle before giving the answer. "Because I promised James that I wouldn't get you involved in any more magic," she blurted out after a long pause.

"What?! When?"

"It was a few days ago, when we thought it was all over. James just sort of cornered me one night and made me promise that if anything weird or dangerous or magical were to happen again, we wouldn't get you involved. At first I just sort of laughed it off, but he was deadly serious. He said that it was our job to protect you, even if it meant lying to you."

"But that's ridiculous," Morton said. "I don't need protecting any more than you do."

"James doesn't seem to think that's the case. He was so serious about it he made me promise on . . . well, on Mum's memory."

Only at these words did Morton realize just how serious James must have been.

"Well, for your information, ten minutes ago I was attacked by a flock of Bat Eyes in my own bedroom," Morton said matter-of-factly.

"You were?" Melissa yelped, her mouth falling open in surprise.

"Yes. So like it or not, I am involved. And from my point of view, it's probably more dangerous if you *don't* tell me what's going on."

Melissa seemed to struggle a moment longer before speaking, but then let out a long resigned sigh, walked over to the satchel, and produced a limp black leathery object from inside.

It was another Bat Eye, only this one was stone-cold dead. Morton stepped over to the small corpse and examined it closely. At first glance Bat Eyes looked a lot like ordinary bats with translucent veined wings tipped with menacing claws, but closer inspection revealed that the creature had one enormous demonic eye where its face should have been, and this specimen had dark oily liquid dripping from around its eye like thick black tears.

"This is a Bat Eye, right?" Melissa asked.

Morton nodded.

"Thought so," she said. "Seems like you're not the only one they're visiting. This one and a bunch of its creepy friends were following me home from school this afternoon."

"How did you catch it?" Morton asked.

"Hit it with my purse," she said casually.

"Wow! You must have hit it pretty hard," Morton said. "It's as dead as a doornail."

"Oh, no, the purse just stunned it. After that I had to skewer it with a sharp pencil."

"Right," Morton said, remembering again just how little tolerance for monsters Melissa had.

"I don't suppose you have any idea why they were following me, do you?"

"Not really," Morton said. "They're mostly just spies. Other than that, they're harmless. They can't sting you or hypnotize you. They can't even bite you because they don't have a mouth."

"No mouth? How can it not have a mouth? Everything has to eat, right?"

"That's not actually true," Morton said. "Mayflies are real insects, and they don't eat."

"Then how do they survive?" Melissa asked.

Morton was about to explain the life cycle of mayflies to Melissa, but she cut him off before he even got a chance to start.

"You know what, I don't need to know that right now. Tell me more about the Bat Eyes. If they're spies, doesn't that mean someone has to be controlling them?"

"Usually," Morton said. "In *Scare Scape* it's mostly just the Zombie Twins who control them. But anyone can use them — I mean, anyone *could* use them, if they knew how to conjure them. They're basically just like flying security cameras."

"And your Zombie Twin toys . . . ?"

"Still sitting on my shelf," Morton assured her.

Melissa shot a glance over her shoulder as if she thought somebody was behind her. "So the question is, who would want to spy on us, and why?"

"I'm not sure," Morton said. "Did you tell James about this?"

"Yes!" Melissa groaned. "He insists it's all part of his echo theory. Says they're not dangerous and we shouldn't worry about them."

"But you don't agree with him?" Morton asked. "You think we should use magic?"

"I wouldn't go that far, but I wanted to find out what our options are. Unfortunately we don't seem to have any. The book is pretty much useless."

Morton felt a twinge of disappointment. "Are you sure?" he asked.

Melissa shrugged. "Take a look for yourself."

Morton hoped Melissa was wrong and made his way over to the book, which was still lying in the middle of the floor. He sat down cross-legged in front of it and stared for a moment at the large black jewel on the cover, once again experiencing flashes of memory from the time when Mr. Brown had first pulled the book out of its green velvet pouch, and half wishing that none of it had ever happened.

Morton pushed the memories aside and spent the next few minutes leafing through the frayed handmade pages. There were over a hundred spells and potions in the book. For the most part though, it seemed to be a random disjointed collection with no particular sense of organization or purpose.

There were spells for conjuring violent thunderstorms, potions to make your enemies literally speechless, several spells involving fire, and incantations for bringing inanimate objects to life. There were also the spells they already knew about, like Brown's spider-walking spell, and a lot of very sinister rituals that allowed you to conjure creatures from parallel dimensions, which is how Mr. Brown had conjured the Galosh. But after only a few minutes of searching, Morton knew that Melissa was right. There was nothing about undoing magic or getting rid of unwanted pests. In fact, the only spell that had anything to do with existing animals was one to make them fatter, which presumably would have been very useful for starving sorcerers in days gone by but hardly helped in the current situation. Despite this, Morton did briefly consider the idea of making the rats hugely fat, wondering if that might make them easier to catch, but then decided that was exactly the kind of spell that could backfire and make matters far worse.

While Morton read, Melissa paced slowly around the attic, clutching her arms around herself tightly, clearly unhappy to be here again. "So?" she said when Morton finally closed the book.

"I guess James was right," he sighed. "Unless we want to conjure a Galosh and get it to eat the rats, this book's not much use."

"Well, we definitely don't want to do that," Melissa said. "Magic is already spreading like fire through Dimvale, and we don't need to add to it."

"Spreading like fire," Morton repeated. "Where did you get that phrase?"

Melissa shrugged. "I think I just made it up. Why?"

"Because I feel like I've heard it before, or read it somewhere . . ." And then Morton remembered exactly where he had read that phrase before, and had a sudden burst of excitement.

"Of course!" he shrieked. "King's diaries! We need to read King's diaries."

"Uh, you mean the ones Brown said he burned right after pushing King down the well?" Melissa said.

"Exactly!" Morton said, leaping to his feet and heading to the stone font in the center of the room. Melissa looked at him with confusion, but Morton pushed his hand into the flakes of black ash that still filled the font and, as he expected, found the charred remnant of a handwritten book, exactly where he'd left it.

"This must be one of King's diaries," he explained. "It's almost completely destroyed, but I remember reading a couple of lines that didn't make sense at the time. They said, 'spreads like ink on blotting paper, or fire in a forest,' and now I think I know exactly what they meant. I think King was writing about magic. I think it was a kind of warning about the way magic works. Which means that this whole diary probably talks about magic. It might be exactly what we need to understand what's going on."

"Uh, am I missing something?" Melissa said, "Because right now that looks a lot more like something Dad cooked on the barbecue than a book."

"Yes, but that doesn't matter," Morton said, carefully placing the blackened fragment on the side of the font and picking up The Book of Portals, "because we have this."

Melissa continued to stare blankly at him.

"There's a spell in here for reversing the effects of fire," he added. "Look." He turned to a page with a drawing of a burning castle.

"'Reversing Effects of Promethean Spoil'?" Melissa said. "What's that supposed to mean?"

"I think Prometheus was supposed to be the god who stole fire from Mount Olympus. Or was he a demigod?" Morton mused.

"Oh, yeah, now I remember," Melissa said. "Why do these ancient books always find complicated ways to say simple things?"

Morton didn't bother answering the question, but instead looked carefully at the spell described on the page. He was surprised at just how simple it looked. It required only that you carve some odd symbols onto a piece of wood before reciting a simple verse. Melissa also read the page quickly over his shoulder.

"Well, that looks easy," she said. "But you're not suggesting we actually do it, are you?"

"Of course, we have to do it," Morton replied. "It's our only hope of finding out what's really going on in Dimvale. I mean, what do we have to lose?"

"You mean, aside from taking the risk that the spell backfires and turns us both into wiener dogs?"

"Can you please be serious?" Morton pleaded.

"I am being serious," Melissa said. "It's dangerous, and I promised James I was going to protect you from magic, so unless you can get him to agree to it, I have no intention of —"

"Get me to agree to what?" a voice from behind them said.

Morton and Melissa both jumped and spun around to look at the open hatch. There, standing on the stepladder, was a very cross-looking James. He clambered the rest of the way up into the attic and shuffled over to them wearing his slippers and tartan robe.

"Come on, then, you might as well tell me what's going on," James said. "I've heard enough to guess, but I'd rather get the story straight."

CHAPTER 7
THE VOICE OF KING

Morton quickly summarized the night's events, and he could see by James's expression that the intrusion of the Bat Eyes came as a shock.

"For the record, I'm with Morton," Melissa said. "I think we should use magic. I only voted against it earlier because you made me promise."

James glanced around the room in agitation. For a moment Morton thought he was about to lecture them again, but he didn't. He simply let out a sigh and said, "Okay. You have a point. This does seem to be getting out of hand."

Morton felt a wave of relief wash over him. He was certain that this was the right thing to do, and he opened The Book of Portals to the spell he'd found.

"But I do have one request," James added. "If we're going to play with magic, can we at least go and do this outside, just in case it, I dunno, explodes or something?"

Both Morton and Melissa agreed that this was a good idea and it didn't take them long to relocate. They ended up huddled around Dad's potting table, which was tucked away right at the bottom of his newly planted garden. Melissa brought a wooden ruler from her schoolbag and a chisel from

Dad's pink toolbox and with surprising skill carved the two complex symbols onto the ruler. They then placed the ruler on top of the charred diary fragment and Morton recited the verse.

> *Take this spark of Promethean spoil.*
> *Take this wood of time's long toil.*
> *Take this charm of reconstruction.*
> *Take this charm of reproduction.*
> *Take them now, as each the same,*
> *And return that stolen by force of flame.*

The very moment the last word left Morton's lips, the ruler cracked loudly and turned a frosty white, the whole thing suddenly covered in a thin coat of crystalline ice, and then slowly shifted from white to a warm shade of orange and, with a sudden crackle, the entire thing burst into red-hot flames.

Everyone stepped back, shielding their faces from the intense heat. Morton was relieved that they'd heeded James's warning.

The ice itself seemed to be burning and melting into a strange blue liquid, which began to flow out, almost like a living entity, enveloping the diary in small rivulets of blue fire. Then Morton saw that which he'd barely dared hope for. Beneath the softly rippling blanket of flame, curled pages were unfolding like flowers on a spring morning, their blackened shells fading to crisp supple whiteness. Morton saw scrolls of King's neat script emerging from the ashes, and with each new page the book grew steadily larger and thicker until at last the soft leather binding spread out over the whole and finally there was the book, in its entirety, presumably exactly as King had left it almost a year earlier.

Morton expected the blue rivulets of flame to subside and die away, but they showed no signs of stopping. James looked curiously at Morton. "So what are we supposed to do now?" he said. "Throw a bucket of water on it?"

"I don't think so," Morton said, and he reached forward and tapped his hand briefly on the blue rivulets of flame. As he had suspected, the fire was cool to the touch. It felt almost like cold water running over his fingers.

Melissa gaped in amazement. "You can actually touch it!"

"More to the point," Morton said, "we can read it." And he lifted the book into his hands and opened it where a frayed ribbon marked a page. He could hardly believe his eyes. There, as plain as day, were what he presumed were the last written words of John King.

"It's . . . it's incredible," Morton said after reading the first few pages rapidly to himself. "I mean, it's not what we thought at all."

"Really, we wouldn't know," Melissa said. "You're hogging it."

"Maybe you could read it out loud?" James suggested.

"I don't know where to start," Morton said, feeling utterly overwhelmed.

"Start at the end," Melissa said. "That way we'll know what his last thoughts were."

"Okay," Morton said. "This is the last entry." And he turned his attention back to the diary and began to read.

November 22nd

Why does fate conspire to bring me such ill luck? Surely I have had more than my share. Yet now, when I must focus all my energies on the task at hand, this buzzing annoyance, this wandering dung beetle of a man who goes by the name of Rodney Brown, has somehow learned that I possess a copy of The Book of Portals.

"Mr. Brown!" Melissa said. "That means he must have written this close to the end of his life."

"Not just close to the end," Morton said. "I think this might have been written the very same night he died. Listen."

When Brown first came to me in search of one of my many books, I tried to play dumb. I told him his notions of magic were pure fallacy. I rather glibly suggested he forget his silly fantasies and find a wife before age stole the last of his opportunities from under his nose, as it is wont to do, but I underestimated the level of his obsession. A few weeks ago he revealed that he has stolen a pagan sculpture, a crude reproduction of a much older diabolical form, but potently magical nonetheless, and I realize now that Rodney Brown could be a danger to himself and others. He has many foolish ideas about magic and understands nothing of its true nature. For one thing, he has the mistaken impression that The Book of Portals is the most powerful magical book in existence. I have no idea where he got such a ridiculous notion and no intention of informing him otherwise. I can't even imagine what devious plans he would cook up in his shallow pan of a brain if he discovered that my library contains a hundred such books, most of which contain far more potent magic than the eclectic collection of mismatched spells in The Book of Portals.

"King's library had hundreds of books on magic?" Melissa said in astonishment. "Books with even more powerful magic than The Book of Portals?"

Morton nodded. "I never really thought about it before, but it only makes sense. I mean he must have had over a thousand books, and there has to be more than one book of magic in the world."

"Wait a minute," James said. "Didn't Wendy say that King's books all got sold off in an auction?"

Melissa nodded. "She's told me several times about the day the auctioneers came and emptied the entire house into two big moving trucks. Everything was sold off."

"Sold off? But that means anyone could have bought his books," James said with a grim look on his face.

Melissa made a snort of annoyance. "Exactly what I was just thinking! For all we know everyone in Dimvale has one of King's books sitting on their shelf. Half the kids in town could be messing around with dangerous magic. It's a wonder any of us are still alive."

Morton thought again about Derek and wondered absently if he might have somehow come into possession of one of

King's books and been experimenting on his own. That might explain what happened to his gun. . . .

"Read some more," James prompted, and Morton turned his attention back to the diary.

For better or worse, Brown is ignorant and completely devoid of imagination. He obviously does not know it was tradition among the cults of that region to perform the sacrificial rites in the same month that the statue was carved, which unfortunately means that Brown is in possession of a truly dangerous talisman. For this reason, I must at all costs get the gargoyle from him. If he learns that it is already capable of granting wishes, he will no doubt use it, and it will almost certainly bring ruin and disaster upon all involved.

But the timing could not be worse. Despite his ignorance, Brown knows that the full moon is the key to his ceremony, so if I am to relieve him of his dangerous toy, then it must be on that night — which, of course, is the very night I intend to attack my true foe.

But I cannot risk putting Brown off for another month. In truth, I cannot even be certain I will live that long. My enemy knows I plan to strike while he is vulnerable, and he will not sit idly by. I will confess that I am afraid.

"What?" Melissa yelped, snatching the book from Morton's hands as if needing to see the words with her own eyes. "Enemy? What enemy? I thought Brown was his enemy."

Morton was equally shocked by this revelation. "It sounds like King was worried about someone much worse than Mr. Brown."

"Worse than Brown!" Melissa said with a shiver. "Now there's a cheery thought."

Morton also felt a shiver run down his own spine and suddenly had a longing to be tucked into his warm bed.

"Is that who's been following us around with Bat Eyes?" Melissa said.

"Maybe," Morton replied, "although I don't see why anyone would want to do that."

"I do," James said, now glancing nervously at the deep shadows under the trees around them. "Think about it. A few kids move into King's house and the very same month there are reports of Zombie Twin sightings, missing cats, toys coming to life, and the strange disappearance of Mr. Brown. If you were King's enemy, wouldn't you keep a close watch on us?"

"I suppose I would," Morton agreed, "but I wouldn't make Derek's Antigravity Laser work like the real thing. That would be pointless."

"Maybe that was a mistake," Melissa said. "I mean, we know magic can go wrong."

Morton wasn't sure about this. It was true that he'd seen plenty of magic going wrong, but if this enemy of King's was as dangerous as King implied, it didn't seem likely that he would accidentally cause Derek's laser to make things float up to the ceiling.

"We should definitely read the rest of the diary," Morton prompted, drawing Melissa's attention back to the still glowing pages.

Melissa sighed wearily, the blue flames casting a flickering glow over her pale face, and leafed through the diary. "Wait a minute," she said, turning to the end of the book. "That wasn't the last entry you read. There's a whole lot of blank pages and then another note right at the back."

Everyone huddled in around the book again and Melissa lowered it so that they could see. There on the second-to-last page was what looked to be a hastily scrawled paragraph written in splotchy ink. Melissa read it quickly.

Again, my luck turns against me, and perhaps for the last time. For certain he played his game well. How foolish of me to not realize that he was using Brown as a pawn in his careful attack. Yet I can hardly punish myself for that. Even Brown himself was unaware that he played a part.

If I were truly brave I would destroy The Book of Parchments here and now to be sure it never falls into his hands, but the Parchments are the most valuable magical artifacts I have ever discovered. Who then am I to cast them into the abyss? No, I will protect them. And more — I will finally use them.

In truth I have been afraid to use the Parchments before now, wary of unleashing their full power, for magic is no inert controllable force. We use it at our peril, for it spreads like ink on blotting paper, or fire in a forest. And the Parchments act on the one same principle as all magic: the opening of the veil between this world and what modern scientists call parallel dimensions, and "borrowing" from alternate realities, for that which is science in one universe is magic in this one. Yet that veil is more fragile than we would wish to believe, and too much magic, as the ancient scholars knew, can irreversibly rupture the fabric between the worlds. I have already been forced to use more magic than I think is safe, and if I turn to the Parchments, I fear that action may cause permanent ripples in this once tranquil town. Yet how can I do otherwise? I see a glimmer of hope. . . . One possible path to defeat him and pass on the legacy . . .

But wait, I see his army of shadows approaching. The time is now. I will use the Parchments. I will risk laying my ink in the eternity of their blank pages, knowing that even if I succeed, this could well be my final hour.

"Ugh!" Melissa growled, getting suddenly angry. "Is it just me or was John King a complete idiot?"

"An idiot?" Morton said, confused by the outburst. "Why do you say that?"

"Well, why did he even bother writing this at all?" Melissa snapped. "Honestly, for a man who made a living writing stories, you'd think he could string two words together so that they made at least a little bit of sense. I mean this is all, 'Ooh, legacy, ah, Parchments, blah de blah, Mr. Brown, thingumy wotsit, mysterious enemy.' For heaven's sake, he reminds me of my math teacher, 'the sum of the square root of weird stuff equals pi times vanilla ice cream.' It makes no sense whatsoever."

"What's so confusing?" Morton said.

"For one thing, what is this Book of Parchments he's so worried about?"

"Well, obviously it's another book of spells," James said. "Like The Book of Portals."

"That's not quite right," Morton put in. "I mean, it's not a book of spells, more just a magic book."

"Now you're making even less sense than King," Melissa said.

"What I mean," Morton explained, "is that according to Scare Scape, the Parchments were magical artifacts that looked like blank pieces of paper. Just by drawing or writing on them, a person could make almost anything happen. With a spell book like The Book of Portals, you're limited to whatever spells are written down. With a Book of Parchments, you wouldn't have any limits besides your imagination."

"Sort of like the blank tiles in a game of Scrabble, then," Melissa said. "You can use them for whatever you want."

"Uh, maybe," Morton said.

"Oh, well, that would at least explain why this enemy of his was trying to steal it. I mean, imagine how great it would be if every time you played Scrabble, all your tiles were blank."

James glanced at Melissa irritably. "It still leaves a lot of questions," he said. "Like when exactly did he write this diary entry? Obviously he must have written it before Brown came over to do the ceremony, but he says Brown was unaware of the part he played, which almost makes it sound like he wrote it after."

Morton had to admit there was something nonsensical about the entry. Why and when would King have written it?

"Keep reading," James said. "Maybe it will make sense eventually."

"Okay, I'll start at the beginning," Melissa said, turning to the first page of the diary. "But I'm going to read quickly. There's a lot to —"

Quite suddenly Melissa let out a loud yelp and dropped the book on the ground.

"Be careful with that," Morton said. He bent to pick up the book, but Melissa stopped him before he could touch it.

"Don't!" she warned. "It just burned my hand."

Morton froze, his fingers a few inches from the flaming book, and at that very instant, the cold blue flame flared into a brilliant orange ball that glowed with blistering heat. Everyone jumped back and shielded their faces. The flame grew rapidly brighter until the book was consumed in white-hot light. James rushed forward and attempted to stomp out the fire, but it did nothing other than cause his sneakers to smoke and give off a strong smell of burning rubber.

Eventually he gave up and jumped away again. The blaze sizzled for a few seconds longer and then, like a dying firework, abruptly went out. For a moment, Morton could see only green splotches in the darkness where the intense white light had burned into his eyes, but when his vision cleared, he saw that nothing of the book remained.

Melissa growled angrily. "Typical. Just when we were getting somewhere, magic goes haywire."

James knelt down and examined the charred square of grass where the book had fallen. No trace of it remained. "Yeah, I don't think any amount of magic will bring it back this time," he said, turning to look at Morton with a frustrated sigh. "Well, at least we've learned something."

"Nothing useful," Melissa exclaimed. "I mean, so what if he had lots of books on magic and some mysterious enemy was trying to get The Book of Parchments from him. It hardly helps us figure a way out of our mess, especially if it does turn out that every kid in Dimvale has one of his spooky books."

"I don't think that's very likely," James said. "Books like that are usually expensive collector's items. It's more likely that one very wealthy collector bought the whole set."

"Of course!" Morton said, realizing that James was right. "That might be the clue we're looking for. King's enemy wanted his books, especially The Book of Parchments, so he would for sure have bought the whole collection after King died."

"Yeah, well, King could have saved us a lot of trouble if he'd just written his name down," Melissa said, still looking annoyed.

"Well, if Morton is right, and I think he might be," James said, "we should be able to figure out who this enemy was just by finding out who bought all of King's books."

"How do you suppose we do that?" Melissa asked skeptically.

"It should be easy. There's probably only one big auction house in Dimvale, so all we have to do is find somebody who works there and get them to look at the accounts to find out who bought King's books."

Melissa's face suddenly dropped.

"What is it? What's wrong?" Morton prodded.

Melissa scratched her head. "You know, this is a weird coincidence, but I just happen to know someone who works at a big auction house."

"You do?" James exclaimed.

"Yes. Jake."

"Jake?" James said. "Do we know him?"

"You met him the other day when he gave Wendy and me a ride to school."

A look of recognition crossed James's face. "Oh, that guy! But that's great! So you can just ask him."

Melissa snorted dismissively. "I doubt it's going to be that easy. He only works there part-time, and all that stuff about who bought what and when and for how much is highly confidential."

"But if he works in the building, can't you just ask him to sneak in and take a look at the files?" Morton asked.

"Are you serious?" Melissa exclaimed. "I hardly know him. I can't very well ask him to risk his job by sneaking into the office and looking at private documents."

"Yes you can," James said in an unusually firm tone. "You just have to spend some time with him."

Morton wasn't sure, but he thought he saw Melissa blushing in the darkness.

"That's not going to happen," she said. "I mean, he's got to be the least cool guy in Dimvale. He wears those lumberjack shirts all the time, and I'm sure his mother irons creases into his jeans."

"So? This is important," James persisted.

"Did I mention he smells of engine oil? I think he sleeps under his car."

James folded his arms and continued to glare at Melissa with an intensity Morton had seldom seen. It was as if the two of them were having some kind of silent staring contest — one that James apparently won a moment later because Melissa finally said, "Okay, fine! I'll try. But let's not stand here all night. My feet are freezing, and it's way past Morton's bedtime."

Morton was actually very relieved to hear this. He was starting to feel so tired that he was having trouble keeping his eyes open, and when he finally climbed into bed for the second time that night, it didn't take him long to drift off into an exhausted, dreamless void. He did, however, have time for one curious thought before falling asleep. Images of John King's neat, flowing script drifted before his eyes and he wondered vaguely how a blind man had been able to write a diary. . . .

CHAPTER 8

THE THING

The next morning, James slept in so late that Morton thought he might have to leave for school without him, but at the last minute he descended the staircase smelling of soap and looking freshly scrubbed, if not entirely awake. Morton lingered in the kitchen for a few extra minutes while James wolfed down a slice of toast and then grabbed a second slice to carry with him to school.

"I guess you didn't sleep," Morton said sympathetically when they finally rushed out of the door.

"Not a wink," James said, and munched his toast in silence all the way to school.

When they arrived about five minutes later, the bell had already rung, and Morton had to race straight to Mr. Noble's biology class. Fortunately Mr. Noble was handing out work sheets for the day's assignment and had his back to the door when Morton crept in.

Morton glanced quickly around the room. By now there were only two seats available, one beside Robbie and another beside Frizz Ferguson. He wondered if he should sit beside Robbie, as he normally did, or beside Frizz. He wanted to make sure Frizz hadn't told anyone about what had happened to Derek, and he didn't want to crowd Robbie, but he also didn't want Robbie to think he was avoiding him. . . .

At that moment Robbie spotted Morton and beckoned him over enthusiastically. Morton felt a smile lift his face and he tiptoed around the far side of the classroom, hoping Mr. Noble wouldn't see him.

"I'm glad you're here," Robbie whispered, rummaging inside his pencil case as Morton hoisted himself onto the stool. "I have something I want to show you." Morton half expected him to pull out a printed schedule for the band's upcoming concerts, but instead he produced a plastic pair of glasses with blue spirals printed on their frosted glass lenses.

"Uh, what are those?" Morton asked.

Robbie was about to reply when Mr. Noble appeared directly in front of them. "Morton," he said, placing two handouts on their table, "if you're going to arrive late, at least do me the courtesy of not distracting your classmates while I'm trying to teach."

"Sorry, sir," Morton said.

Robbie and Morton fell silent, and Mr. Noble launched into a long lecture about carnivorous plants, which at any other time Morton would have found fascinating. At this particular moment, it felt like an inconvenient interruption.

Robbie seemed to feel the same way and kept casting frustrated glances at Morton. After a couple of minutes he pushed the strange pair of spectacles over to Morton's side of the table and wrote on his notepad in large letters: *Try them on!*

Morton glanced cautiously at the glasses. He recognized them now as X-ray Specs from the advertisements that cluttered the back pages of *Scare Scape* — ads that featured a variety of tricks and trinkets that ranged from plastic fried eggs to exploding cigars and . . . Antigravity Laser Cannons.

He'd tried on a pair of X-ray Specs in a joke shop once a couple of years ago. All they did was make everything look fuzzy, which, if you applied enough imagination, sort of resembled the way X-ray images looked, but on the whole they'd been disappointing in the extreme. Something told him that was not going to be the case now.

He braced himself and then slipped the glasses on. The effect was overwhelming. The room and everything in it changed instantly, and this time, there was nothing fuzzy or vague about what he was seeing. There, before his very eyes, was an entire class of pale skeletons, all sitting in translucent chairs in a room with transparent walls.

Morton could see every detail around him. He could see the braces on Kelly Talbot's teeth, even though she was sitting with her back to him. He could see the sprinkler pipes in the ceiling and the wires in the wall. He could see the books in his bag, which was under the bench. He could see Mr. Noble's lunch box in his desk, and he could even see right through the wall to Mrs. Punjab's math class, where more skeletons slouched lazily at translucent desks.

Morton whipped off the glasses and tucked them quickly out of sight in the front pocket of his sweatshirt. "That's . . . that's incredible," he whispered out of the corner of his mouth.

Robbie nodded in agreement with a look of worry on his face. Morton scrawled quickly on the notepad: *How did you find out about them?*

Robbie scribbled back: *I was going to wear them onstage.*

And he held his hands out and made a funny smile. Morton had a comic image of Robbie singing atonal songs while wearing these nerdy glasses, and he realized it was exactly the sort of thing Nolan would love.

Robbie then wrote something else: *Does this have something to do with what you were going to tell me yesterday?*

Morton sighed. He wasn't quite sure how to respond. He'd already made up his mind not to get Robbie involved, but now that Robbie had made this discovery on his own, Morton knew he couldn't possibly lie to him outright.

He didn't believe that was any way to treat a friend.

A few minutes later Mr. Noble finished his lecture and told them to work in pairs and draw a full-color diagram of a carnivorous plant, being sure to label all the parts that he'd written on the board. Fortunately this meant that everybody started talking, and Morton and Robbie were able to continue their conversation without attracting Mr. Noble's attention.

"So?" Robbie prompted. "Do you have any idea what's going on?"

Morton decided to tell Robbie everything and let him decide what to do with the knowledge. He filled him in on the bathroom encounter with Derek, and the Bat Eyes in his bedroom, and all the details he could remember from King's diary.

"So you think somebody else is doing magic?" Robbie asked.

"It's starting to look that way, and with King's library of magic books out there somewhere, it's hardly surprising."

"At least Melissa knows Jake. That's one piece of luck."

"Yeah, but she's not very hopeful that he'll want to help her."

Robbie made a little chuckling noise. "Oh, he'll want to help her. Don't worry about that."

Morton was surprised by Robbie's response.

"What makes you so sure?" he asked. "I mean, he hardly knows her. And I don't think he likes her much. I've noticed he gets very nervous around her."

Robbie made a funny smile and winked at Morton. "You're kidding, right?" he said.

Morton didn't think he was kidding about anything and stared back at Robbie with a blank expression.

Robbie frowned. "Look, don't worry about it. She'll get Jake to find out. She can just — be nice to him."

"Nice!" Morton exclaimed. "You have met my sister, right? I mean, being nice is not exactly her specialty."

Robbie puffed his cheeks in frustration. "Well, she doesn't really even have to be nice. She just sort of needs to smile at him and do that thing that girls do when they want boys to do something for them."

"*Thing?*" Morton said. "What thing?"

For some reason Robbie started to look very uncomfortable. "It's sort of like . . . Well, they kind of . . . Look, I don't know how they do it, but they do it all the time."

"Do what?" Morton said, starting to feel exasperated.

"The *thing!*" Robbie replied, sounding equally frustrated. "You know, they just sort of get you to do stuff for them even when you don't want to. Like one time, I said I was going to sell a set of collectible cat's-eye marbles to this girl in seventh grade and she made me give them to her for free."

"She did?" Morton exclaimed, utterly shocked by this revelation. "How did she do that?"

"She just sort of . . ." Robbie's face went suddenly very red and he trailed off. "Look, I can't explain it," he said under his breath. "You just have to trust me on this one."

Morton scratched his cheek. "So, it's a bit like magic, then, this *thing*?"

"Yes, I guess it is," Robbie said.

"And you think Melissa knows how to do it?"

"Like I said, all girls can do it."

Morton lapsed into silence for a moment, trying to make sense of what Robbie was telling him, but then thought of another question.

"What if Jake found out Melissa was doing the *thing* to him? Wouldn't he get angry?"

"No!" Robbie said, now clutching his head. "Even when boys know girls are doing it to them, they don't care. And Melissa's very pretty, so she'll be really good at it."

Morton almost fell off his stool at these words. Were his ears deceiving him? He'd heard people say that Melissa was pretty before. Mum, of course, had always told her how beautiful she was, and the boys who used to hang around outside their old house in the city used to say nice things about her. But Morton had never taken it seriously. Melissa was just sort of skinny with a long, beaky nose and a funny pointy chin.

"Did you just say Melissa was pretty?" he asked.

Robbie squirmed in his seat and glanced away. "Yeah, kind of," he said in an overly casual voice.

"Pretty, like the way Julie Bashford is pretty?" Morton said.

Robbie shot Morton a strange look. "Julie's not pretty," he said in a stiff tone of voice that Morton had never heard him use before.

Morton scratched his head. "She's not?"

"No! She looks like an albino turtle."

"She does not look like an albino turtle!" Morton blurted out. Unfortunately at that very moment Mr. Noble was walking by, and he stopped at Morton's desk and gave him a reprimanding stare.

"Morton, not only did you arrive late but you've obviously been spending more time talking than working. Please be so kind as to visit me after class to receive extra homework," he said, and then returned to the front of the class.

Morton groaned inwardly and returned his attention to the diagram of a Venus flytrap he was supposed to be drawing. He and Robbie didn't speak again for the rest of the class, which Morton was actually relieved about. Carnivorous plants, it seemed, were far simpler to understand than people.

As soon as Mr. Noble's class was over, Robbie told Morton that he had a quick meeting with Nolan in the music room and asked Morton to come and meet him there as soon as Mr. Noble let him go.

Morton said he would and wandered to the front of the class to speak with his teacher. Mr. Noble didn't seem to be in any hurry and made him wait a long time before he finally gave him a five-hundred-word essay on the evolutionary origins of carnivorous plants.

"Five hundred words!" Morton gasped. "But that's like a tenth-grade assignment."

Mr. Noble pulled open the top drawer of his desk and removed the lunch box that Morton had seen earlier while wearing the X-ray Specs. "It's not *like* a tenth-grade assignment; it *is* a tenth-grade assignment. Hand it in to me this time next week," he said.

Morton stood for a moment longer, not quite sure what to say, but Mr. Noble simply opened up his lunch box and began placing its contents on his desk. Morton presumed he'd been dismissed and shuffled out of the room and went in search of Robbie. As he ventured up the stairs he lamented the fact that the last thing he needed right now was extra homework, but then, he could hardly complain. He *had* been talking in class. And at least the essay was a subject he was interested in.

When Morton arrived at the music room the door was closed, so he sat on the bench across the hall to wait. The bench just happened to be directly opposite Nolan's locker, which stood out from all of the others because it was papered from top to bottom with pictures and magazine cutouts of famous musicians.

As Morton examined the images on the locker, which included everything from classical composers to modern pop singers, he noticed something colorful poking out from the bottom. It was the corner of a glossy page with very familiar lettering. Curious, he wandered over to get a closer look and confirmed his suspicion that it was an issue of *Scare Scape*. Morton thought this was very strange. As far as he knew, Nolan had no interest in anything that wasn't strictly to do with music, so why would he have an issue of *Scare Scape*?

A nervous twinge ran through Morton's body. He hadn't forgotten that when all the cats had gone missing, Nolan hadn't believed the official explanation. He distinctly remembered him saying that he'd heard about the Zombie Twin sightings and even went so far as to say he thought something "bigger" was going on. Since then Morton had presumed that Nolan had lost interest in the subject, but now he was beginning to wonder if he'd been wrong about that.

Morton looked again at the corner of the comic protruding from the bottom of the locker. Only the lettering for the title was visible, and it wasn't quite possible to read the issue number. He crouched down and tugged gently on the edge. If he could inch it out a little farther . . . Quite suddenly the whole comic slipped right through the gap beneath the door and Morton found himself holding the tattered issue in his hands. At that very moment, the door to the music room burst open and Morton jumped to his feet, still holding the comic. Julie appeared in the doorway, but instead of coming out into the hall she stood there with her back to him.

"Give me one good reason why I shouldn't walk out this door and straight back to Scorch Harrison's band?" she barked angrily.

Nolan's tired voice rang out from inside the room. "I will, if you'll calm down," he said.

Julie turned, as if she intended to ignore Nolan's request, but as she did so she spotted Morton staring directly at her and stopped in her tracks. She glanced down at the comic in his hand and then back up to his face. He felt a bead of sweat break out on his forehead, but fortunately she didn't seem the least interested in the comic or where it had come from. "What are *you* doing here?" she said gruffly.

"I . . . ," Morton began, but Julie apparently wasn't interested in his answer either, because she turned around again and stomped back into the room, slamming the door behind her.

Morton breathed a small sigh of relief and was about to squat down to slip the comic back into Nolan's locker when his eyes fell on the cover for the first time. This was a special collector's edition of *Scare Scape*, called King's Gold. The cover showed a man looking up at a tall crane that had just lifted a giant coffin from an equally giant hole in the lawn of an old stately home. Morton knew the image all too well. It was from the sequel to the original Wargle Snarf story. Could it be a mere coincidence that Nolan had a reprint of that particular story?

Morton glanced quickly at the inside cover. There was a full-page illustration of what looked like a pirate's treasure chest, but instead of gold and jewels, the chest was full of bones, maggots, and monsters. A short introduction was written beneath:

Dare to lift the lid on this chest of ill-begotten plunder and you will find pestilence on every page, sin in every shadow, and death in every deed, for here are gathered a host of the darkest tales ever scribed by human hands. The grim, the ghastly, and the wantonly gory await you inside. But be warned, you will find no gleaming gems of wisdom, no silver threads of hope or gilded acts of kindness beyond this point. For this is not the gold of riches and wealth, but King's Gold, a treasury of pure, raw terror.

He then turned to the Snarf story closer to the back, just to be sure it was the same one. It was. The story was called "Return to the Wild Place" and followed the plight of a scientist who discovered a Snarf corpse and became infected by its poison-tipped barbs, even though the creature had been dead for over a hundred years.

One thing Morton distinctly remembered about this story was that it actually listed all the ingredients for the only spell that could apparently reverse a Snarf transformation forever. Another thing he remembered was that the spell involved bat's blood and, rather coincidentally, a blank page from The Book of Parchments that King had mentioned in his diary.

Morton gazed at the cover for a moment longer and then suddenly realized that he'd better put the comic back where he'd found it.

He was about to slide it back into the locker when the music room door burst open again. Morton jumped to his feet and this time he managed to stuff the comic up the front of his shirt before anyone emerged, which was just as well because Nolan was the first to step into the hall. He had dark circles under his eyes, as if he hadn't slept in days, and seemed to lack his usual upbeat energy. Robbie and the twins followed him out and they too seemed a little perturbed. Only Julie appeared to be in good spirits. She swaggered out of the room wearing a smug smile.

"Melvin, you're *still* here?" she said.

Morton felt his face flush. "It's Morton," he said firmly.

Julie made a dismissive sniffing noise. " 'Morton'? What kind of name is that anyway? Is that even a real name?"

"It's a lot more real than 'Scorch,' " Morton said, clenching his teeth.

"Yeah, well, when you're the most talented songwriter in Dimvale, you can have any kind of name you like," Julie replied.

Nolan, who had meanwhile opened his locker and retrieved several sheets of music, flinched visibly at this comment, but Julie didn't seem concerned. She just chewed nonchalantly on her gum.

Robbie made a nodding gesture to Morton and, even though break time was almost over, they headed out to the school yard to get some air.

"Why is Julie so angry at Nolan?" Morton asked.

"Oh, she's all full of herself because Scorch offered her a spot in his band. She wants to be the lead singer now."

"What? But *you're* the lead singer."

"I know. It's ridiculous. I mean whoever heard of a drummer who sings lead vocals? That's so eighties."

"So what happened?" Morton asked.

Robbie shook his head and frowned. "Nolan said he'd let her try singing lead on one of his new songs. He didn't seem to care much one way or another. He hasn't been himself these last few days. To be honest, I think he's really upset about his grandma."

By now they had arrived in the school yard and were standing in their usual corner, beside the gate to the sports field. Morton stood there awkwardly fumbling with the comic that was still tucked up his shirt.

"Is something wrong?" Robbie said, noticing Morton's unusual mood.

Morton thought again about Julie's words and wondered if he shouldn't just come out and tell Robbie what she'd said before. But now hardly seemed like the best time to discuss something so trivial.

"No, it's nothing," Morton lied. "I was just thinking about Derek's laser."

"Speaking of Derek," Robbie said in a hushed tone, "check that out."

Morton followed Robbie's gaze to a large circle of kids on the far side of the school yard.

"Looks normal to me," Morton said.

"No, it's not normal," Robbie said. "Look who's in the center."

Robbie led them closer and Morton saw that the circle of kids was clustered around Derek, who was talking in an animated fashion, as if he were giving some kind of lecture. Morton had to admit this did look a bit unusual, but not so unusual that it warranted the look of panic on Robbie's face.

"So Derek's a popular kid," Morton said.

"But he's *not* a popular kid," Robbie shot back. "And look who's in the group: Barry Flynn, Timothy Clarke, even Simon Bean. Last time I checked, they all hated Derek. Now it looks like they worship him."

The more Morton examined the scene, the more he realized that Robbie might have a point.

"Maybe we should go investigate," he suggested, and they walked briskly over to the gathering. Curiously, just before they got there, Derek saw them coming and immediately stopped talking. The kids all turned to see them and then, as if on cue, the whole crowd dispersed. Derek, however, stood his ground and scowled.

"Come to break more of my toys, have you?" he said.

"Of course not!" Morton replied, annoyed by the attitude. "We just came over to, uh, to see what the fuss was about."

"You'll be the last to know," Derek said, and then walked off and joined another group of kids not too far away.

"Tell me he's not up to something," Robbie said.

"You may be right," Morton agreed, watching the second group of students cluster around Derek. "But up to what, exactly?"

Robbie sighed. "Nothing good. And just when we'd finally gotten everything back to normal too."

Morton made a slight nod. He wanted to say that he didn't think things had ever truly gone back to normal; that, in fact, he was pretty sure that whatever was going on had started long before they moved to Dimvale, and maybe even long before there was a Dimvale, but that was just a wild theory for which he had no proof. But something told him that very soon he would have proof, and that when he did, the idea of a normal life might be lost to them forever.

CHAPTER 9

THE DRAWN CURTAIN

Morton arrived home from school later that day to find the house eerily quiet. Usually at this time there was some activity in the kitchen — either Dad would be cooking frantically, Melissa and Wendy would be gossiping about the day's events, or James would have all his books sprawled on the table while he did his homework. In fact, it wasn't uncommon to have all three of these things happening at once.

Morton slipped off his shoes and padded into the living room. "Hello?" he called. "Anyone home?"

There was no answer, so he bounded up the stairs and was about to call again when he heard voices coming from Melissa's room.

"I thought we promised we were never going to look at that book again," came the first agitated voice, which Morton recognized at once as Wendy's.

"I know, but that was then and this is now," Melissa replied in a controlled but irate tone.

"So? It was dangerous then and it's dangerous now."

"Look, aside from the rats, that Bat Eye thing was following me, and some kid was floating on the bathroom ceiling at Morton's school. Who knows what might happen next?"

"I understand," Wendy said, her voice growing softer, which somehow made it sound even angrier. "And I'm not saying what you did was wrong, just that we should have all talked about it first. We have to be honest."

"Don't lecture *me* about honesty!" Melissa snapped.

"What's that supposed to mean?" Wendy retorted.

"Look, it's easy for you to stand there and suggest we arrange a committee meeting every time somebody wants to open a box of cookies," Melissa hissed back. "But if things go back to the way they were, it won't be *your* brother chomping his way through the streets like a meat-eating Weedwacker."

"He might not be my brother, but he is my b —" Wendy's voice stammered to a sudden stop.

"Well, go on, finish your sentence," Melissa said in a goading voice. "You were going to say, 'James is my boyfriend.'"

Wendy gasped in outrage. "I was not! He's far too young to be my boyfriend. I was going to say he's my friend."

"Nice try, but *friend* doesn't start with a *b*."

"*Best* friend. Aside from you, that is," Wendy corrected, although even to Morton's ears she didn't sound very convincing.

"Well, I'd like to believe you, but since you've been lying to me for days now, I honestly don't think I can."

"Lying? I haven't been lying."

"Oh no?" Melissa said, now forgetting to keep her voice down. "Are you sure? Because you and James have been play-ing a lot of tennis recently, which is pretty weird considering that the tennis courts closed down for the season at the end of October."

"Look, I . . . It's not . . ." Wendy floundered.

The room went completely silent, and Morton decided he'd better sneak back downstairs before he was discovered, but he was too late. Melissa's bedroom door burst open at that very instant and a flushed, teary-eyed Wendy thundered out onto the landing. She spotted Morton at once, and her already miserable face twisted into an even more uncomfortable expression.

Morton had never before wanted so badly to be invisible.

Wendy paused for the briefest of moments and then shot down the stairs, brushing past him without a word. Melissa rushed to the doorway and looked like she was about to call after her, but she saw Morton and her jaw dropped in shock and outrage.

"You . . ." she began, but she seemed incapable of finding any more words and simply retreated into her room and slammed the door.

Morton stood exactly where he was for what felt like a very long time, unsure what he was supposed to do now. He really hadn't intended to eavesdrop on their conversation, but then again, he hadn't exactly torn himself away either. He also didn't quite understand what he'd heard. Could it be true that James and Wendy were actually dating? Surely James would have said something. . . .

Eventually he sauntered down the stairs and ambled around the kitchen, feeling useless and somewhat ashamed of himself, until James arrived home a few minutes later.

"Where is everybody?" he asked.

"Uh, Melissa's in her room," Morton said. "Not sure about Dad."

James accepted this news with a shrug and started setting out his homework on the kitchen table.

"Uh, you're late," Morton said, deciding not to mention the argument. "Anything, uh, weird happen?"

James sat down at the table and turned to face Morton. "I don't know," he said. "Probably not."

Morton found this to be a very strange answer. "What does that mean?" he prodded.

Instead of answering the question, James asked Morton another. "Have you seen Brad recently?" he said.

Morton suddenly remembered their previous encounter and slapped his head. "Oh, I completely forgot! I did see him, and I was supposed to tell you he was looking for you. I guess he found you, then?"

"Kind of," James said. "He left this note in my locker."

James produced a crumpled piece of lined paper from his pocket and handed it to Morton. It had a brief note in very splotchy, untidy handwriting, which read:

Meet me at the pARK (u know where) AFteR school OR u will Be SORRY. I Know All ABOut ColBy's cAT.

SIGneD: BRAD

PS u CAn BRing yOR BRuther. But not thAt DORK RoBBie.

"Colby's cat?" Morton said. "That's weird. Do you think he's figured out what happened to all the cats and knows we were involved?"

"That's what I thought at first, but then I started asking around, and it turns out there's nobody in school named Colby. So I decided I'd better go meet with him and find out what he meant."

"What!" Morton shrieked, utterly shocked by the calm nature of James's revelation. "You actually did what he asked?"

"I wanted to get to the bottom of it," James said with a shrug. "Anyway, he didn't even show up. I waited for half an hour and finally decided it was a prank."

"Oh, so that's it," Morton said, suddenly angry. "He's playing mind games with you. Robbie always said he used to enjoy finding new ways to bully him, but I never thought he'd be this bad. You should give that letter to Finch."

"Maybe," James said, seemingly unruffled by the whole affair. "So, what about you? Anything interesting happen to you today?"

Morton was about to say no, but then remembered the X-ray Specs, which he still had tucked in his sweatshirt pocket. "Oh, yeah," he said, pulling the glasses out and handing them to James. "Robbie found these."

At that moment Melissa stormed into the room, her face angry and hard.

"Let me guess," she said in a sardonic tone. "Flesh-Eating Spectacles. You put them on and they eat your brains out."

James gave her a quizzical look. "What's wrong with you? Snarf ate your homework?"

"No, stole my best friend actually," Melissa shot back snidely.

James was clearly confused by this comment, but before

he could respond Morton pressed the glasses into his hands, hoping to distract him.

"Really, you should try them on," he said.

James paused a moment and then put them over his eyes. His mouth opened in astonishment. "Wow! These are actually cool," he said, suddenly jumping to his feet and looking all around the kitchen. "I can see everything! I can see what's in the cupboards. I can even see through the walls." James walked out into the dining room and stared up at the ceiling. "Look I can see my bedroom, and . . ." He paused.

"And what?" Melissa said.

James walked back into the kitchen and stared directly at Melissa's stomach. "And I can see that you stopped off at the bakery on the way home and bought one of those extra-large chocolate chip cookies. Wow! You must have been hungry. You practically swallowed it whole."

"Oh, grow up!" Melissa said, snatching the glasses from his face. "This is serious. That's two completely random acts of magic in two days."

"Actually, I don't think it's random," Morton said. "Both the glasses and the laser are things you can buy from the back pages of *Scare Scape*. So maybe somebody just did one spell, or made one wish, and that's affecting all the toys."

"It's possible," James said. "But I still can't see why anyone would want to make *all* that junk from the back pages real. Anyway, at this point, it's all just guesswork. What we really need to do is find out for sure who bought King's library." At this James turned to Melissa. "How did it go with Jake?" he asked.

"I'm working on it," she replied.

"Meaning you haven't found out anything?"

"Rome wasn't built in a day, you know," Melissa said, rolling her eyes.

"Yes, but you're not building Rome; you're asking Jake for a simple favor. How hard can it be?"

"If it's so easy, why don't you just ask him yourself?" Melissa retorted, her anger bubbling to the surface again. "In fact, why don't you invite him to play tennis with you?"

This comment clearly hit home, and James's whole body went suddenly very still. Morton tried to think fast and come up with a way to defuse the inevitable and monumental argument, but thankfully didn't need to. Dad breezed through the door at that very moment, carrying a large basket bundled in his arms and wearing an excited smile.

"There you are," he said. "You'll never guess what, but I just found the remnants of a vegetable patch in the back garden. Just look at what I dug up."

Morton peered into the basket, which was filled with a dozen rather stunted and disfigured vegetables.

"Uh, they're kind of lumpy," he said skeptically.

"Ah, they're real vegetables," Dad said proudly. "Not those factory-farmed, over-bloated, cosmetically altered, gene-modified things you get in the supermarket."

"That's nice, Dad," James said. "But what are you going to do with them?"

"I'm going to make a fresh vegetable stew," Dad replied, and he went straight to the sink and started scrubbing.

Melissa, who had been glowering at James, turned toward the door. "We'll finish this later," she said, and she headed back up to her room.

Aside from the fact that Dad's stew, when it finally materialized, appeared to contain more grit and gravel than the driveway, the rest of the evening passed without incident, or even argument, and even after Dad left for work, Melissa and James kept their distance from each other. Morton dared to hope that maybe they'd both decided to steer clear of the whole subject, but unfortunately that wasn't the case. Sometime after he'd gone to bed, he heard raised voices coming from James's room. He couldn't hear what they were saying, and he had no intention of making the same mistake twice and going to listen, but it was clear that this was one of the worst arguments James and Melissa had ever had. He lay awake for a long time, wondering if they would ever truly be friends.

Despite Melissa's argument with James and her apparent reluctance to spend time with Jake, on Saturday morning she seemed to have a complete change of heart. She appeared soon after breakfast wearing one of the few leftover outfits from her closet, and Morton overheard her talking to Jake on the phone. She laughed and joked and, if Morton hadn't known otherwise, he would have sworn she was talking to one of her oldest and closest friends. Shortly after the call, she announced to Dad that she would be gone all day and not to expect her home until early evening.

Not long after that, to Morton's surprise, Wendy rang the doorbell. Morton greeted her and was about to explain that Melissa had gone out, when James ran to the door wearing his coat and scarf, and without any explanation the two of them left together. For some reason this left Morton feeling unusually lonely, and even though Dad was home, working away in his study, the house felt much bigger and emptier than Morton remembered it ever feeling before.

After about two cups of hot chocolate and a lot of loafing around, Morton finally faced the fact that he was going· to have to do the rather sizable homework assignment Mr. Noble had given him, although he knew it was not going to be easy. Even though he was genuinely fascinated by carnivorous plants, his mind was in far too much turmoil to settle down to one thing. In fact, the way he looked at it, the whole of Dimvale was in too much turmoil, and he wondered how James and Wendy could simply go off and have fun when mysterious magic was spreading like measles through the streets. At least Melissa was trying to help solve the problem.

Morton tried to push such thoughts out of his mind, settling down at the small desk in his bedroom and dragging out his schoolbooks. As he did so the tattered edition of King's Gold that he'd found in Nolan's locker slid to the floor. He'd stuffed it in his bag and completely forgotten about it. He bent down to retrieve it and discovered a small strip of yellow cardboard slipped in between the comic's pages. He plucked it out and saw it was a bookmark. On one side were printed the words:

Sydenham Crooks. Collectible Books. Odd, rare, and curious reading for those of odd, rare, and curious breeding.

Morton presumed this was the bookstore where Nolan had bought the comic. Something about it rang a bell, though

Morton couldn't quite understand why. He definitely had never been there. In fact, he hadn't been to any comic shops in Dimvale because he hadn't had the time to seek any out.

He began leafing through the comic absently, and when he reached the back, he noticed that one of the pages had been torn out. At the sight of this his stomach lurched, and not just because someone had abused a valuable collector's edition. He knew exactly what had been on the torn-out page. Just to be certain, he quickly retrieved his own, mint-condition copy of King's Gold from his shelves and flipped to the same spot. Sure enough, he was right. Both sides of the page that had been torn from Nolan's comic were plastered with ads for toys, tricks, trinkets, and other whimsical items. Among them, of course, were X-ray Specs and the Antigravity Laser Cannon.

Morton started to feel queasy. Surely this was too much of a coincidence? A couple of weeks earlier Nolan wouldn't have even laid his eyes on a *Scare Scape* comic, and now he not only owned a fairly valuable collector's edition, but he'd also torn out a page featuring items that in the last few days had been enchanted by some unknown spell.

Morton now felt certain that he was missing something and he looked again at the bookmark. *Sydenham Crooks. Collectible Books.* It had already occurred to him that if anyone's books could ever have been described as collectible, it would have been John King's. It was entirely possible that this store could have ended up with some of his collection, but that wasn't the clue his mind was grasping for. It was something else. . . .

It suddenly hit him like a blast of cold air, and chills ran through his entire body.

Morton pushed his chair away from his desk, spilling his pencils across the floor, and dashed to the attic stairs. He bounded up the steps three at a time and burst through the door and headed directly to the small wooden box he'd previously tripped on, throwing it open and quickly locating the photo of the young John King standing in front of the store. He turned to read the writing on the back, just to be sure he was remembering it correctly. He was. The words clearly said *My brother Syd and me, age 14.* And the sign on the front of the store read *Crooks Collectible Books.*

Sydenham Crooks. It was a very unusual name. Was it possible that this was the person in the photo, the person King called his brother? If so, was it then also possible that he would know something about what was happening in Dimvale?

Morton knew that he had to find out, and he dropped the photo back into the box and practically flew down the stairs.

"I'm going out!" he called to Dad as he raced past his study.

"What? Where?" Dad began, looking up from his papers, but Morton didn't linger to explain himself and continued out of the house and down to the shed where they now stored all the bikes. Morton's scooter was there too, gleaming like new, and he realized he hadn't even touched it since they'd moved in. At one time he'd used it every day on his paper route, which he loved, and when they first moved to Dimvale he had fully intended to get another paper route as soon as he could as a way to get to know the people in his neighborhood. But it hadn't worked out like that at all. He'd been so wrapped up in strange magical events that he hadn't had time to do anything normal.

This had to change, he thought. They couldn't hope to settle in to a new life in Dimvale while Two-Headed Mutant Rodents were breeding in the sewers and Bat Eyes were following them around. No. They had to put an end to these mysterious events once and for all, and he hoped more than anything that this Sydenham Crooks might be able to help them achieve that goal.

It took him a little longer to get downtown than he'd hoped, mostly because he still wasn't completely familiar with Dimvale, but eventually he ended up on Main Street and quickly located Wardle Lane, which was the address printed on the back of the bookmark.

The street turned out to be a very narrow lane with only a few small neglected-looking stores.

Morton dismounted his scooter and walked slowly along until he came to a store with a peeling old wooden door and a large cracked window. Despite the decrepit facade, the sign itself looked new and appeared to be hand painted in flowing gold letters. It read:

SYDENHAM CROOKS, COLLECTIBLE BOOKS

Morton peered in at the display and was surprised to see only three books propped up on a makeshift shelf. The books were nautical journals of some kind and they were covered in fine gray dust. When he'd seen the bookmark he'd imagined a large, brightly lit store, with a cozy corner that sold fresh-baked muffins and had a constant flow of well-dressed customers. He couldn't have been more wrong.

To his own surprise, Morton started to feel afraid. There was something unnerving about the isolation of this store, the way the window was almost empty, and the way the sign, though freshly painted, seemed somehow to lean to one side. And then Morton suddenly realized that he'd left the house without telling anyone where he was. If something happened to him . . .

Morton shook himself. He knew better than to let his imagination run away with him. He had no reason to fear going into a bookstore in broad daylight, although now that he was here he wasn't sure exactly what he was supposed to do.

He decided to play it by ear and pushed through the door without further delay. A small brass bell jingled above his head and the thick, damp aroma of mildew and old coffee wafted over his face. Despite the sparse display in the window, the store itself was crammed to bursting with books. It was also much larger than it looked from the outside, with several separate rooms linked together, all with very tall ceilings. Each room was lined with high, densely packed shelves that were sagging under the immense weight of the books upon them. Not only that, but many of the books seemed to have tumbled like falling rocks into sloped mounds at the foot of each stack of shelves, leaving a maze of narrow pathways winding through the store.

Morton turned to close the door. The bell over the door jingled a second time, and a short, stocky man appeared from behind a heavy velvet curtain at the end of a narrow alcove.

Morton couldn't help noticing that the curtain, which was a lush royal green and hanging from brightly polished brass rings, looked out of place in this dim, dusty store. Morton also noticed that mounted directly above the curtain was a clock, which obviously wasn't working because both hands were pointed directly up at the number twelve, and it was long past lunchtime.

The man who had emerged from behind the curtain was wearing a loose-fitting cotton suit and a slightly crooked red bow tie. He was carrying a large leather book, which he snapped shut the moment he saw Morton. Morton examined him closely, trying to decide if he in any way resembled the teenager in the photo he'd found. There was a certain roundness to the man's face that vaguely resembled that of the boy in the picture, but aside from that, it was difficult to say.

"Yes?" the man said, carefully pulling the curtain closed behind him, giving Morton a brief glimpse of a small dark room beyond.

"Uh, do you have any comics?" Morton said, suddenly wishing he'd thought more carefully about what he intended to say.

The man sniffed disapprovingly and adjusted a paper note pinned to the curtain that read *Staff Only Beyond This Point.*

"This is a specialty bookstore," the man said, staring down at him as if he were a beetle on the floor. "We don't sell comics or children's picture books."

Morton felt his lips go dry and for a moment was lost for words. He'd hoped to bring the conversation around to King casually, but if this store didn't sell comics, that might be difficult.

"Are you sure?" he persisted. "A friend of mine said he bought an old *Scare Scape* comic here. You know, they're famous around here because John King was one of the artists and he used to live in Dimvale."

The man, who Morton now presumed had to be Sydenham Crooks, froze on the spot. His cloudy gray eyes grew wide and his breath seemed to stifle in his throat. For a fleeting moment Morton imagined a deep anger swelling inside him. But then the moment passed and Crooks turned his back on Morton and climbed a tall stepladder to arrange books in a high display cabinet.

"I don't know anything about a John King, or anybody else who draws comics for that matter," he said, without even looking at Morton. "As I already told you, we don't sell children's books here."

Morton was as shocked by the answer as he was by Crooks's brusque manner. He had been certain that this person had to be King's brother. What were the chances that someone with the same name just happened to have opened a bookstore in Dimvale? Very slim, to say the least, Morton thought, but then, why would he lie?

"Was there something else?" Crooks snapped rudely, now turning to stare at Morton.

Morton felt a lump in his throat. "Oh, uh, I'll just look around, if that's okay," he croaked, not sure what else to say or do.

Crooks merely shrugged and continued arranging books.

Morton felt a great sense of relief the moment the man's eyes were no longer on him, and he ventured deeper into the store, partly to avoid his unsettling gaze, and partly to give himself time to think.

A curious thought entered Morton's head. If Crooks didn't sell comics, then why did Nolan have one of his bookmarks? He wondered if Crooks, whether or not he was King's brother, might have ended up with part of King's lost collection of books. If so, was it possible that Nolan had stumbled on a book and that he was somehow involved in the mysterious happenings at school?

Morton began to scan the shelves carefully in search of anything that might have once been part of King's collection. The closest he could find to books of magic was a New Age section, which was mostly books on silly stuff like how to interpret your dreams or how to make friends by drinking the right combination of herbal teas. There was nothing at all serious, or even very old, which Morton found odd, because most of the other sections had piles of older books, and some sections even had additional glass-fronted cases to protect the rarest, most valuable books.

Morton scoured the rest of the store as best he could but soon realized that aside from a few local history books there was very little here that might have belonged to King's collection. He did, however, notice a very large section of classical sheet music, which, he realized, would be a much more likely explanation for Nolan's visit to the store than anything to do with dark magic.

Morton couldn't help but feel disappointed and was just deciding to leave, when Crooks descended from his ladder with a pile of books in his arms and made his way down the narrow alcove to slip behind the green curtain. Once again, Crooks took great pains to adjust the curtain behind him, as if wishing to conceal what lay beyond, and Morton had a sudden thought. He knew that some antique book (and comic) sellers kept their most valuable items tucked away for viewing only by appointment. Was it possible that Crooks had just such a collection?

Morton peered around the corner and listened for sounds of Crooks moving beyond the curtain, but it was strangely silent. He ventured down the alcove to get closer and listened again. Still nothing. Morton then stepped right up to the curtain and pulled it aside ever so slightly, but what he saw was so unexpected it almost made him stumble backward in surprise.

There behind the curtain was a smooth, solid wall — which made no sense because he was sure he'd seen Crooks vanish through there moments before. What was even stranger was the fact that the wall itself had an almost completely lifelike painting of a green curtain identical in every detail to the real one that hung in front of it, right down to the *Staff Only* sign.

He was so shocked that he simply stood there, trying to make sense of what he was witnessing, and was still standing there when something sharp and bony dug into his shoulder, startling him out of his trance. He turned to see Crooks leering down at him. Somehow, impossibly, he'd snuck up behind him, trapping him at the end of the alcove.

"If you can't read, then why come into a bookstore?" he said, pointing at the sign with a malevolent grin.

Morton stared up at Crooks and had the sudden feeling that there was something decidedly unnatural about him. His skin seemed too gray and the proportions of his face were somehow wrong, and even his teeth, which were yellowed and coffee-stained, looked false, as if they were too large and didn't fit properly in his head.

But Morton didn't have time to dwell on these strange impressions. Crooks dug his fingers even deeper into his shoulder, causing him to yelp with pain.

"Don't think I don't know who you are," he hissed, leaning in closer to Morton's face, his dry, musty breath wafting unwanted into his nostrils. "You're the thief! Came back to steal more books, did you?"

"I . . . I haven't stolen anything!" Morton choked, attempting to pull free of Crooks's bony grip, but Crooks squeezed tighter and began to shake him violently.

"You think I'm a fool? Do you? Think you can steal from me twice and get away with it?" he shrieked.

"N-n-no!" Morton stammered. "I've never been here before, honest."

"A thief and a liar, then!" Crooks said, and to Morton's absolute horror he saw that Crooks was holding a rope in his free hand and realized he intended to tie him up.

At that moment something clicked inside Morton's head and with a sudden burst of enraged strength he twisted his body around so that Crooks lost his grip on his shoulder. He then dropped to the floor and dove at Crooks's legs. Crooks stumbled forward and careened into an immense pile of paperback books, which avalanched over him, and he crumpled to his knees under the sheer weight.

Morton flew out of the alcove, yanked open the door, then leaped onto his scooter and tore down the street as fast as his legs would propel him. In the distance he heard Crooks calling out for him to stop, but he didn't look back. He'd already seen more of Sydenham Crooks than he cared to, and as he raced away he felt that he would be happy if he never again laid eyes on him as long as he lived.

CHAPTER 10

TWO-HEADED TROUBLE

Morton had never been so relieved as he was twenty minutes later when he rounded his scooter onto Hemlock Hill and saw the conical turret that had once been John King's study peeking above the trees.

His whole body was still trembling, and his brain was struggling to process what he'd just seen and learned. Obviously somebody had been stealing from Sydenham Crooks, and Morton had a very strong suspicion that it was Nolan. But there was something more happening — something about that secret door. . . .

Morton caught sight of James and Dad sitting on the porch deep in conversation, and he dismounted his scooter and walked slowly toward them, giving himself a little extra time to steady his breathing.

Both Dad and James appeared to be very serious. James had a particularly deep frown, and Morton wondered if something terrible had happened, but the moment they saw him they looked up and smiled broadly.

"Morton, we were just talking about you," Dad said.

Morton propped up his scooter and walked over to join them. "You were?" he said. "You looked very serious."

Quite unexpectedly Dad let out a peal of laughter. "Yes, yes, I have no doubt we did," he said. "It's not exactly easy trying to solve the riddle of Morton's mind."

Morton thought this was a very odd thing to say and hoped that Dad would explain himself, but he quickly changed the subject.

"By the way, I have some bad news. I have to rush in to the observatory this weekend. I know I don't usually go in on weekends, but we're watching a supernova and we want to get regular luminosity charts, obviously. I drew the short straw for both tonight and tomorrow, I'm afraid."

"That's okay," Morton said as he always did when the subject of Dad working nights came up, even though he secretly always felt a lot happier when Dad was home.

"Yes, but the really bad news," Dad continued, "is that I don't have time to cook, so I'm afraid I'll have to order pizza for supper."

"Pizza!" James and Morton exclaimed excitedly.

Dad laughed and ruffled both James's and Morton's hair. "Well, you might try to sound a little disappointed," he said, getting to his feet. "Come on, then. You can choose the toppings."

They all stood up and were about to go into the mudroom, when a loud grating metal sound rattled from the direction of the street. They stopped and turned to see Jake's old yellow car pull up at the bottom of the driveway. Jake and Melissa climbed out.

"Hello, what's all this, then?" Dad said. "A boy on the scene?"

"Oh, he's just a friend," James said. "Don't worry, there's

nothing —" James spluttered to a stop because at that exact moment Melissa put her arms on Jake's shoulders and kissed him squarely on the lips.

Dad turned suddenly and began ushering James and Morton into the kitchen. "Oops! I don't think we were supposed to see that," he said.

James, however, was frozen to the spot, staring with his jaw open wide. "I can't believe it," he said. "She told us —"

James didn't have time to finish because Dad leaned over from the doorway and literally yanked him into the house.

"James!" he said very firmly. "I want you to promise not to tease her about this. Heaven knows she's had a hard enough time settling into Dimvale as it is."

"Yes, but, Dad —" James began, but Dad cut him off.

"I don't want to hear it," he said. "I want you to promise you won't tease her."

James finally managed to close his jaw and he mumbled something that sounded like a promise just before Melissa bustled into the kitchen humming happily to herself.

Morton, James, and Dad stood in a mute row, staring at her. She gave them a broad smile and continued humming as she breezed through the kitchen and up to her room.

Dad looked at his two sons. "Was she humming?" he said.

James and Morton nodded, and Dad made the tiniest smile.

Later, when they sat down to eat pizza, Morton wondered if Melissa was just pretending to be happy, but her buoyant mood continued through supper and she didn't bicker with James at all. She even started washing the dishes without being asked.

Morton noticed that Dad was also watching her very closely, though of course he didn't say anything about Jake or her mood, and it suddenly dawned on him that Dad was remarkably good at minding his own business. This made him wonder if this wasn't the first time Dad had pretended not to notice when strange things had been happening to them. . . .

Very soon after supper, Dad gathered his papers and headed for the observatory. Morton half expected Melissa to stop what she was doing and revert to her usual stompy, grumpy self the moment Dad was out of sight, but she didn't at all. She finished the dishes without a word of complaint and then drifted up to her room, still humming tunelessly to herself.

"Well, she's obviously had an exciting day," James said. "How about you? Where did you get off to on your scooter?"

Morton had been so confounded by Melissa's behavior that only when James said this did he start thinking again about his chilling encounter with Sydenham Crooks. Of course, he had to tell James and Melissa about everything that had happened. But then even as he thought this, he realized that they might not be very happy with him for going off alone, and also, he still didn't really know what exactly had happened. He knew he was still missing some crucial piece of information.

"Oh, I uh, just went out, you know."

"Out where?" James asked with a skeptical tone.

"Uh, well, looking for used comic shops and stuff like that."

"And did you find any?" James persisted.

Morton started to feel flustered and tried to think of a way to change the subject, but as it happened, he didn't need to. At that very moment, Melissa returned from her bedroom wearing a tight skirt, high-heeled shoes, and a very glossy layer of lipstick.

James turned his nose up the moment he saw her.

"*What* are you wearing?" he said, part surprise and part revulsion.

"Clothes," Melissa said, oblivious to the insulting tone. "Most people wear them. It tends to be less embarrassing than wandering around naked."

James continued to look confused. "No, but I mean, you look like you're going somewhere."

Just as James said this they heard the distant honking of a car horn and Melissa ran to grab her purse from the coat-rack by the front door.

"I am. I'm going out driving with Jake."

A look of total panic crossed James's face. "But you spent the entire day with him!"

"So?"

James seemed genuinely upset that Melissa was leaving, which Morton found surprising. He personally hated the idea of Melissa going out and leaving the two of them home alone, but he didn't think James would have cared one way or another.

"Look, you asked me to get Jake to find out who bought King's books, so I'm doing it," Melissa said, getting cross.

"But does it have to be tonight?" James said, now almost in a pleading tone.

The car horn sounded again. Melissa glanced back toward the window. "First you say this is urgent, then you say you want me to delay it until tomorrow. Honestly, sometimes I think you're intentionally trying to drive me crazy. I'll be back by ten, okay? It's no big deal." And with that she strutted out the door and vanished into the twilight.

James watched her go and then turned back to Morton. "I'm pretty sure she doesn't really have to go out with him again tonight," he said irritably.

"Maybe she just wants to have some fun," Morton suggested.

James made a begrudging smile. "I guess you're right," he agreed. "And I don't suppose we can blame her for that. The closest thing she's had to a night out since we arrived in Dimvale was that night we spent in the backyard when the cats ate Mr. Brown."

Morton chuckled in spite of himself. Even though the memory of that night still sent shivers of dread down his spine, James always had a way of making things sound not as bad as they really were.

"Speaking of living normal lives," James said, "I think I'm going to turn in early. I really need to get some sleep."

Morton agreed and the two of them brushed their teeth and went to bed.

Unfortunately, as so often happened, even though he'd been exhausted just minutes before, the moment Morton's head hit the pillow a nervous energy seemed to spring up from the depths of his unconsciousness and his brain clicked into overdrive and he lay awake churning questions around in his head.

About an hour later, he was still lying awake, thinking, when he became aware of an odd scratching noise coming from the hallway outside. He sat bolt upright. In any normal house at any normal time Morton might have dismissed a faint noise like that as a mouse, but after the recent intrusion of the Bat Eyes, he wasn't about to make any such assumption.

He slid silently out of bed and glanced around his room, wishing for one of Melissa's swords or even Dad's trusty frying pan, but he'd left his baseball bat in Dad's study the night he'd found Melissa in the secret attic, and he could see nothing else that would be of much use as a weapon. He was going to have to take his chances unarmed.

Steeling his nerves, he gripped the white ceramic doorknob, ready to yank it shut if anything attempted to push its way in, and silently opened the door. The hallway was a patchwork of shadows, but it appeared to be empty. The sound, it seemed, was coming from the bathroom down the hall.

Morton took a deep breath, trying to force himself to remain calm, and tiptoed along to the bathroom door. He then turned the handle, inched open the door, and pushed his eye up to the crack. He saw at once what was making the noise.

There, in the gray shadows, were three truly enormous Two-Headed Mutant Rodents, one chomping into the toothpaste, another chewing the toilet paper, and the third scampering around in the bathtub, chasing a slippery bar of soap.

Morton wondered how they had managed to get in, and then answered his own question a split second later when he saw a fourth rat in the toilet bowl. He knew that even normal rats were sometimes smart enough to find their way up from the main sewer and slither around the U-bend in the toilet to get into houses. Tonight, four had found their way into his bathroom.

Morton gasped, and the rats turned their heads toward him. Their black eyes targeted his own and, as if with one mind, they let out a resonating chorus of high-pitched shrieks.

Morton slammed the door closed.

His first thought was to get Melissa, but she was still out, so instead he tore along the hall and burst into James's room without even a thought of knocking.

"James! Wake up!" he yelled, fumbling for the light switch. "It's the Rodents — they crawled in through the toilet pipe."

Morton continued to grapple along the wall until he finally found the switch and flicked it on. The bare bulb hanging from the ceiling burst into life and Morton squinted, momentarily blinded. He looked over to the bed to see a motionless lump. James could sleep through anything!

"James, will you wake up!" he said, running over to the bed and reaching for the covers, but the instant he touched them he realized something was wrong. The motionless lump was not James but a crumpled-up pile of blankets. Astonishingly, James was not there at all.

Morton became paralyzed. If James wasn't in bed, then where was he?

Squashing down a rising sense of dread, Morton dashed through the house, checking every room and calling out for James. His heart sank with the realization that the house was in fact utterly empty.

There were only two possible explanations. One was that James had left the house to do normal human things, like get a breath of air. The other was that James had left the house to do something else. Something entirely *not* human . . .

Morton bounded out through the mudroom and onto the dusty porch. He'd expected to find the yard empty and silent, but this is not what he found at all. Dark shapes writhed and hissed and crawled about in the shadows of Dad's garden. He reached up and yanked the pull cord on the porch light above him, and a dim yellow haze spilled out over the surrounding darkness, confirming his fears. The lawn was swarming with Two-Headed Mutant Rodents, thousands upon thousands of Two-Headed Mutant Rodents.

He retreated hastily into the house, slammed the door, and stood panting, unable to decide what to do next. Melissa was out there, possibly surrounded by rats, and James . . . was he out there too?

A high-pitched shriek followed by the sound of claws scraping on wood brought Morton back to the immediate problem of the rats that were already in his bathroom, and he realized that, alone or not, he would have to deal with them right away. But how?

Morton thought for a moment and then he grabbed two of Dad's biggest cooking pots and a large metal colander. He also retrieved oven mitts and quickly but carefully taped them to his hands with duct tape. Finally he pulled on Dad's oversize gardening boots, which lay like deflated inner tubes in the mudroom, and decided he was ready for action — at least, as ready as he'd ever be.

He clambered back up to the bathroom, thinking he must

look a little bit like an astronaut from an old black-and-white movie, and paused at the door to listen. The scratching and screeching sounds were louder than before, and when Morton finally dared to peer in for a second time, he realized why. There were now half a dozen Rodents gnawing away at towels, soap, toilet paper — anything that was vaguely edible. In some distant part of his brain he made a mental note that he probably should make a habit of putting the toilet seat down after all, but then he jumped bravely into the bathroom, turned on the light, and slammed the door behind him.

A dozen bristly pink noses sniffed hungrily in his direction. Morton suspected that even though the Rodents were notorious for being able to eat anything, they would still find him more appetizing than soap and old cotton — and he was right. Without warning, several of the creatures leaped at him from all directions. He had to act fast. In a flash he grasped the handles of the two large pot lids and dropped the pots themselves to the tile floor with a loud metal clang. Using the lids as shields he managed to deflect two of the rats, which bounced away and landed at his feet, but two more landed on his head and immediately sank all four sets of teeth into his unruly hair. Morton yelped in shock more than pain but kept his eyes on the two rats that were now gnashing at the ankles of Dad's heavy rubber boots. He tried shaking them off, but their jaws were strong and no amount of jumping would jar them loose. Then, as he was stomping his feet, two more rats leaped for his arms, and he realized with some significant sense of gloom that they weren't just attacking him randomly. They were immobilizing him one limb at a time.

Just as he was thinking this, the two rats on his head leered down at him from above, and suddenly he could see nothing but yellow teeth against a backdrop of pink fleshy mouths — mouths that were eager to devour him. For one brief second he hesitated, but then he crashed the lids in his hands together like a pair of heavy cymbals right over the rats' heads. Stunned, they dropped to the floor in two limp clumps of fur, and Morton quickly bent down and scooped them into one of the pots. Then, using his padded hands, he boldly yanked the two rats from his boots and stuffed them into the same pot, slapping on the lid an instant later. He placed one foot over the lid to hold it down and then quickly scanned the room.

There were only two rats left, clinging fiercely to his wrists and doing a very effective job of yanking the stuffing out of Dad's oven mitts with their rock-hard teeth. Morton swung his arms out wide, slamming the two rats' bodies against the wall with the full momentous force of the swing. The rats let out loud wheezing squeaks, like two deflating bagpipes, and dropped unconscious to the floor.

Morton only allowed himself a few seconds to recover from his brief battle and, although his heart continued to pound, he quickly unwound the duct tape on his wrists, threw the unconscious rats into the second pot, and used the tape to fasten both lids firmly in place. Savage hissing and scraping noises came from inside, but he was barely concerned with that. What troubled him now were the whereabouts of James and the safety of Melissa.

He kicked off Dad's boots and made his way downstairs, but he hadn't even reached the bottom step when he heard the front door open, followed by a familiar and welcome voice humming happily.

"Melissa?" he called, a sense of relief washing over him.

The humming stopped and Melissa stuck her head into the hallway and squinted in Morton's direction. "Morton, are you still awake?" she said.

Morton turned on the landing light, causing Melissa to gasp at the sight of him. Only then did he realize that he had a large graze over his left cheek and his pajama shirt was shredded like an old flag.

"What happened?"

"The rats, they got in through the toilet, but . . ." Morton trailed off. Melissa looked absolutely fine. Her clothes weren't ruffled, her lipstick wasn't smudged, and not a single hair was out of place. "You look, uh, normal."

Melissa gave Morton a questioning look. "Were you expecting me to look somehow abnormal?"

Morton didn't wait to explain. He raced past Melissa back through the kitchen and out onto the porch. Somehow, impossibly, the lawn was deserted. Where before there had been a dense sea of Two-Headed Mutant Rodents, now there was absolutely nothing.

Melissa appeared beside him, a look of consternation on her face. "Did I miss something?"

"Yes!" Morton exclaimed, both annoyed and relieved. "There were Two-Headed Rodents everywhere. Didn't you and Jake see them?"

Melissa shook her head. "We didn't see anything."

"Well, that's not the only problem," Morton went on. "James is missing. I think . . ."

Morton's voice suddenly failed him and he stood, staring dumbly at Melissa.

"What? What is it?" she asked, shaking him on the shoulder.

Morton still couldn't find his voice. He'd avoided any mention of Robbie's Snarf sighting and his suspicions that James might be out prowling again because he'd hoped it wasn't happening, but now, faced with the facts on hand, he could think of no other explanation for James's behavior.

"You don't think he's . . . ," Melissa began, seemingly as reluctant to put it into words as Morton was.

Morton nodded.

Melissa's expression turned to one of pure terror. "Are you sure?" she said in a breathless whisper.

"I'm not sure of anything. But Robbie saw a Snarf on Halloween, and James is definitely not in the house."

Melissa didn't wait to hear any more. She kicked off her high heels and bounded up the stairs like an Olympic athlete. Morton scurried after and followed her into James's room. She turned on the light, just as Morton had done earlier, only this time, there was a cry of distress.

"Ow! Turn that off, I'm trying to sleep!"

Morton looked on in disbelief. There was James lying in his bed, tangled in his sheets, as usual, with a very drowsy look on his face.

Morton was speechless.

Melissa walked right over to him and looked directly into his bleary eyes. "Where have you been?" she demanded.

James covered his face with his hands. "What are you talking about? I've been here, fast asleep. What happened?"

"Morton nearly got eaten alive by Two-Headed Mutant Rodents is what happened."

All trace of James's sleepiness vanished and he sat bolt upright. "What? When?"

"Just now!" Morton exclaimed. "I came in looking for you but you weren't here."

"Were you hurt?" James asked.

"Of course he was hurt!" Melissa exclaimed, pointing to the scratch on his cheek. "Which makes me repeat my question, where were you?"

James dropped his head and stared guiltily at the floor. "I . . . I was under the bed," he said.

Melissa placed her hands on her hips. "Really? You expect us to believe that?"

"It's true!" James pleaded. "I woke up a few minutes ago and found myself under the bed. I must have fallen onto the floor and somehow rolled under. It's not the first time it's happened — Morton will tell you that."

Melissa looked questioningly at Morton. He realized that this was in fact true. James had rolled under the bed at least twice before that he remembered.

Morton shrugged and held up his palms, and Melissa started wandering around the room looking over everything with a suspicious eye.

James sighed in frustration. "Please don't tell me you think I'm still turning into a Snarf, because that's a ridiculous idea."

Melissa pulled back the curtains and inspected the windows. Like most of the house's upstairs windows they were painted shut and probably hadn't been opened in twenty years.

At last she too let out a big sigh, as if to clear the air, and let the curtains fall. "Sorry," she said. "We're all a bit too worked up, just like you said."

"Well, I'm sorry too," James said, looking at Morton. "I won't let that happen again, I promise."

Melissa smiled and turned to the door. "I suppose we should at least try to get some sleep."

"What about the rats?" James said, still sitting up in his bed.

"Leave that to us," Melissa said, and she headed out of the room.

Morton turned to follow. "Good night," he said, and he closed the door behind him. He paced off down the hallway and stopped beside Melissa, who was lingering outside her own room.

"He's lying," she whispered crossly. "I don't know how he did it. But he did. Somehow he snuck back into the house without you seeing him."

"What makes you so sure?" Morton asked.

"Look, James is very smart, but he'd make a terrible spy," Melissa said. "He had dirt on his face and leaves in his hair."

Morton nodded silently. He hadn't been close enough to see the dirt, but something else had occurred to him. Something must have scared away the rats, something that even a swarm of giant Two-Headed Mutant Rodents would be afraid of, and only one creature came to mind: the Wargle Snarf, with its fear-inducing pheromone.

"What are we going to do?" Morton sighed.

"Watch him like a hawk," Melissa said.

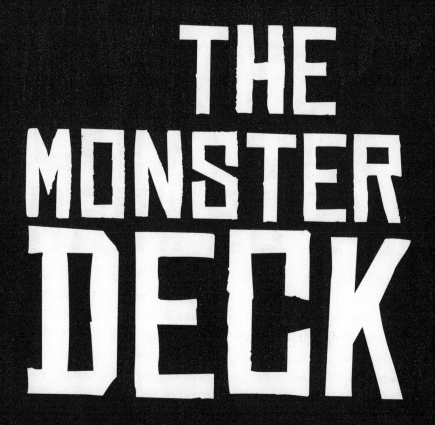

TOXIC
VAPOR WORM

Small, fast, and venomous, this partially winged serpentine creature is not to be toyed with. Its ability to dissolve instantly into a blue vapor makes it not only capable of passing through air ducts and keyholes but also renders it impervious to physical attack. In fact, it is virtually indestructible. Attempts to diffuse the vapor have met with little success since the Worm can reform itself into smaller replicas even at microscopic sizes. The toxic venom secreted through the fangs of this creature is equal in strength to that of a black mamba. Specimens must be stored in airtight containers and treated with extreme caution.

ACID-SPITTING FROG

Rarely found in populated areas, this seemingly ordinary frog is deadly. Its secret weapon is a constantly replenishing bladder of highly corrosive organic acid. Larger adults of the species can spit a distance of up to fifteen feet, and just one teaspoon of frog acid is sufficient to melt a hole through two inches of plate steel.

The acid-spitting bladder makes for a formidable defense, but is also used for hunting. In normal conditions this carnivorous frog will use the acid to incapacitate only small animals, such as birds or rodents, but remains of bigger mammals have been found in some larger frog colonies.

KAMIKAZE COBRA

This fearsome snake is in fact no relation to the typical cobra. Though it shares that snake's slight flattening of the head and it does have fangs, that's where the similarity ends. Unlike the cobra, which has a venomous bite, this snake's defense mechanism is entirely unique. If the sharp fangs and hissing don't scare away attackers, the Kamikaze Cobra has one final and fatal tactic: It explodes, usually taking the attacker with it. The snake does this by detonating an explosive capsule in its skull.

Skillful snake charmers have been known to successfully behead this creature before it manages to self-destruct, neutralizing the explosive, but there are also many stories of tragic mishaps. This temperamental beast should be avoided at all costs.

FLESH-EATING SLUG

This infamous pest is similar to other slugs, in that it lives in moist soil, often near vegetable gardens or other domestic spaces. Unlike the common slug, however, the Flesh-Eating variety is almost entirely carnivorous. It has small but powerful teeth and will regularly attack mice, moles, and other small land-dwelling creatures. While little more than an annoyance to humans in small quantities, infestations can become dangerous or even deadly. For reasons not fully understood, large numbers of Flesh-Eating Slugs will sometimes adopt a frenzied feeding pattern, causing them to attack larger animals en masse. Feeding frenzies happen only at night, but many family pets have been lost this way, and some human fatalities have been reported.

ELECTRIC KILLER EEL

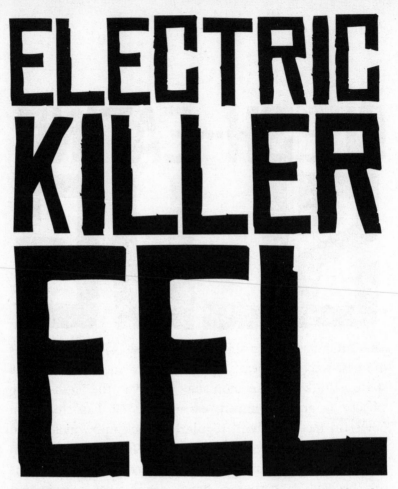

Though it prefers swampy lakes and stagnant ponds, this slithery vermin is more than capable of moving on land.

Eels usually stick together in swarms of about two dozen and, for the most part, avoid humans. However, beware: A single eel packs a six-thousand-volt shock at two amps when threatened, which is enough electricity to power a small house and stun an elephant.

Thick rubber gloves and boots will offer some protection, but avoidance is always the best defense.

BAT EYE

From a distance, this transdimensional creature looks like an ordinary bat, but closer inspection reveals that, in fact, it has no mouth or nose. Its "face" is simply one large eye.

Though it is not dangerous per se, the Bat Eye can be used by unscrupulous individuals as a surveillance tool through the establishment of a low-level psychic bond, which can be strengthened with relatively simple spells. Since the Bat Eye does not appear to eat or reproduce, it must be generated by supernatural methods. Many of these methods are described in detail in The Book of Portals.

HYDRA SNAKE

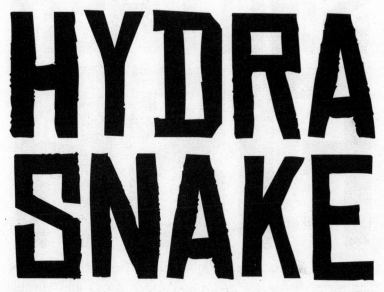

This venomous four-headed snake is named after the mythical many-headed beast slain by Hercules. Fortunately this snake does not sprout two heads every time one is cut off. It can, however, survive with only one head intact, making it four times harder to kill than a regular snake. It is especially aggressive when guarding its eggs, which it does very well on account of its 360-degree vision. This may be the reason Hydra eggs were once considered to be gifts worthy of a king.

SMOTHER FISH

Sometimes called Paper Wights, these paper-thin creatures flap through the air and pass under doors and through small openings with little trouble. Some strains also have chameleon-like properties and can hide in plain sight on walls, floors, and other flat surfaces.

Though individuals are mostly harmless and feed on smaller insects, they have been known to travel in shoals of up to a hundred. Such numbers enable them to smother larger prey, which they then slowly digest, usually over a period of months.

Fortunately Smother Fish are easily disposed of with a good sharp pair of scissors.

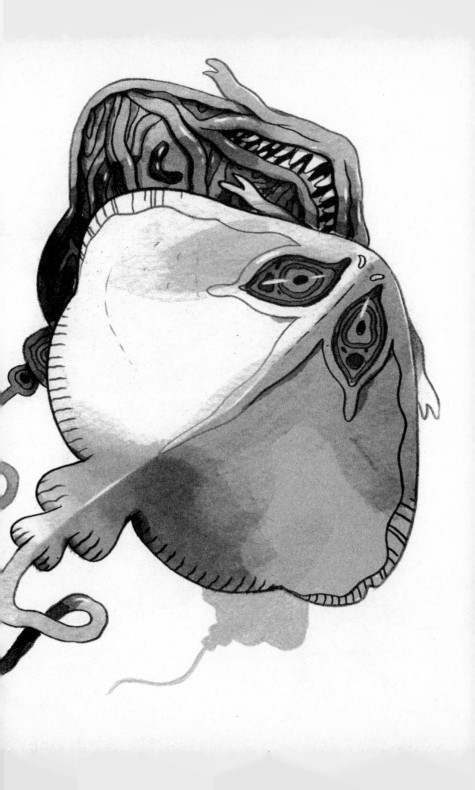

VISIBLE FANG

The defining characteristic of this rare creature is its reclusive nature. It avoids being seen by taking advantage of its translucent body and confining itself to shadowy places. Despite its diamond-hard fang, from which it gets its name, it has never been known to attack conscious prey, instead first using some as yet unverified hypnotic technique to place its victims in a trance. Though it will eat anything, it is believed that it prefers dense muscular organs, particularly the heart.

It is also said that the Fang avoids crowds, seeking out houses where people live in solitude. This is almost certainly true, though some debate continues about why the Fang adopts this habit. Some claim it is a purely defensive strategy, while others suggest that the hypnotic powers of the Fang are more effective on vulnerable and lonely souls.

THE ZOMBIE TWINS

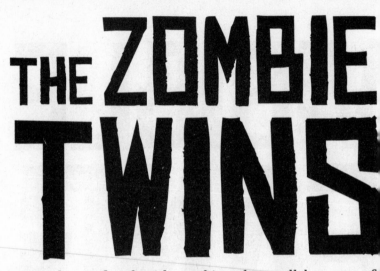

Not to be confused with zombies, the small but powerf[ul] Twins are named for their ability to gain psychic contr[ol] over other beasts, living or dead. The Twins' influence ov[er] living creatures is limited to animals with lesser intelligenc[e,] but they are capable of controlling the cadavers of an[y] creature, including those of recently deceased humans.

It is believed that the Twins are more powerful when i[n] proximity to each other, enabling them to create some kin[d] of psychic feedback loop.

Despite having no physical strength or defenses, the[ir] extraordinary intelligence and strategic brilliance, combine[d] with their ability to raise armies at will, makes them a f[oe] of truly formidable proportions. What is not clear is wh[at] motivates the Twins. They have been known to battle bo[th] for and against otherworld interdimensional powers. Leadi[ng] theories suggest that the Twins originate from their ow[n] dimension and it is therefore impossible to interpret the[ir] actions on the "mortal plane."

GRISTLE GRUNT

Small, sinewy, walking walls of muscle. What you see is what you get with this myopic creature. It has no head, most likely because it has very little brain. Its preferred weapon is a club, and its preferred hangout is a very damp, smelly cave.

Grunts live only in rocky, mountainous regions and hunt in packs of about five, tracking down larger game such as goats, deer, and stray humans. They do not, however, eat raw meat, instead roasting their food over an open flame. Many experts believe that only the female Grunts are intelligent enough to actually light fires, and though it is almost impossible to tell male and female Grunts apart, several independent reports support this theory.

FLESH BULB

Often found hanging in caves, this tennis-ball-size creature has a unique attack technique in which its opalescent skin flashes so brightly that it can cause temporary blindness. The Bulb then quickly attaches itself with its four leglike tentacles to its prey and feeds through the mouth on its underbelly.

The Flesh Bulb is a large parasite and, like ticks or other bloodsucking parasites, once it is attached it is almost impossible to remove. Acetone or lighter fluid has shown the best results. Though the Flesh Bulbs do not intentionally kill the host, they are occasionally found in large swarms and human fatalities have been reported.

INK BLIGHT

Extremely rare, almost nothing is known of this strange, creeping, oily entity. It looks like slow-moving black tar and consumes everything with which it comes into contact, thus no effective studies can be done. In fact, it is uncertain whether the Blight is even an organism at all. Some experts believe it is a manifestation of dimensional collapse, and that any apparent mobility is dictated by random fluctuations in some unknown ether. Contact with the Blight has proven fatal in all known incidents, and there is absolutely no known remedy for occurrences. Any areas infected must be evacuated until the Blight naturally subsides, which usually takes one to two weeks.

KING-CRAB SPIDER

This giant arachnid has a bony crablike carapace that makes it impervious to most predators. Adults can weigh as much as four pounds. It has strong venom, which, while not lethal in small doses, will render most people unconscious for several hours.

Though it does spin an incredibly tough web, it does not use the web for capturing its prey, merely for storing and immobilizing it. Like many larger spiders, it hunts by hiding in holes and leaping directly onto its intended victim, which it then neutralizes with its venom.

GREATER SPOTTED
WARGLE
[RHYMES WITH GARGLE]
SNARF

Few creatures boast the raw power of the Snarf. Up to fifteen feet long, with an impenetrable bony carapace and a double ring of razor-sharp, metal-ripping teeth, this behemoth is tough enough to tackle a tank . . . and win. Like its smaller cousin, the Lesser Spotted Snarf, the Wargle can paralyze its victims by secreting a fear-inducing pheromone from glands distributed all over its body.

This nocturnal creature has perfect night vision, and its sense of smell is ten times more acute than that of a bloodhound. Few humans can survive an encounter with a Snarf, and the unfortunate ones who do discover that exposure to the Snarf's poison-tipped barbs causes a slow, painful transformation into a hybrid human-Snarf creature.

Legend has it that the Snarf draws its demonic power from the brimstone in its stomach, which it gets by drinking from the boiling rivers of Hades.

FLESH-EATING COCKROACH

These creatures are almost identical to the familiar domestic pests, but with two significant distinctions: They are at least five times the size of an average cockroach, and they are completely carnivorous.

The only good news about these pests is that they are rare, and reports seem to indicate that they are naturally repelled by clean, bright environments, preferring derelict homes and slums.

However, if you do get an infestation, be prepared to move out in a hurry. Each roach eats twice its body weight every day, and females reproduce at a fearsome rate, capable of laying several pods in a month. Each pod in turn is capable of holding more than one hundred eggs.

TEN-EYED SALAMANDER

This seemingly harmless creature is, in fact, one of the deadliest pests in the arcana. Despite its name, the Ten-Eyed Salamander can have any number of eyes, ranging from six to twenty. It is commonly accepted that the extra eyes are a by-product of its extremely advanced regenerative abilities for, like all salamanders, this creature is capable of regrowing lost limbs. Unlike regular salamanders, this one can regenerate limbs in a matter of seconds. Some have even been observed to regrow large portions of their bodies.

In addition to their resilient regenerative abilities, these Salamanders have highly toxic skin, which can cause instant paralysis, and are exclusively carnivorous. They also have an unsettling habit of jettisoning their poison-saturated tails when under extreme stress. The tails continue to move, usually twitching and jumping violently, distracting or paralyzing would-be attackers while the Salamander itself escapes — or strikes.

SHARK HOUND

Sometimes referred to as a Land Shark, this savage creature is a four-legged nightmare, bringing the ocean's worst terror to dry land. It can outrun a human with ease, and its ferocious teeth make it a match for most other wild creatures.

Though it has a highly acute sense of smell, its one weakness is its vision. It has a blind spot both directly in front of and directly behind it.

Legend has it that the Shark Hound hunts only on the full moon, but in fact this is a myth, no doubt propagated because it hunts exclusively at night, depending as it does on scent rather than sight.

DRAGON FLY

This large flying insect is one of the few true fire-breathers. Despite being little bigger than a hummingbird, it can belch out a shaft of flame six to eight feet in length and generate temperatures of up to 700 degrees.

Though fire breathing is a highly effective defense, it may serve another purpose. Some experts believe that Dragon Fly eggs can hatch only after exposure to high temperatures and that the insects build small nests from twigs and incinerate them to catalyze germination. No studies have been able to verify this.

TWO-HEADED MUTANT RODENT

This unique strain of wild rodent has two heads and hence twice the ferocity of the meanest sewer rat. It will eat anything, from old rope to old bones, and it is *always* hungry. Like many plague beasts, the rodents have rapidly growing populations, which, in the right environment, can double in size each week. They are also impervious to traditional pest control techniques. Most traps don't seem to work and poisons have no effect on the Rodent's seemingly indestructible digestive system.

It is also rumored that these creatures are more intelligent than average rats, which might explain why traditional trapping techniques are ineffective.

GALOSH

Often called the foot soldier of the underworld, this humanoid creature is not of earthly origin. However, history documents many incidents involving this being and there is no doubt it is a powerful and formidable foe. It is obedient and fearless and very strong.

Its thick leathery skin forms a tough natural armor, and like many other-dimensional beasts it cannot be killed by normal methods. It is commonly accepted lore that the only certain way to stop a Galosh is to hack it to a thousand pieces, which is almost certainly true since the Galosh is not actually alive in any natural sense of the word.

SWAG SPRITE

Though completely harmless, these small marsupial creatures are aggravating and infuriating. Capable of appearing and disappearing at will, they seem to spend all of their time stealing small items that they stuff into the pouch on their backs. They are also known to occasionally replace stolen objects with other items, presumably stolen from some other location. No reasonable explanation has been proposed for this behavior. Swag Sprites seldom stay in one place for long, but folk remedies claim that burning a potpourri of bergamot oil will discourage their appearance.

CHAPTER 11

THE REAL MRS. SMEDLEY

When Morton ambled into the bathroom the next morning, he found it spotlessly clean, with no sign of the previous night's battle. Melissa had sent him off to bed hours before, insisting she would handle the cleanup on her own, and to her credit, she had done an impressive job. The bathroom was now possibly even cleaner than it had been before the rat invasion.

Morton washed his hands and face with a sense of relief, and then shuffled down the stairs to the kitchen. As he did so, he heard Dad's voice echoing up to the landing, and even before he heard what he was saying, Morton could tell by his tone that something had upset him. He found out exactly what a moment later when he stepped into the dining room.

"It's a total disaster!" Dad was saying to a stunned-looking James and a pale and disheveled Melissa. "My spring bulbs have been ravaged, and so has half the town by the sound of it."

A familiar sense of doom squeezed out the last drops of Morton's sleepiness.

"Uh, what happened?" he asked, although he knew exactly what Dad was complaining about.

Dad dropped the Sunday paper on the table. "Apparently Dimvale is infested with a mutant strain of two-headed rats."

"Oh, uh, right," Morton said, faking a yawn. "I think we knew about that. We saw the pest control van on the way to school the other day, didn't we, James?"

"Oh, yeah. I think we did," James said, also feigning disinterest.

"Yes, well, the blasted things swarmed right through the north end of Dimvale last night," Dad went on, "which very unfortunately includes our garden."

Dad took a large swig of tea, draining his cup, and immediately poured himself another. "I spent a fortune on that garden, not to mention all the time digging and planting, and then I get home this morning to find it looking like somebody had just finished a reenactment of the Battle of Hastings right over my perennials. Of course, the veggies are all gone too."

James caught Morton's eye and made a "be thankful for small mercies" shrug. In spite of the dire situation Morton felt a smirk creep to the corners of his mouth.

Dad meanwhile had finished his second cup of tea and poured himself yet another. "This article makes it sound like these horrid things might be a real problem," he went on. "Apparently some woman was walking one of those little Chihuahua dogs, and they swarmed out of the drain and went straight for it. The poor woman tried to fight them off, but they chewed right through the leash and then scampered back into the sewer, taking the dog with them. And the authorities think there might be thousands of them living in the sewers."

"Are you sure you didn't read this in one of those fake newspapers?" Melissa said, still maintaining a facade of disinterest.

Dad shook his head and tried to pour himself a fourth cup of tea, but the pot was now empty. "I assure you this is a real newspaper, Melissa," he said. "And you might not be too happy about this, but I've decided I'm not comfortable leaving you kids home alone while these things are roaming the streets, so Mrs. Smedley has very kindly offered to babysit until this blows over."

"What?" Melissa yelped, a look of genuine outrage on her face. "I thought we agreed I was old enough to be in charge?"

"We did," Dad said, "but these are extenuating circumstances."

"They're just rats," Melissa protested.

"Nonetheless, I'll feel a lot safer knowing there's a fully grown adult on the premises."

"I don't think I'd describe Mrs. Smedley as a fully grown adult," Melissa scoffed. "More like an overripened adult."

Dad gave her a reprimanding look. "Regardless of her age, she's coming," he said firmly.

"She'll have a heart attack at the first sign of trouble," Melissa went on, changing her tone as if to appeal to Dad's reason. "Something shocking like that might traumatize Morton. He's really quite fragile, you know."

Dad got to his feet and began clearing away plates. "If Morton's fragile, then I'm a chocolate rabbit," he said. "In any case, I wasn't inviting a discussion. I was merely informing you. She'll be coming after supper tonight."

Dad then hastily piled the dishes into the kitchen sink and retreated up to his office.

Melissa turned up her lip and scowled across the table at James and Morton. "Great, that's all we need, Medley Smedley keeping tabs on us."

"Well, you can hardly blame him," James said.

"I don't suppose it matters," Melissa replied in a miserable tone. "The whole situation is hopeless anyway. Things are getting worse by the minute, and we still don't have a single clue about why any of it's happening."

As Melissa said this, Morton realized he still hadn't had time to mention his visit to the bookstore or the photos of King he'd found in the attic. He cleared his throat sheepishly.

"Uh, actually, there's something I've been meaning to tell you."

Melissa and James both craned their necks around suddenly and locked their eyes accusingly on Morton.

"I don't like the sound of that," James said.

Morton glared back at them defensively. "What's that supposed to mean?"

"It doesn't mean anything," Melissa put in quickly.

Morton knew this wasn't true and found himself feeling annoyed. Despite this, he sighed and told them about the comic he'd found in Nolan's locker and how it, and King's photos, had led him to the bookstore. He did his best to play down the scary parts, hoping that they'd be more interested in what he'd learned and not so concerned with how he'd learned it. Unfortunately this strategy didn't work at all. James was practically purple with rage by the time Morton had finished, and he jumped up from the table and began waving his arms up and down like an angry scarecrow.

"What is wrong with you?" he screeched. "You find out that King might have a brother and then go off alone to some strange store, and don't even think to tell one of us? And you wonder why I made Melissa promise not to get you involved in anything dangerous!"

"It was just a bookstore!" Morton protested. "And it was broad daylight. I didn't think it was a big deal."

"Not a big deal?" James echoed. "Morton, do you have any concept of danger? Honestly, you are hopeless sometimes. I just don't know what we're going to do with you."

"Do with me?" Morton exclaimed, now feeling very angry. "I'm not some pet you get to push around and tell what to do."

"I don't mean it like that," James said.

"Yes, you do!" Morton shot back. "You mean it exactly like that. You and Melissa expect me to sit home like a good puppy dog and wait for your instructions. Well, for your information, that's not the kind of person I am. And more to the point, while you were out snuggling with Wendy on some park bench, I was actually trying to do something to get us out of this mess before the whole town gets eaten alive, so don't start telling me what I can and can't do."

"Wendy and I were not snuggling!" James protested, but Morton wasn't in a listening mood. He stormed out of the dining room to head up to his room. Before he could reach the stairs, however, the phone in the hallway rang, and he rather foolishly snatched up the receiver on his way past.

"Hello?" he said gruffly.

"Morton!" came Robbie's voice over the phone. "Is everything okay? You sound upset."

"Upset?" Morton said, his anger now very much in control of his mood. "Why should I be upset? My family doesn't trust me and my best friend doesn't want to hang out with me anymore."

There was a long silence on the other end of the line, and then at last Robbie responded.

"What are you talking about?" he said.

"Julie told me that you don't want to hang out with me anymore," Morton replied.

"Julie said what?" Robbie asked, his voice pained.

"It's okay, I get it," Morton said. "Life's been way too complicated for you since I moved here, and you want your normal life back."

"Normal life?" Robbie said. "What are you talking about? Look, I don't even know why Julie would say something like that."

"Maybe because it's true," Morton said.

"It's not true! It's . . ." Robbie trailed off, and Morton heard him breathing nervously on the other end of the phone. "Look, we can't talk about that now. I have some important news. Nolan's gone missing."

Morton felt his anger drain away rapidly to be replaced by a crushing sense of dread. "Missing? You mean he didn't show up to rehearsal again?"

"No, it's much worse than that," Robbie explained. "Inspector Sharpe came to our house this morning and asked if anyone had seen him. Apparently he vanished yesterday afternoon, and his parents called the police. Sharpe's been to interview all the band members, but nobody's laid eyes on him since Friday."

"Did Sharpe ask you anything else?" Morton asked nervously, knowing only too well that if anyone were going to connect them with the strange events in Dimvale, it would be her.

"No, only questions about Nolan," Robbie said, and the two of them lapsed into an uncomfortable silence.

"Listen, I have to go," Robbie said at last. "See you in school tomorrow, okay?"

"Yeah, sure," Morton said, and he hung up and turned to face James and Melissa, who were watching him from the dining room doorway with looks of concern on their faces.

"We heard you mention Inspector Sharpe," James said.

"Nolan's gone missing," Morton said.

James's face drained to a chalky white. "How? When?"

"All they know is he went missing on Friday night," Morton answered, and then he continued up the stairs, still in no mood to talk to James.

For the rest of the day Morton holed up in his room on the pretense of tackling the very large assignment given to him by Mr. Noble. Unfortunately his thoughts were now even more fragmented than they had been the day before, and somehow the hours slipped by without him achieving anything. All too soon it was suppertime, and Morton finally gave up any hope of finishing the assignment and went back downstairs to join the others.

When he arrived in the kitchen, he found Melissa washing dishes at the sink with a sulky expression, and James drying, while Dad was throwing laundry into a hamper.

"Ah, Morton," he said. "There you are. Can you help clean up? Mrs. Smedley will be here any minute, and I don't want her to get the wrong impression."

"If you don't want her to get the wrong impression, then we should leave the house messy," Melissa quipped.

Dad sighed tiredly at her comment but didn't respond. Instead he simply turned to Morton. "Just pick up your things as quickly as you can and take them back to your room," he said, then headed upstairs with the hamper tucked under his arm.

Morton didn't really understand what the fuss was about, but he did as he was told and started collecting the schoolbooks, socks, and other odds and ends that seemed to sprout like mushrooms all over the house.

After about twenty minutes of earnest tidying, the doorbell rang.

"That will be her," Dad yelled from upstairs. "Can you let her in?"

Morton ran to the door, but when he arrived, instead of the elderly lady he'd seen shuffling up and down the driveway of the house across the road, a complete stranger was standing on the porch. It was a very petite woman with pale green eyes and dark wavy hair, wearing a light woolen dress, a string of freshwater pearls, and canvas shoes. Morton had no idea who she was.

"Oh, hello," she said a little nervously. "Is James home?"

Morton turned to call James, but James had already appeared and was now standing beside Melissa, and it was clear by his expression that he had no idea who this person was. Both he and Melissa looked baffled and simply stared at her.

"Oh, pardon me," the woman added. "I mean James, your father, not James, your brother."

Instead of running to get Dad, all three of them continued to stand there as if hypnotized. Fortunately Dad joined them at the door a moment later.

"Mrs. Smedley, so glad you could help out," Dad said in a very formal voice. "We can't begin to thank you enough."

James practically jumped out of his skin. "Mrs. Smedley?"

The woman raised her eyebrows and looked questioningly back at James. "That's me. Were you expecting someone else?"

"We . . . We thought . . . ," James said, fumbling badly for words, and looking suddenly very worried. "We saw an old lady collecting your mail and thought . . ."

"Oh, I see," Mrs. Smedley said, with a soft, sympathetic laugh. "That would be my mother. She visits sometimes on weekends."

James inched backward and a strange, almost frightened look crossed his face. At the same time, Melissa was now looking at Dad with an equally strange expression, although not one of fear. Morton couldn't really read Melissa's expression, but if he'd had to guess he would have said it was one of realization, or recognition. In a peculiar way, Melissa seemed to be looking at Dad as if she were seeing him for the first time. None of this made any sense whatsoever to

Morton, and he had the distinct feeling that he was missing something.

"Is everything all right?" Mrs. Smedley said, clearly also aware of the odd behavior. "I hope I haven't confused you."

Dad stepped forward. "I'm just realizing there *was* some confusion," he said, putting a hand on Melissa's and James's shoulders, "but I think we're on the same page now, aren't we?"

Melissa made a nervous smile and nodded politely, but James, for some reason, began rubbing his hands anxiously and looked away.

Dad cleared his throat. "Well, I suppose I should introduce you. This is Melissa, James, and Morton."

"Lovely to meet you at last," Mrs. Smedley said, shaking each of their hands in turn. Morton couldn't help noticing that Mrs. Smedley's hands were buttery soft and that she smelled ever so slightly of violets.

"Well, do come on in," Dad said, still sounding a little nervous. "I'll show you the ropes."

Dad spent the next twenty minutes showing Mrs. Smedley around the house while the kids lingered in the kitchen. Both James and Melissa were unusually silent and sat at the table without saying a word.

"Is everything all right?" Morton asked, his sense of confusion mounting.

"Yes, fine, of course it's fine," Melissa said, with a distant smile. James, however, didn't respond, and the room fell immediately back into silence.

"Uh, Mrs. Smedley seems nice," Morton persisted.

"Yes, very nice," Melissa said.

James nodded in agreement, but Morton could tell there was something he wasn't saying.

A few minutes later, Dad and Mrs. Smedley returned to the kitchen.

"Hopefully those rats won't pay a second visit to my garden," Dad was saying. "But don't hesitate to call me at work if there are any problems."

"We'll be fine," Mrs. Smedley said. "I wouldn't dream of interrupting your work. I'm sure it's very important."

"Well, hardly," Dad said, "but it does pay the bills. And I don't like being away when things are so . . ." Dad struggled for words. "Unusual," he said at last.

"I assure you, I will take care of everything," Mrs. Smedley said, and Dad seemed to relax visibly at these words.

"Well, the good news," Dad said, "is that it sounds like they've found a quick way to get rid of the rats."

Morton jumped to his feet. "They have?" he exclaimed, completely surprised by the pronouncement.

"Yes, I heard it on the radio. Apparently your teacher Mr. Noble has helped devise some method to get rid of them by releasing poisonous gas canisters in the sewers."

Morton had a sudden horrible dizzy sensation and had to grab on to a nearby chair for support. "Did you say gas canisters?" he asked, knowing full well that was exactly what Dad had said.

"Yes. It's some special kind of gas though. Something to do with rapid chemical decay, so as not to contaminate the ground water. Sounded very clever actually. They hope to use it this week."

Morton could hardly believe what he was hearing and

now had to sit down. Despite what Dad and Mrs. Smedley, and no doubt everyone else believed, using poisonous gas was the worst possible thing they could do.

"Are you all right?" Dad said, noticing Morton's sudden change in mood.

"Oh, yes, it's just that I have a big assignment to write for Mr. Noble," he said, forcing a smile.

Dad wandered over to Morton and put his hand on his forehead and looked directly into his eyes. "Are you sure that's all it is?"

Morton nodded. "Really, I'm fine," he said. "You'll be late for work."

Dad glanced up at the clock and realized that Morton was right. "Good gracious!" he exclaimed, and immediately began his last-minute bluster of pre-departure confusion.

A few minutes later they all walked Dad to the car and waved good-bye to him as he shot up the driveway, skidding his tires on the gravel as he went.

"Well, it's certainly going to be fun to get to know you all," Mrs. Smedley said as they returned to the house.

"Uh, it would be, but I have homework," James said, and walked straight out of the kitchen. Melissa watched him go with a scowl and then turned back to face Mrs. Smedley.

"Actually, very sorry, but I have homework too," she said, and despite the fact that she used a much politer tone than James had, she didn't waste any time following him up the stairs.

Mrs. Smedley's face dropped. "I didn't realize I was such a scary ogre," she said lightly to Morton.

"Oh, uh, no, you're not at all," Morton stammered, feeling very awkward. "They're just . . . Well, things are a little weird right now."

"Yes, I suppose this two-headed-rat thing is a bit out of the ordinary," Mrs. Smedley said. "And right after that odd affair with the missing cats too. You must think Dimvale is the strangest place in the world."

"Well, it's not just that," Morton replied.

Mrs. Smedley frowned and smiled at the same time, which up until that very moment Morton hadn't realized was even possible. It made her look sympathetic and kind. "No, I suppose it's a lot more complicated," she responded. "I imagine none of this is easy. Your mother passing away so suddenly. Moving to a new town. Starting a new school and making new friends. Your father tells me you've all been very strong and brave, and I can see exactly what he means. It's a tough little chestnut of a family you have here."

"Chestnut?" Morton said, surprised by the odd choice of words. His mother had always recited a little poem about chestnut trees when she tucked him into bed at night, and he knew that the chestnut had always been her favorite kind of tree. "Why a chestnut?" he asked.

Mrs. Smedley shrugged. "I don't know. It just popped into my head. Maybe because chestnuts are hard and strong on the outside but very sweet on the inside." She laughed out loud at her own words, revealing delicate white teeth that matched the pearls around her neck. "Oh, don't listen to me! I spend far too much time reading poetry. I'm sure you've got better things to do. I know you have homework, so why don't I set to making something nice for tomorrow's breakfast and you can go finish it off."

"It's true I have a big project," Morton said, although the assignment was now the furthest thing from his mind. "I guess I'll see you later," he added, and bounded off after his siblings.

When Morton arrived at the top landing he saw that James's room was empty and heard angry whispers coming from behind Melissa's bedroom door. He poked his head in without knocking to see James and Melissa standing with their noses almost touching in what appeared to be a stand-up fight. The moment they saw him they stopped their heated whispering and backed away from each other.

"Well, you might as well come in," Melissa said in a stiff voice, "and close the door."

Morton stepped in and pushed the door firmly shut. James sniffed and sat down heavily in the swivel chair at Melissa's desk and spun it around so that he had his back to them.

"Look, I don't know what you guys are fighting about," he said, "but I hope you realize we have a real problem."

"We have lots of real problems," Melissa said. "Which one are you talking about?"

"The gas canisters, of course."

James scratched his chin. "I thought that was good news. I mean, it sounds like the authorities have got it under control after all."

Morton clutched at his head in frustration and groaned loudly. "No! You don't get it. It's not going to work. In fact, it's going to make things worse, much worse."

James and Melissa stared blankly at him and he realized that neither of them had a clue what he was talking about.

"I've told you before, the rats can't be poisoned," he said.

"Not with normal poison, no," James responded. "But Dad said this is some special kind of poison."

"But, it's not going to work!" Morton repeated. "That's exactly what happens in the story. They try to kill the rats by putting poisonous gas in the sewer, but the poison doesn't kill them, it just drives them all out onto the streets."

James and Melissa stared at each other, both looking suitably shocked.

"So what do we do?" Melissa asked, a slight tremor in her voice.

"We stick to the plan," James said.

"What plan?" Morton said in an exasperated tone. "We don't have a plan!"

"We can't do anything until we find out who bought King's books," James stated, clenching his teeth in mild anger. "And Melissa is going to find that out very soon, right?"

"I'll find out," Melissa said, "but if Morton is right, then it might already be too late. It looks like we're going to drown in a sea of yellow teeth before the end of the week."

CHAPTER 12

THE CRY OF THE SNARF

Morton lay awake in bed, rolling from side to side. A faint sliver of moon was visible through the window, and he had already watched it creep halfway across the black November sky. It had been several hours since they had all said good night to Mrs. Smedley, but he'd long ago given up on the idea of sleep, and he had no idea what time it was when he heard the soft padding of feet shuffling along the corridor toward his room. His door drifted silently open and Morton looked up, wondering if Mrs. Smedley had come to check on him, but when he saw the blue nightgown with matching fuzzy slippers he realized it was Melissa.

"What are you doing awake?" he asked.

"It's James," Melissa said. "He's gone again."

Morton felt a surge of adrenaline run through his body and sat instantly upright.

"Are you sure?" he said.

"Of course I'm sure. And this time I checked under his bed."

Morton jumped to his feet and was about to bound down the hall to James's room, when Melissa put her hand on his chest.

"Just remember to keep it quiet," she said. "We don't want to wake Mrs. Smedley."

Morton nodded and continued on his way more quietly, followed by Melissa. When they arrived at James's door, it was already partially ajar. Morton pushed it open all the way and peered into the blackness beyond. It was silent. Utterly silent.

"James!" Morton whispered. "You in here?"

Melissa pushed into the room. "I already told you, he's not," she said, and she flicked the light on, momentarily blinding Morton. When his eyes adjusted he saw what his ears had already confirmed: the room was completely empty.

Morton shook his head. "This makes no sense. I've been awake all night. There's no way he could have snuck out without me hearing him."

"Not to mention the fact that Smedley's on guard down there," Melissa said, creeping over to the windows to inspect them, just as she had done the night before.

Morton looked around too. He noticed that James hadn't really finished unpacking, despite the fact that they'd been living in the house for some time. His model airplanes, which once hung from the ceiling of their shared bedroom, were still lying jumbled in open cardboard boxes, and his books were spilled haphazardly on the floor in front of the small inset bookshelf. Morton thought this very out of character for James, because he usually kept them neatly arranged in alphabetical order. In fact, now that he thought about it, he was sure he'd seen James arranging his books on the shelf just a few days earlier. . . .

Recognition came to Morton in a flash. He'd known since they moved into the house that King had drawn many of its rooms and hallways into his stories, and he suddenly remembered that he'd seen a narrow inset bookshelf just like this in a harrowing tale about a boy whose parents wouldn't let him own a dog, so he ended up raising a baby Shark Hound in a hidden part of his basement.

"It's a secret passage," Morton said. "I should have realized there'd be at least one in this house."

Melissa looked closely at the bookshelf. "That can't be a secret passage. It's on an outside wall. Where would it go?"

"Down," Morton said, stepping over to the shelves and examining them closely. "There should be a release catch here somewhere."

It didn't take him long to spot a small bronze lever at the back of the unit. He pressed the lever down and there was a metallic clunk and the whole unit swung open. Melissa rushed over to Morton's side and they both peered through the newly opened door. There, in a narrow passage jammed between James's bedroom and the outside wall, was an unusually narrow staircase that descended steeply into the darkness.

"So James has been sneaking out all along," Melissa said. "Now what are we going to do?"

"We follow him, of course," Morton said, and he stepped closer to the narrow stair and peered down into the swallowing darkness.

"Wait!" Melissa whispered, tightening her long fingers on his elbow. "There's no light. At least let me get a flashlight."

Morton agreed that this was probably a sensible idea, and Melissa ran swiftly back to her room and returned a moment later with a small key-chain flashlight.

"You'll still have to go first," she said, shining the inadequate blue beam down into the dusty shadows. Morton was quite happy to do so. He was certain that James had taken these stairs minutes, if not moments before, and he trotted confidently down, gliding his hands along the wall for guidance.

After a dozen or so steps, Morton felt the air grow suddenly cooler, and a musty dampness wafted over his face. Melissa's tiny light revealed what looked to be a wider landing of hard-packed dirt below and Morton felt, rather than saw, the narrow wooden passage open up into a larger space. They stopped when they reached the bottom, and Melissa held the flashlight out in front of her, as if willing the miniature beam to shine farther. They were now standing in a narrow brick tunnel with an arched ceiling. The bricks were old and covered in patches of white lime, and here and there Morton saw rusted metal brackets with frozen rivulets of wax hanging beneath them.

"Candles," Melissa said with a snort of recognition. "John King's favorite form of lighting."

"Well, we know he's been down here," Morton said. "This tunnel is just like one he drew in a story."

Morton crept cautiously forward and Melissa followed, holding the key-chain light above her head. Their footsteps echoed from all directions as they made their way along the passage, and the heavy musty air grew staler with each step. For a moment, Morton had the illusion that they were floating along in a bubble of light on an endless river of darkness, but then something changed. Morton caught the scent of fresh night air. Quite unexpectedly they arrived at a heavy arch-shaped oak door studded with metal bolts, like something from a castle or an old dungeon. The door was wide open, but all Morton could see beyond the frame was a dense thicket of thorny branches and tightly wound vines.

"Well, go on," Melissa prompted. "We're not going to turn back now, are we?"

Morton glanced up at Melissa with a frown. He wasn't sure exactly how he was supposed to keep going beyond what appeared to be an impenetrable tangle of brush. But Melissa didn't seem in the least perturbed by this. "Here," she said, "I'll go first this time." And even though she was wearing her silken nightgown and fluffy slippers, she squeezed through the door and crept sideways along the exterior wall until she, and her light, vanished from view. Morton followed quickly and soon realized that it was much easier than it looked, although he did feel a few sharp thorns snag at his legs as he pushed his way through the branches.

At last he was outside gazing up at the starry night sky and Morton saw that they were standing at the back of the house. This part of the yard was still overgrown with bushes and small trees, and looked out over another field of clumpy, overgrown grass that surrounded their property, which was in turn surrounded by a hedgerow of shrubby trees. Beyond that Morton could just make out the silhouettes of distant rooftops.

"I guess that settles it," Melissa said. "James has been night-prowling again."

"Yes, and I think he went this way," Morton said, pointing out a well-trodden path that cut through the long grass.

"Are you sure you want to go out there?" Melissa said.

"No," Morton said, but he began walking anyway, and Melissa followed.

The path led to an opening in the hedgerow and Morton crawled through to find himself standing on a dark and narrow road. There was just enough light to see that he was on Spruce Street, not far from their house.

"I never realized our backyard was so big," Melissa said, crawling through the gap behind him.

"I wonder if it's all our property," Morton said.

Melissa shivered. "Well, either way, there's no sign of James," she said, "and I'm not about to let you go off looking for him, so we might as well just go back."

Morton nodded and he was about to return through the gap in the hedgerow, when a horrific screech filled the night air. He knew at once what it was. Robbie had described it as an angry whale, but to Morton it sounded like a giant, rusty ship scraping along rocks in a fierce storm. It was loud, painful, and easily the most terrifying sound Morton had ever heard.

"That wasn't the rats, was it?" Melissa said, looking around nervously.

"No," Morton replied. "Not rats."

"Quickly! Back to the house!" Melissa commanded, and she turned and scampered hastily back through the hedge.

"But James is out here," Morton said, still lingering on the street. "What if he's in trouble?"

Melissa, who was now peering at him through the hedge,

made an annoyed snorting sound. "I think we both know the only kind of trouble he'll be in is the kind where he's eating somebody else's pet spaniel, or worse. . . ."

The distant shrieking sound came again, and this time Morton felt a jolt of irrational fear course through his entire body. His heart doubled its pace, his hands and face broke out in a cold, clammy sweat, and his legs began to tremble. "It's a Snarf," he said. "No doubt about it."

"What do we do?" Melissa said, clearly also affected by the strange airborne scent of dread.

"Run!" Morton screeched, and he leaped back into the field and tore off across the long grass toward the house. But now it was Melissa's turn to linger, and she stood rooted to the spot, looking around fretfully in all directions.

"Melissa!" Morton yelled. "It's the fear pheromone. Keep running!" Morton had barely finished speaking when suddenly an immense white, fleshy, wormlike creature came crashing through the hedge. The creature glared directly at them, and Morton had the strangest sensation that he recognized its dark and fearsome eyes.

The Snarf shrieked yet again, a horrific keening that tore through the cold night air, and Morton felt the ground tremble at the power of its cry. He bounded the few paces that separated him from Melissa and tugged violently on her arm. "Run!" he yelled at the top of his voice.

The creature made an odd, bony rattling, and its teeth vibrated like a series of electric bread knives arranged geometrically in its mouth. Unable to think of what else to do, Morton kicked Melissa hard in the shin. She yelped in pain, but this at least seemed to snap her out of her trance, and then they were both running for the thicket of trees and the heavy oak door hidden behind it. Morton struggled through the long grass, several times stumbling on dense tufts of undergrowth, and Melissa very quickly took the lead.

Morton heard the sudden cracking of branches and knew without looking that the Snarf had pushed right through the tall hedge and was now in close pursuit. Fear crashed down on him with such force his legs almost buckled.

Another cry ruptured the night behind him, this time so close that he felt the hot rancid air blast over the back of his neck from the depths of the creature's brimstone-filled stomach. Scenes from a dozen *Scare Scape* stories flashed unbidden into his head. Stories in which naive children were eaten alive by savage creatures with hollow, merciless eyes.

At last he was scrambling through the thicket that concealed the arched doorway but then there was another cry — this time from Melissa — and before he really knew what was happening, she placed her hands on his back and pushed him into the passage ahead of her. He stumbled onto the packed-dirt floor inside and turned to see the creature's head burst out of the darkness, its immense mouth open wide and its terrifying array of teeth gnashing hungrily at the air.

Morton glanced quickly around for a weapon — something, anything to drive the Snarf away — but at that very same instant, Melissa did the unthinkable. She flung herself into the path of the charging Snarf, shutting the door from the outside as she did so.

Morton let out an involuntary cry of terror, leaping to

the door, but even as he approached it he heard a latch on the outside drop into place and he knew that Melissa had locked him in.

Morton lunged at the door, pounding on it with his fists. "Melissa! Open up!" he screamed, even though he knew it was futile. The Snarf would waste no time in devouring her, swallowing her whole, like a giant featherless gannet. But Morton continued to pound and kick anyway, cursing himself for not being faster and Melissa for being stupidly brave and James for . . . for . . .

Suddenly the Snarf sounds outside stopped and Morton fell to his knees, his fists bruised and grazed from the hard oak door. Hot tears seared his eyes. Surely it couldn't end this way. Not like this.

The silence seemed to rise around him like black water, choking out all his senses, and for a moment, he crouched there in the absolute darkness and imagined that being dead would not feel much different to the way he felt in that very moment.

But then a sound cut through the darkness, a sharp metallic click from outside and, impossibly, the door swung open to reveal a slender silhouette against the faintly moonlit sky.

"Melissa?" Morton whispered, his voice trembling from the tears that still soaked his cheeks. "How . . . ?"

Melissa staggered into the passage, clearly exhausted from terror, and turned on her small key-chain flashlight to dilute the darkness. "I knew he wouldn't eat me. Not his own sister."

"But . . . but what happened?" Morton asked in a tremulous voice.

"He . . . he cried," Melissa said.

"Yes, I heard that, but . . ."

"No, I don't mean that kind of cry. He came right up to me and sniffed me all over and then sort of looked at me and tears started running out of his eyes. Big yellow tears that sizzled when they landed on the grass. I just stayed really still and then he turned and ran off, just like that."

Morton was speechless. He had been fairly certain that Snarfs did not cry.

"I . . . I don't understand how he . . . how he transformed so quickly," Melissa stammered, still obviously in shock. "I mean, we just saw him a couple of hours ago and he was normal. How is that possible?"

"Anything's possible when it comes to magic," Morton said, unable to provide a better answer.

"I know. That's what I hate about all this magic," Melissa whispered, a little of herself returning to her voice. "Anything *is* possible. It's enough to make you crazy."

Morton knew exactly how Melissa was feeling. He'd once thought that magic would be fun, that a world in which anything was possible would be exciting. But now, more than ever, he just wanted a normal world, like the one he'd grown up in.

"Come on," he said at last. "There's nothing more we can do here tonight."

Melissa nodded solemnly, and the two of them ventured back toward the narrow stairs.

A few minutes later, Morton emerged into James's brightly lit bedroom. Melissa sidled out behind him, brushing twigs and leaves from her hair, when her face suddenly twisted and she pushed her fist into her own mouth to choke a scream.

Morton froze for the briefest moment, wondering what in this world, or any other, could possibly bring such a look of pure terror to Melissa's face.

Whatever it was, he decided, he didn't want to have his back to it any longer, and he spun rapidly around to see . . .

"James? Wendy?" he said, feeling certain that he must now be dreaming.

James and Wendy were sitting on the bed, both with dirt on their clothes. They jumped instantly to their feet when they saw Morton and Melissa, obviously equally surprised to have this midnight rendezvous, but neither of them spoke.

Melissa pulled her fist from her mouth and stared in confusion at James.

"But . . . but I just saw you. You're a Snarf. You turned into a Snarf."

James made a tired, annoyed sigh. "That wasn't me, you idiot. It was Brad. Brad's turned into a Snarf."

CHAPTER 13

BATS' BLOOD

Melissa recovered quickly from her shock. Within moments she was marching back and forth in James's bedroom like a prisoner in a cell.

Morton, meanwhile, was sitting on the bed feeling completely stupid. He, of all people, should have guessed that Brad turning into a Snarf was a possibility all along, but he had been so terrified at the thought of it happening to James that he just hadn't been thinking clearly.

"I just . . . I don't understand this at all," Melissa was saying. "I mean, who is this Brad anyway?"

"Brad used to be the lead singer in Nolan's band," Morton said. "He tried to beat us up, remember?"

"But why is he a Snarf?"

"Because when I was turning into a Snarf, he cut himself on my spines," James explained.

Melissa started rubbing her temples with both hands as if her head was aching very badly. "How does that explain anything?"

"The Snarf spines are venomous," Morton said. "Anyone who gets cut by them slowly turns into a Snarf. I should have guessed right away. It's just like the rats. Reversing my wish got rid of my rats but not Timmy's, so reversing James's wish turned him back into a human but obviously it didn't stop Brad from changing into a Snarf."

Melissa, who was still pacing, suddenly stopped dead in her tracks and stared accusingly at James and Wendy.

"Okay, fine, so that makes sense, kind of, but why did the two of you feel the need to go skulking around like night ninjas and keep this whole thing a secret from us?"

James clenched his jaw. "Can you blame me?" he growled. "After what you two got up to in the attic? Chasing after a Snarf is a dangerous business. I didn't want Morton taking risks on my behalf, and you didn't seem to be very good at keeping promises."

"I didn't break my promise!" Melissa retorted. "Morton found me. What was I supposed to do?"

"You weren't supposed to go in the attic in the first place," James shot back.

Melissa sniffed angrily and was about to respond when Wendy cut in. "I think we'd better just put that behind us," she said. "We've all been doing what we thought was for the best, right?"

Melissa and James calmed down, glancing guiltily at each other, as if they both realized this was hardly the time to bicker, although Morton could tell Melissa was seething inside at the thought of Wendy and James making plans behind her back.

"So is there more to the story?" Morton asked. "Or is that everything?"

"Oh, no. That's only the half of it," James said.

"Hmpf! What's the other half, then?" Melissa said in a sulky tone. "Wendy's turning into a Flesh-Eating Butterfly?"

Wendy blushed and cast a hurt glance at Melissa.

"I'm sorry," Melissa said. "I'll shut up now."

James sat down on his chair and pulled off his shoes. "The other half of the story is that Nolan has been collecting ingredients for some kind of potion, and I'm not sure, but I think he might be feeding it to Brad."

"So Nolan *is* involved!" Morton exclaimed.

"Yes," James said, rubbing his feet as if he'd been walking for hours. "A couple of nights ago, Wendy and I waited outside Brad's house to see if he was up to something, and sure enough he snuck out after dark. We followed him, and for some reason he went to the old Wall of Noise rehearsal space. We had heard that Nolan was using a new space to practice with his new band, so at first we thought maybe Brad had rented the old space, that he was starting his own band, but then about an hour later, Nolan showed up too. He was carrying two grocery bags, and even from where we were hiding across the road we could smell rotten meat. He seemed very nervous, which is totally not like Nolan."

"I admit that sounds weird," Melissa said, "but it's hardly proof that Brad has turned into a Snarf."

"Oh, we have proof," James said. "We saw him with our own eyes. Well, actually, not quite our own eyes. We saw him with these." James rummaged in his pocket and produced the pair of X-ray Specs that Robbie had given to Morton.

"Hey, where did you get those?" Morton protested.

"You left them in the kitchen. I was going to destroy them, but the first time I tried them on I found the secret passage behind my bookshelf, so I figured they might be useful and decided to hang on to them for a while. Good thing I did too. After Nolan went inside the rehearsal space, Wendy and I crept over to the door and I put them on. I saw everything. I saw Nolan go down the stairs into a little room in the basement, and by this time there was a full-grown Snarf in there. Brad must have turned completely in just two hours."

"Are you sure it was a Snarf?" Morton asked, trying to imagine the scene.

"Trust me. I know a Snarf when I see one," James said adamantly, and Morton realized that this was, of course, true. "Anyway, Nolan poured some kind of liquid onto the food and threw it into the room and then locked the door again and ran back up the stairs."

Morton was shocked by this strange turn of events. He was trying to figure out firstly why Nolan would want to feed Brad and secondly why he wasn't eaten alive.

"It gets even weirder I'm afraid," Wendy added, obviously noting the horrified looks on Melissa's and Morton's faces.

"It does," James said. "We followed Nolan after he left. It was easy with these on. I could see exactly where he was going. I could even see him right through the buildings. At first I expected him to go home, but he didn't. He went to that old church, down behind the graveyard; you know, the one with the big sign asking for donations to repair the roof."

Morton nodded.

"Somehow, we didn't quite see how, he managed to get into the church and started to climb a narrow spiral staircase that led up to the top of the spire. And then he started catching bats with his bare hands. Literally, he started plucking them off the ceiling."

Morton felt the hairs on the back of his neck bristling. He was fairly certain he knew what James was about to say next.

"At first I thought he was eating them alive," James went on. "I saw all these little bat skeletons flapping around and I thought they were in his stomach, but then he turned to his side and I realized he was holding a bag. He was stuffing live bats in a bag."

"I'm not sure I want to hear the rest of this story," Melissa said with a sickly expression on her face, but James kept talking anyway.

"After he left the church we presumed he was going to take the bats back to the Snarf, back to Brad, I mean, but he didn't. He went home and went into the shed at the bottom of his yard."

"We didn't need the X-ray glasses after that," Wendy said. "We could see him right through the window of his shed."

There was a moment of silence, and Morton could tell that nobody really wanted to finish the story, but Melissa finally spoke up. "So what did he do?" she said faintly.

"It was really horrible," Wendy said. "He . . . he . . ." Wendy went suddenly pale. "Let's just say he . . . collected their blood in a pot."

"He didn't stop with the bats' blood either," James said.

"He started adding other things from jars on his shelf. I mean, there's no doubt about it. Nolan's doing magic."

"What kind of magic?" Melissa asked, as if she didn't really want to know the answer.

"I think I might know," Morton said. "There's a recipe for a Snarf cure that uses bats' blood in the comic I found in Nolan's locker. I think he might actually be trying to help Brad."

"Well, he's not doing a very good job," Melissa said. "I mean Brad's most definitely still a Snarf."

"That's true," Morton said, perplexed by the whole series of events. "But the weird thing is, you need The Book of Parchments to make that potion work, or at least a page from it."

"The Book of Parchments?" Wendy said, her eyes wide with alarm. "Didn't you say that was what King's enemy was trying to steal from him?"

Morton nodded.

"You're not suggesting Nolan was King's enemy? Surely he's too young."

"Well, if he's as good at magic as King seemed to think, he could probably make himself look young," Melissa said.

"Yeah, but I doubt he could give himself parents, and spend years in school creating a false identity," James replied, clearly skeptical of the whole notion.

Melissa paced nervously again around the room. "Well, if he hadn't conveniently vanished, we could ask him," she said, and then suddenly stopped pacing and turned to face the others with a look of horror on her face. "You don't think Brad ate him, do you?"

James grimaced and made a sucking noise with his teeth. "I admit, that was my first thought," he said. "That's why Wendy and I went out again tonight. I wanted to go back to the rehearsal space to see if there were any signs of, well, you know, bits of Nolan."

"And?" Melissa said, her eyes still wide with horror.

"Nothing," James replied. "The place was deserted."

"Which doesn't mean no," Melissa added.

"At this point, no news is good news," Wendy offered, trying to be optimistic.

"Anyway, there's not much more we can do tonight," James said. "I suggest we turn in. Maybe tomorrow we'll find out what happened to King's library. That might help make sense of some of it."

Everyone was in agreement that bed was a good idea, and James got up to escort Wendy home through the secret passage so as not to waken the sleeping Mrs. Smedley.

That night Morton dreamed he was in the school cafeteria trying to strike up conversations with the other kids, but every time he sat next to one, a Ten-Eyed Salamander or a Toxic Vapor Worm or some other monster would come and scare them away. Annoyingly the dream seemed to go on all night and by morning pretty much every monster from *Scare Scape* had scared away pretty much every single person he knew, and he awoke feeling not in the least rested or refreshed. In fact, when Dad called him for breakfast he thought he would feel tired for the rest of his life. But as he shuffled down the stairs, clinging to the banister for support, he smelled something so delicious that he actually started to get excited. He'd forgotten that Mrs. Smedley had promised to bake something the night before, and when he arrived at the table he saw that Dad was serving hot apple strudel with whipped cream and maple syrup. James and Melissa were already eating, both still in their pajamas, ravaging large slices of strudel like hungry Shark Hounds.

"Hey, save some for me!" Morton said, running over and attempting to grab the serving plate from the middle of the table.

"No need to forget your manners," Dad said. "There's plenty more in the oven."

"There is?" Melissa exclaimed, looking like she'd just found the best shoe sale in history.

"Yes, so slow down before you choke yourself."

Dad helped Morton to a generous serving and then, as promised, retrieved a second strudel from the oven. The smell of cinnamon and sweet apple percolated through the entire house and for a few brief minutes Morton forgot everything about the previous night's troubling revelations, and his mind drifted back to an earlier time, a time when tasty meals were frequent occurrences and his biggest challenge had been tracking down back issues of *Scare Scape*.

"I must say, it doesn't feel right eating Mrs. Smedley's food without her being here to enjoy it," Dad said, chewing happily on his own dwindling portion.

"Why didn't she stay?" Morton asked.

"She said something silly about not imposing on our little family unit, which I told her was of course ridiculous. We'd be happy to have her anytime. In fact, I was thinking of inviting her to —"

Quite suddenly James broke into a coughing fit so extreme that he spilled his milk all over the tablecloth. Melissa and Dad both jumped to their feet.

"Gracious!" Dad exclaimed, running into the kitchen to grab a tea towel. "Good thing I didn't serve cranberry juice this morning."

"James!" Melissa hissed under her breath. "You did that on purpose!"

"What? Don't be ridiculous!" James said, folding the tablecloth over to stop the pool of milk from dripping onto his lap.

"Did it ever occur to you," Melissa went on, "that you're not the only one with feelings?"

"I don't have a clue what you're talking about," James said.

"Yes you do," Melissa shot back in a reprimanding voice. "And you know what I think —?"

Dad rushed back into the room and began dabbing at the damp spot on the tablecloth before Melissa could finish her sentence.

"What do you think?" Dad said, smiling brightly.

"Oh, nothing, Dad," Melissa said.

"Really?" Dad said, his smile wavering.

There was a moment of tense silence and then Melissa turned on her heel. "I have to go," she said, and ran back upstairs to get dressed.

James glanced at the clock. "Yeah, I should get going too," he said, getting up from the table and following Melissa.

Dad watched them both go, his smile now replaced with a puzzled frown. "Did I just miss something?" he asked.

Morton shrugged. "I think we both did," he said, eating the last piece of strudel, which somehow no longer seemed so sweet.

When James and Morton arrived at school later that morning, Morton wasn't the least surprised to find that Derek's ever-growing fan club was dominating the scene and a crowd that appeared to include well over half the kids in school was gathered around him. What did surprise Morton, however, was the fact that Robbie was waiting for him at the gate standing beside a very irritable-looking Julie Bashford.

The moment he saw Morton, Robbie nudged Julie on the elbow and the two of them approached.

"Julie's got something she wants to say to you," Robbie said.

"Oh," Morton said, suddenly very confused about his emotions. "What's that?"

Robbie turned to face Julie, and she chewed her lip reluctantly. "I'm not saying it in front of *him*," she said, glancing at James.

James seemed to understand that this was a personal matter and made some flippant remark about needing to sharpen his pencils, then wandered off across the school yard.

Robbie nudged Julie on the elbow for a second time.

"I'm sorry for saying those things about Robbie," Julie finally said in a flat monotone voice. "I shouldn't have said them."

"And . . . ," Robbie prompted.

"And Robbie really is your best friend and he likes you a lot."

Morton was so caught off guard that he couldn't really think of a response. As it turned out she didn't give him chance to respond anyway. She simply looked at Robbie and said, "Satisfied?" and marched gruffly away, leaving the two of them standing in awkward silence.

"I'm sorry," Robbie said at last. "She shouldn't have said those things. They're not true."

Morton wandered over to the nearest bench and flopped down tiredly. "No, I'm sorry," he said. "I was the one that shouldn't have said anything. I guess I was a bit spooked out by everything, and I'd just had a fight with James."

"Really? But you and James never fight," Robbie said. "What was it about?"

"It's complicated," Morton said, and then did his best to fill Robbie in on all he had missed. By the time Morton had finished, the first bell had rung and the two of them made their way into school.

"Wow!" Robbie said at last. "I guess that explains why Nolan has been acting so weird recently. But I can't believe Brad is a Snarf."

Just as Robbie was saying this, James spotted them from across the hallway and meandered over. "Everything okay?" he asked.

Robbie nodded and looked up at James. "I was just saying I can't believe Brad is a Snarf," he repeated.

"I know, it's a bit of a shock," James said.

Robbie nodded thoughtfully and then added, "Still, I suppose it's fitting. I mean, he always was a bit of a beast."

James seemed unpleasantly surprised by this comment and scowled at Robbie.

"What?" Robbie retorted, staring back at James. "It's true."

"There's a big difference between being a bully and being a Snarf," James said.

Robbie made a snorting sound and appeared ready to argue the point, but suddenly a group of kids they'd just seen hanging out with Derek spilled into the hallway, all giggling so loudly that it was difficult to ignore them.

"I wonder what's so funny," Morton said, turning his back on Robbie.

The laughter grew suddenly even louder, and one laugh in particular seemed to drown out all the others.

"You know, I think I've heard that laugh before," James said, looking around nervously.

"I definitely haven't," Robbie said. "In fact, it sounds more like a donkey than a person."

"A donkey with a sore throat," Morton put in, strangely amused by the persistent laughter.

Robbie began to chuckle at Morton's comment, but James looked at them both sternly.

"This is hardly the time for brevity," he said.

Morton giggled. "I think you mean *levity*."

"Yeah. *Brevity*?" Robbie said. "What's that? Some kind of underwear?" And he burst quite unexpectedly into hysterics.

James scowled even harder, a deep furrow appearing between his eyes. Morton stared up at him, trying not to laugh, but for some reason the more he tried not to laugh the more he wanted to laugh, and before he knew it he too was laughing hysterically at Robbie's joke. In fact, now that Morton thought about it, the whole situation was quite ridiculous. Brad turning into a Snarf; John King falling down his own well; Mr. Brown getting eaten by cats.

"Will you stop giggling like schoolgirls!" James said sternly.

Robbie, who was now doubled over laughing, put his hand on Morton's shoulder and managed to pause long enough to speak. "Did he say 'giggling like schoolgirls' or 'wiggling like schoolgirls'?" he said, and then burst into an even bigger belly laugh. Morton also found this to be painfully funny and started laughing so hard that he fell to the floor gasping for air.

As he rolled around on the floor he wondered dimly why all the other kids in the hall were also laughing, falling down one after the other and flapping around like fish on a beach. Somewhere, in a deep corner of his brain, Morton thought this was very, very odd. And then he realized he could hardly breathe.

Quite suddenly Morton's stomach was beginning to ache, and gray clouds were crowding in around the edges of his vision. James appeared over him, his hands firmly clamped over his ears. He was shouting something, but Morton couldn't hear a word he was saying. He just thought how unfortunate it was that James had no sense of humor. . . .

CHAPTER 14

MUTINOUS MAGIC

Morton awoke to the sensation of cold water sloshing down his back and an immense pain in his stomach muscles. Opening his eyes, he found he was staring up at what appeared to be a janitor's closet. He could no longer hear the cackling laughter, but he could hear some kind of commotion. He sat up to find James holding a now empty bucket and Robbie sitting in a dazed state beside him, his clothes also dripping wet.

"The Evil Laughing Clown," James said simply. "I'll never forget that irritating cackle. We used to hide it under Melissa's bed and set it off, remember? It used to make her so angry, even though she couldn't stop laughing."

Morton did remember, and it suddenly all made sense. He'd seen one of the kids in the hall holding a clown doll, which he now realized must be another magically enchanted toy from the back pages of *Scare Scape*. It had never occurred to him that laughing uncontrollably could be so dangerous.

"I couldn't breathe," Morton said, taking several gulps of air.

"Not surprising," James said. "Didn't the ad for that thing say, 'You'll laugh yourself to death'?"

"Sounds right," Morton said. "What happened to the others?"

"They'll be fine. I took the batteries out as soon I realized what was going on," James said. "But that's the least of our worries right now."

Morton listened again to the noises coming in from the hallway. It sounded like a crazy carnival with shouting and laughing and, perplexingly, the constant barking of dogs.

"Is there some kind of riot?" Morton asked, even though he was fairly sure he knew the answer.

"Yes, a *Scare Scape* riot. It looks like *everybody* has something from the back pages. Annoyingly, so far the silent dog whistle seems to be the most popular."

"That explains the barking," Robbie said. "But where are the teachers? Why hasn't Finch gotten the situation under control?"

"That's a good question," James said. "Firstly, I have to presume Derek wasn't the only one with an Antigravity Laser Cannon because a bunch of teachers are stuck on the ceiling in the staff room. Mrs. Punjab and Mrs. Wallis passed out laughing, but the rest of them have completely vanished, Finch included."

"It sounds like everyone's gone crazy," Robbie said, getting to his feet and pulling the door open a crack to listen to the riotous noise outside.

James nodded thoughtfully. "Yep! That's pretty much it. You know, the irony is, we're reading *Lord of the Flies* in English class, but it really doesn't seem to have made an impact at all."

Morton hadn't read *Lord of the Flies* and didn't really know what James was talking about, but made a mental note to get the book out of the library the next chance he got.

"What are we going to do?" Robbie asked, getting to his feet and pressing his ear to the door.

"Well, for starters I think we'd better get somewhere safe, like out of the school," James said. "After that, I'm out of ideas."

Morton and Robbie agreed that getting away from the carnage was probably the best first step.

"Just stick close," James said as he inched open the door. "It's pretty insane out there."

James wasn't exaggerating. The hall was crammed with stray dogs and wild children. The moment they emerged from the janitor's closet, two very giddy girls ran up to them and blew great plumes of flame at their heads. Morton felt the heat singe his eyebrows and covered his face with his hands. The girls seemed to think this was hilarious and laughed loudly before running off to perform the trick on their next victims.

"Hot Pepper Candies," Morton said. "I should have known those would be popular."

"Yeah, I'll tell you what else is popular," James said. "Fog Pellets. Visibility's down to zero on the whole second floor."

"Uh-oh," Morton said. "What color is the fog?"

"White," James said. "Why?"

Morton sighed with relief. "Lucky it's not green," he explained. "Monsters are supposed to come out of the green fog. The white fog is pretty harmless, except people get lost in it and lose their memories, which might explain where most of the teachers are."

"Good thing we don't have to go to the second floor, then," James said. "Come on, we better run."

James led the way past barking dogs and running children

as they headed toward one of the side doors, since the front door was apparently blocked by some kind of volcano, which Morton thought was most likely the Vesuvian Lava Lamp. They were halfway there when the door to a nearby bathroom burst open and a vast wave of white foam sprayed out, covering Morton from head to toe and knocking James and Robbie flat on their backs.

"Exploding Soap," Morton said, wiping the viscous white froth from his face and shaking great globs of it from his arms. "Suddenly it doesn't seem as funny as it did when we used it on Melissa."

"Just keep running," James said, slithering back onto his feet and attempting to sprint for the now visible exit but immediately falling over again.

Morton helped James and Robbie to their feet and they settled into moving with a kind of sideways slide, but before they'd gotten far, a couple of overfriendly dogs came skidding and bounding onto the scene and knocked all three of them down yet again like a row of bowling pins.

At that point, Morton heard someone calling his name. "Morton, help!"

Morton rolled over to look in the direction of the voice and saw a small girl with frizzy blond hair bouncing on the ceiling like a helium balloon. It was Willow, the girl whose cat he had retrieved the day after the Zombie Twins released their control on the town's feline population.

"I can't get down!" Willow said tremulously.

Morton suddenly realized just how dangerous this situation was. If Willow were to get blown out the window, who knew what would become of her.

"Hold on to the lights and stay away from the windows," Morton bellowed, but no sooner had he said this than a fierce wind howled down the hall and Willow rolled like a tumbleweed across the ceiling and shot out of sight around the corner, screaming as she went.

"We have to help her!" Morton said.

"How?" Robbie said, grabbing on to a nearby fire extinguisher for support.

Before Morton could answer he saw a swirling triangle of dense black smoke racing toward them from the far end of the hall.

"A miniature tornado?" James said, staring in complete shock at the rapidly approaching vortex.

Morton wasn't sure exactly which toy or combination of toys might be causing a tornado, but he didn't want to stand around talking about it. The fearsome artificial cyclone was wrenching drawings from the walls and picking up everything else in its wake, including a dozen stray dogs and several children.

"Quick!" Robbie said, heading in the opposite direction. "Follow me!"

James and Morton followed Robbie as he slithered down the hall and took a sharp left into an adjacent hallway. Robbie quickly slammed the heavy fire doors behind them, just as the cyclone tore past, howling like a small jet engine. The boys all huddled around the square window in the door and peered at the devastation beyond.

"We've got to stop this!" James said. "Somebody's going to get hurt."

"You can say that again," Robbie said. "It's like they're all possessed by a clown with a very bad sense of humor."

"You know, something tells me this is Derek's doing," Morton said, and as he did so a whining voice droned from behind them.

"Talking about me behind my back again?"

The three boys spun around to see that there, completely blocking the passage ahead, was a large group of teachers, among them Mr. Noble, Mr. Rickets, Mrs. Houston, and, most alarmingly, Principal Finch. This sight itself was strange enough, but what made it utterly bizarre was the fact that Derek Howell was standing at the front of the group like the captain of a small army.

The boys stood staring with complete incomprehension. Morton wondered for a moment if Derek had told Finch and the other teachers that he and James were somehow responsible for the current mayhem, but Principal Finch wasn't even looking at them. He was looking directly ahead with an unusually docile expression on his face.

"It *is* you," James said accusingly. "What have you done to the teachers?"

"Nothing," Derek said in an oily voice. "Or at least, nothing they'll remember."

"What's that supposed to mean?"

Derek made a gloating smile and held up what looked like a pocket watch hanging from a silver chain around his neck. Morton noticed immediately that instead of a numbered face, the watch had a black and white spiral that turned lazily behind the glass.

"It's the Mesmer Disk," Morton said. "He's hypnotized everyone!"

"No keeping secrets from you, is there?" Derek said.

"Are you mad?" James sputtered. "This whole situation is completely out of control. Somebody could get hurt!"

"From where I'm standing it doesn't look out of control," Derek said. "In fact, I seem to be in perfect control of everything."

"Really?" James said. "You mean you actually intended to get a school full of barking dogs, tornadoes, and wild children?"

"That's exactly what I wanted," Derek said confidently.

"Why on earth would you want that?" Robbie said, his face a mixture of revulsion and confusion.

"So you'll get in trouble, of course," Derek snapped, as if this was somehow obvious.

James, Morton, and Robbie were dumbfounded by this response and simply stared back at Derek.

Derek sighed impatiently. "I thought you were supposed to be smart, but obviously I was wrong," he said. "I've hypnotized everybody in school and they're all going to wake up tomorrow with no memory of what happened. But when they get here in the morning the school will be a complete wreck. And you three are going to confess to having done it."

"And why would we do that?" Robbie asked.

Derek held up his Mesmer Disk again and this time the spiral face started spinning at a more rapid, dizzying speed. "Because you'll do anything I tell you to do," Derek said.

"And the best part is, you won't even remember doing it, which is why the first thing you're going to tell me is how you've been doing all this magic in the first place."

"Us tell you?" Robbie said. "We thought you were the one doing the magic."

Derek made a small jump of surprise at this comment and eyed the three boys suspiciously. "You're just saying that to trick me into thinking you don't know how to do magic."

James groaned and clutched his head. "We don't know how to do magic, you idiot!"

Derek flushed angrily. "I'm *not* an idiot! I've outsmarted you and the whole school. And it's obvious you're responsible for all this stuff that's been happening. I know you've got magical powers, and I want them. Now, if you'll watch the disk . . ."

"Don't look!" Morton shouted, holding his hand up to block the spinning silver object from his sight, but James had already caught a glimpse of it and his eyes were going a little misty. Morton rushed at him and turned him around so he had his back to Derek. James quickly shook his head and seemed to recover, but Derek merely snorted derisively.

"We can do this the hard way if you prefer," he scoffed, then in a more commanding voice he said, "Hold them!"

To Morton's horror, Principal Finch, Mr. Rickets, and Mr. Darcy responded at once to Derek's command and stepped forward with outstretched arms.

Morton dove out of their reach while James produced the X-ray Specs from his pocket, put them over his eyes, and lunged for Derek. Derek held up the spinning Mesmer Disk like a defensive amulet and yelled for James to stop, but James obviously wasn't affected by it while wearing the glasses and he crashed into Derek a split second later. Derek lost his grip on the disk and it went swirling up out of his hands.

Derek screeched in outrage, "Stop them! Stop them!" And Mr. Darcy rushed at James and wrestled him to the ground at the same time Mr. Rickets dove at Robbie.

Only then did Derek look up in search of his precious hypnotic disk — which, strangely, had gone up but not come down. Morton followed his gaze to find Willow on the ceiling. She was holding the disk so that its face was pointing directly at Derek.

"You are feeling very sleepy," she said, presumably because she didn't know what else to say. Derek was so outraged that he didn't think to look away and almost instantly his eyes took on the familiar glassy vacant look.

"You will tell Mr. Darcy and Mr. Rickets to let Robbie and James go," she said, and quite remarkably Derek turned to the teachers and said in a monotone voice, "Release them."

They did exactly that, and Robbie and James pulled themselves to a sitting position.

"What should I do now?" Willow said, accidentally turning the disk to face them all. They all quickly threw up their hands to shield their eyes.

"First you should put the cover on the disk," Morton said.

"Oops! Sorry," Willow said, closing the silver cover over the pendant.

"So, what *should* we do now?" James said, getting to his feet.

Morton looked around at the wreckage that only a few hours before had been a perfectly orderly school environment. Derek had single-handedly hypnotized every teacher and almost all of the kids and managed to destroy half the school. Just how could they ever hope to recover from this?

CHAPTER 15

THE MIDNIGHT DOOR

After a brief debate, Morton and the others agreed that they couldn't just abandon the school and had to at least try to minimize the damage done by Derek's hypnosis, but it took almost an hour for them to figure out a plan of action. This was largely because they were interrupted by barking dogs and the still rampant tornado on several occasions so they had to keep moving to different parts of the school. Despite this, they finally managed to lay out what Morton thought was a pretty good solution to the nightmare circus that Derek had created.

It was Morton who figured out that since Derek had already hypnotized everyone to forget everything the next morning, all they had to do was get everyone to stop causing mayhem and go home. And since they would all do exactly what Derek told them to do, and Derek would do exactly what Willow told him to do, then in theory Willow just had to tell Derek to tell everyone to go home with symptoms of a cold and go straight to bed. The next morning they'd all arrive at school with no clue as to what had happened.

In practice this seemingly simple plan was difficult to execute and took them several more hours. First they had to get Willow and several other students down from the ceiling, which involved tracking down the second Antigravity Laser Cannon and dragging one of those big blue gymnastic mattresses around to cushion everyone's fall. Next Willow gave Derek very careful instructions, and Morton, James, and Robbie followed him around the school, cornering each student, confiscating their toys, and sending them home. They also set to work driving out the stray dogs and opening windows to clear the fog from the second floor as they worked their way along. (Things went a little more quickly after they managed to stop Nelly Stark from shooting the Tornado Spinning Top down the hallways.)

It was almost the end of the day by the time they'd emptied the school of students and at last turned to the teachers. Under Willow's instruction Derek mechanically told the teachers to go home, one after another, until only a single teacher remained. It just so happened that the last teacher there was Mr. Noble.

"Wait!" Morton said, interrupting Willow before she could instruct Derek once more. He suddenly realized he had a golden opportunity — he could make Mr. Noble forget all about the difficult homework assignment he'd given him. That would certainly take a load off his shoulders, and right now he had more than his share of problems without having to worry about extra homework.

"What is it?" Willow asked, looking up at Morton patiently.

But Morton had second thoughts. Mr. Noble hadn't really been unfair in giving him the assignment. He had been talking in class, after all, and he suddenly realized just how tempting it was to use magic for selfish purposes. He also realized that giving in to that temptation would make him no better than Derek . . . or even Mr. Brown.

"Never mind," he said quickly. "Go ahead."

Willow shrugged, and moments later Morton watched Mr. Noble pace out of the school with a determined focus, just as all the other teachers had done.

Finally there was nobody left except for Derek, and the school had an eerie, ghostly feeling. It reminded Morton of a *Scare Scape* story about a boy who had the power to make anybody who annoyed him vanish . . . which of course ended up being everybody, including his parents and siblings.

"Be sure to give Derek an extra dose of amnesia," James said. "Make him forget all about that Antigravity Laser Cannon and getting stuck on the ceiling. Otherwise we'll just have to go through this all over again."

Willow did exactly as James suggested, and Derek simply turned away and sauntered out the door as if everything were completely normal.

"So, I guess that's everybody," James said. "We should get out of here too before the cleaners show up."

"I suppose I should give you this," Willow said, holding up the Mesmer Disk.

"Yeah, we should probably put it with the others," Morton said.

"You promise you won't hypnotize me," Willow said, looking a little nervous.

"I promise," Morton said with a warm smile. "But you

have to make a promise too. You have to promise not to tell anyone what happened. Magic is a dangerous thing and we're trying to stop it, not make it worse."

Willow played thoughtfully with her long golden hair. "So, are you like some kind of secret anti-magic police?" she asked.

"Uh, yes, I suppose we are," Morton said, feeling somehow pleased with that title, as if it satisfied something deep inside of him that he had never been fully aware of before.

"Can I join?" Willow asked. "That sounds like fun."

Morton glanced at Robbie, who was frowning and shaking his head. "Maybe when you're older," Morton said. "I think it's a bit too dangerous for you now."

Willow sighed and handed over the disk. "I knew you'd say that," she said, blinking rapidly and smiling up at Morton. "I guess I'll see you tomorrow, then."

"Yes, see you tomorrow," Morton said, although even as he said that, he wondered if he really would. With all the magical insanity that was surrounding them, he was starting to feel very pessimistic about the prospect of there even being a tomorrow.

Robbie and James seemed to have the same thought and the three of them stood in silence for a few seconds until James nudged Morton on the arm. "Come on," he said. "Let's get out of here."

A few minutes later they were walking home in the crisp, cool sunshine, which at least brought some warmth to Morton's mood.

"I'll say one thing for Derek," James said. "He's not stupid. Although, he obviously doesn't know anything about magic, which I guess makes Nolan our number one suspect again."

Robbie sighed. "Yeah, but I still can't imagine why Nolan would make all the *Scare Scape* toys magic. What does he gain from that?"

"Well, we have to find him and ask him," Morton said, with an air of determination.

"In the meantime, let's hope Melissa has learned something about the missing books. That should shed some light on this whole crazy mess," James said as they plodded tiredly along the driveway toward the back porch.

As soon as the house came into view, Morton saw that several of the windows on the ground floor were open and a nasty-smelling smoke was billowing out.

"Oh no! What's happened?" Robbie said in sudden panic.

Morton and James, however, remained calm. This was not the first time they'd witnessed such a scene.

"Don't worry about it," Morton said. "It's probably just supper."

Sure enough, when they entered the kitchen Dad was on his hands and knees in front of the oven, wafting acrid black smoke out into the room. The smell was so bad Morton could hardly breathe.

"What are you doing?" he said, holding his scarf over his nose.

"I don't understand it," Dad said, coughing and choking. "I haven't even put anything in the oven yet!"

"Maybe you left the mitts in there again," Morton suggested, remembering the last time Dad almost set fire to the kitchen.

"Not this time," Dad said, holding up a very tattered pair of red polka-dotted mitts. "There must be something else in here that — aha!" Dad reached for a pair of metal tongs and pushed them into the smoky blackness of the oven. A moment later he pulled out what looked like a charred hairy potato, billowing with wretched smoke so dense that it stung Morton's eyes.

"It's one of those blasted rats!" Dad exclaimed, leaping to his feet and running for the door.

Morton, James, and Robbie jumped aside quickly as Dad pushed past them to throw the smoking carcass out onto the lawn.

"The blighters are getting into everything," Dad went on, stomping on the smoldering lump. "I found one in the car this morning on my way home. It bit me on the ankle. I must say, it's getting quite out of hand. Thank goodness they're going to release the gas in the sewers tonight."

"What?" Morton shrieked.

"You don't sound too happy about that," Dad said, still stomping.

Morton quickly changed his tone. "No, I mean, wow! That's great news! Uh, what time tonight?"

"Midnight," Dad said. "They want to do it when there's nobody on the streets, for obvious reasons."

"Let's hope it works," James said.

Dad finally stepped away from the smoldering carcass and looked back up at the house. A gray smog was still billowing out the door. "You better stay here while I go and open some more windows," he said, and went back inside, immediately coughing and choking again.

Morton, Robbie, and James did as Dad asked and waited outside, standing well clear of the windows to avoid the smoke. Nobody said anything, and an odd tension seemed to hang in the air. Morton was sifting through a list of worries in his head when Jake's old yellow car suddenly squeaked to a halt at the end of the driveway.

Jake jumped out and ran around to open the back door like a well-trained chauffeur, and both Wendy and Melissa climbed out and smiled politely at him. Morton noticed that this time there was no kiss. In fact, Melissa behaved as though Jake was nothing more than a kind stranger who had given them a ride.

As Jake drove away, Melissa and Wendy walked toward the house and both got a whiff of the smoke.

"What is that disgusting smell?" Melissa exclaimed.

"Never mind the smell," James said. "We've had a bit of a rough day, and we're really hoping that Jake told you who bought King's library."

"Oh?" Melissa said. "How rough?"

"Well, Derek hypnotized almost every kid in school and organized a riot, and Dad just told us they're releasing the gas in the sewers tonight."

"You're right, that is a bad day," Melissa said. "Even by our standards."

"So?" James prodded.

Melissa sighed and looked at Wendy. "I'm not sure it's

good news," she said. "But it turns out King's creepy maybe-brother bought his entire collection."

"Crooks!" Morton said. "Somehow that doesn't surprise me."

"We should set a watch outside the store," Wendy suggested. "We could use the X-ray Specs to find out what he's up to."

"That could take days," Morton said, "and we don't have days. The rats are going to swarm the streets at midnight tonight!"

"Midnight!" Melissa said, as if she hated the very word. "Why does it always have to be midnight? What's so great about midnight? Why can't it just be half past ten?"

Morton had often wondered that himself. Just what *was* the fascination with midnight? Almost every issue of *Scare Scape* had a story where something happened at midnight, as if there was something magical about both hands of a clock lining up to the number twelve. In fact, even the special edition that he'd found in Nolan's locker had a story called "The Midnight Door" in which . . .

At that very moment Morton had the overwhelming sensation that his brain had started spinning in his skull, and thoughts and memories started flashing around in his head like arcs of lightning. Visions of his encounter with Crooks raced before his eyes, and he suddenly remembered the fact that there had been a clock right above the velvet curtain and that the clock had been set to midnight. . . .

"I think I know where King's library is," he said, his whole body going numb.

Everyone turned to face him expectantly, but he couldn't think quite how to explain it, so he ran to grab Nolan's tattered copy of King's Gold from his bag in the mudroom.

"It's easier if I just show you," he said when he returned, and opened the issue to the story he'd noticed before but not bothered to reread. "The Midnight Door" told the (as always, tragic) tale of a fugitive who was hiding out in an abandoned train station where he found a painting of a door on the wall at the end of an alcove.

One night while hiding from the authorities, he discovered that whenever the station clock was set to midnight he could pass through the painting into the world beyond.

"I didn't think about it until now," Morton explained as the others pored over the comic, "but there was a clock over the velvet curtain and the first time I saw Crooks go behind it, it was set to twelve o'clock. I thought it was just broken, but now I think it must be magic. I think that might be where Crooks is hiding King's books."

James, who was now holding the comic, made an odd grimace. "I think you might be onto something," he said. "Listen to this: King's comments at the end of the story."

And so you see, our tragic hero, like so many before him, was trapped by his own lack of knowledge. He did not understand that the power to bring a mere illustration to life is perhaps the purest, most coveted magic of all. For as I have said many times, magic is the act of opening the veil to another dimension — but where most magic is a mere pinprick to let a drop of another world seep through,

**this power to bring drawings to life is like opening
a river. So it is with the power of the Parchments:
with infinite creativity, comes infinite danger!**

"The Book of Parchments again!" Melissa said. "How
often does that show up in stories?"

"To be honest, almost never," Morton said. "I only even
remembered it because I'd reread the Snarf story just
recently."

"So if you're right and Crooks has this secret curtain, then
does that mean he'd also have to have The Book of
Parchments to make it work?" Wendy asked.

"According to King," Morton said. "But there's only one
way to find out for sure."

Wendy frowned and looked down at Morton. "Are you
suggesting we break into Crooks's bookshop?"

"We don't have any choice," Morton said. "We have no
other clues and the rats are going to swarm the streets
tonight."

"You know what I hate?" Melissa said, "I hate the fact
that you're right."

"Are we sure about this?" Robbie said, licking his lips
nervously. "Because this sounds like it could be very
dangerous."

"Dangerous and stupid," James said, "but Morton's right.
We've run out of options."

"Oh well," Melissa said. "Just another fun Clay family
outing. Bring lemonade and a sharp sword."

Nobody laughed, and Morton could tell by the look on
Melissa's face that despite her flippant words, she too was

afraid, and with good reason. He can't have been the only one to consider the possibility that Crooks might not only be King's brother but also the mysterious enemy King had written about in his diary. And if that was true, then Crooks would be far more dangerous than anything they'd encountered before.

CHAPTER 16

COLBY'S CAT

After the kids had happily wolfed down a makeshift supper of canned spaghetti, Mrs. Smedley arrived wearing a white cable-knit sweater and a pair of faded jeans. Wendy and Robbie had left a couple of hours earlier, and they'd agreed to meet up at the park at ten o'clock, by which time they hoped Mrs. Smedley would be asleep.

Dad seemed embarrassed about the lingering smell of charbroiled rat in the kitchen and apologized profusely. Mrs. Smedley insisted it didn't bother her in the least, and she ushered him out of the house with assurances that everything would be fine.

"Well, you all look like you need cheering up," she said to James, Melissa, and Morton as Dad's car pulled away. "Why don't I bake you some cookies?"

"That would be nice, if the oven didn't smell of dead rat," Melissa said.

"Good point," Mrs. Smedley said, pulling open the oven door and turning up her nose. "I guess I'll have to give it a good clean first."

"You can't do that!" Melissa shrieked. "You'll ruin your sweater."

Mrs. Smedley laughed. "That's also a good point, but I think I should make the effort. James — I mean, your father, has a lot on his plate right now. It can't be easy running a household, raising three kids, and working a full-time job. He needs all the support he can get, so I'm not about to worry over a few stains on an old sweater."

James, who had been fiddling with his tennis racket in the mudroom, cleared his throat and stepped forward. "I'll, uh, I'll help you clean the oven," he said.

Melissa turned and stared at James with a look of complete surprise.

Mrs. Smedley seemed particularly happy about this and smiled warmly at James, even though he was still looking down at his feet. "That's very nice of you, James, but honestly, I don't think youth should be wasted on menial chores. Heaven knows you'll spend most of your life doing them anyway, and there must be more fun to be had in this big old house." Mrs. Smedley glanced around as if she were in a museum. "Tell me, do you still have bat problems in the attic? John always seemed to have an infestation of the things when he lived here."

James, Morton, and Melissa let out simultaneous squeaks.

"You . . . you knew John King?" Melissa said.

Mrs. Smedley looked curiously at them. "Of course. He was my neighbor."

There was a long moment of silence and Morton guessed they all looked shocked or disturbed, because Mrs. Smedley's expression changed to one of sympathy.

"I'm guessing you heard how he died," she said.

They all nodded.

"A terrible tragedy," Mrs. Smedley went on. "He was such a nice man —"

"He was a nice man?" Melissa interjected. "I thought he was a spooky hermit."

Mrs. Smedley pursed her lips thoughtfully. "Well, I can see why some people might have thought that," she said. "But really, he was a very sweet man underneath. He used to help out at local charity events, and he did a lot for children's literacy. I think he let people think of him as a spooky old man because it was good for business. He used to be a comic book creator, you know."

"We do know," Melissa droned. "Morton reads his ghastly comic."

"Oh, really?" Mrs. Smedley said, giving Morton an encouraging smile. "Well, I've never read it myself, but I've heard it's very good. I think his only problem was that he spent too much time working. He was always working, day and night. They say that's why he went blind, but you know, I never quite understood that."

"Why not?" Morton asked. "We read a magazine article that said he worked in the dark too much."

"Yes, I think I read that too, but it never sounded right to me. I mean, that kind of thing is usually a degenerative disease, that is, it comes on slowly. But with him, one day he could see perfectly, and the next, he was completely blind."

"You never asked him about it?" James said.

"I thought it would be impolite," Mrs. Smedley said with a regretful tone. "We weren't that close. I mean, I'd check up on him every once in a while, to make sure he was okay, but it's true he liked to be alone. Poor man."

The three kids continued to stare at Mrs. Smedley, waiting to see if she would continue, but she simply shrugged. "Well, I wish I could tell you more," she said, "because by the looks on your faces I'm quite sure I could talk about him all night and you'd listen. Unfortunately that's all I know about the mysterious Mr. King and, as you know, I do have an oven to clean."

James made a point of offering to help Mrs. Smedley clean the oven one more time, but she repeated her insistence that she do it alone, and the three of them shuffled up the stairs and ended up pacing restlessly in James's bedroom.

"So, imagine that. Our very own babysitter baking cookies for King," Melissa said.

"I wonder what else she knows about him," Morton said.

"She said she doesn't know anything," James said.

"Nothing she thinks is important," Morton said, "but she probably knows things that might be useful. Like the whole thing about King going blind suddenly."

"I don't see how any of that matters," Melissa said. "King's dead, and if we don't get down to business, we'll soon be joining him. I say we get armed and ready."

James and Morton reluctantly agreed with her and set to preparing for the night's expedition. Melissa decided to wear all black and retrieved three swords from under her bed and offered one each to the boys. Morton declined because they were too heavy, and James declined because he was fairly certain that if he had a sword the only person he'd injure would be himself.

Shortly after nine o'clock they said good night to Mrs. Smedley and went through the charade of going to bed. All three of them stuffed pillows under their blankets just in case she popped her head in, then James led the way down the hidden staircase and out through the oak door.

A moonless sky scattered with deep blue stars stretched to the horizon, and a cold breeze caused bare branches to wave their gray skeletal arms overhead, as if warning them away from danger. All three of them looked out and shivered.

"I guess there's no turning back now," James said.

"There never was any turning back," Melissa said. "What's that thing Mum always used to say, about going forward?"

"The only way forward, is through the truth," Morton said.

"That's it. So, here's hoping we find some truth," Melissa said.

"Here's hoping we come back alive," James said, and they set off at a trot for the park. Once there, they were greeted by the eerie sight of two dark figures sitting alone on the swings, whispering in the dark.

"Robbie, is that you?" Morton called, unable to see much of anything in the almost total blackness of Dimvale's night. The two figures jumped up and ran toward them.

"We were worried you wouldn't be able to sneak out," Wendy's voice said a moment before Morton was able to make out her profile. "It's past ten."

"Yes," Morton said. "Which gives us less than two hours before they release the gas."

"How far is it to Crooks's shop?" James asked.

"About twenty minutes, if we move fast," Wendy said,

and she set off in the lead, taking them up side streets and through parking lots, much as she had done on Halloween.

Morton found that all he could see in Dimvale's deep night were the silhouettes of buildings, dark hollow forms with hazy outlines, which reminded him of King's black sketches from countless macabre tales.

"It's so dark," Morton said to James as they bustled along, trying to keep up with Wendy.

"Here, try these," James said, handing him the X-ray Specs. "They work just as well at night as they do in the day."

Morton put the glasses on and was amazed to see the streets light up like a neon sign. Just like when he had tried them on in Mr. Noble's class, suddenly he could see everything. The buildings and trees all fluoresced brightly in a way that reminded him of an old video game, and Wendy and Melissa, who a few moments before had been indistinguishable in the dark, suddenly appeared as bright blue wiry forms on a black background.

"Wow! I think they're even more useful at night," Morton exclaimed. "I can see everything."

Just then Wendy came to a sudden stop. Through the glasses, Morton saw her skull bobbing about in a curious way, and he guessed that she'd heard something. Melissa stopped at her side, and the three boys caught up to them.

"Now what?" Melissa asked.

"Shh!" Wendy commanded.

Everyone obliged and stood silent, barely breathing. Morton peered out ahead to see if he could spot anything unusual. They were passing beside an old industrial strip on the south side of town, which consisted of derelict brick buildings with rows and rows of broken windows. With the glasses on, Morton could see their outlines clearly and could even see what looked like large pieces of abandoned machinery inside, but there was no sign of movement. He looked right through the buildings to the streets beyond, which also appeared to be deserted, but then, very low to the ground, he did see something. At first it looked like a faint mist rolling slowly toward them, but as it grew closer he realized that it wasn't a mist at all. It was a densely packed clutter of fine-boned, four-legged skeletons stretching as far as his eyes could see.

He whipped the glasses off instantly and turned to face Wendy.

"Rats," he said. "They're behind that factory."

"How many?" Wendy said.

"Thousands!" Morton said. "Hundreds of thousands."

"But it's too early!" Melissa said. "We're supposed to have more time."

"Well, never mind that now!" Wendy said. "We should get off the streets." And she turned and ran back in the direction they'd just come.

Everyone followed at an accelerated pace, and Morton kept glancing behind to see if the rats were in pursuit. Unfortunately they were, countless scores of them, and they were rushing along the road like a turbid river that had burst its banks in a storm.

Suddenly Wendy stopped again, and everyone practically skidded to a halt beside her. This time nobody spoke, because the reason Wendy had stopped was obvious. There was a loud metallic rattling, almost as if an earthquake were shaking the ground. But this was no earthquake. Morton saw that several of the metal manhole covers on the street ahead were vibrating like lids on a pan of boiling water. With the X-ray Specs on, he could see a mass of tangled skeletal forms pushing feverishly up at the heavy metal disks. Suddenly the manhole cover nearest to them burst open and a swarm of long-tailed Two-Headed Mutant Rodents bubbled up and spread across the street like a grotesque hairy lava.

At that same moment, the swarm that had been chasing them from the rear closed in at the top of the street, and before they could react they were completely surrounded, trapped on a rapidly diminishing island of asphalt in a sea of carnivorous teeth.

Morton removed the glasses. He no longer needed them to see the nature of his impending doom.

Melissa pulled her sword out of the makeshift sling on her back and held it up in a futile defensive gesture. Morton suddenly wished he'd taken her up on her offer of a sword, although he knew it wouldn't have made the slightest difference. What was one extra blade against a million needle-sharp teeth?

The circle of rats tightened steadily around them, like a living noose, and they each instinctively took a step toward one another.

"Okay, Morton," Melissa said. "This is the point where you come up with a brilliant idea to get us out of this mess."

Morton swallowed hard and tried to concentrate. As he'd

feared all along, the real problem was one of sheer numbers. There were so many Mutant Rodents now that Morton couldn't imagine any non-magical solution, short of burning the city to the ground.

"We're waiting," Melissa said as their island of asphalt continued to shrink.

"I . . . I can't think of anything," Morton said.

"What, no musical note that dissolves their brains, or special food that turns them into friendly pets?"

Before Morton could answer, a paralyzing shudder of intense fear rippled through his entire body. At the very same moment, Melissa and Wendy gasped and Robbie made a desperate choking sound. Only James remained silent and motionless.

The Two-Headed Rodents seemed to feel something too. They stopped creeping forward and began squeaking so loudly that Morton clasped his now trembling hands to his ears.

"What's happening?" Wendy shrieked.

"I know that feeling," Robbie yelled. "I've felt it before, when I saw —"

Robbie's words were cut off by a sound so terrifying that if Morton hadn't already heard it before, he would have run in the opposite direction, regardless of the sea of rats waiting for him.

"It's the cry of the Snarf!" Morton shouted. "Whatever you do, stay calm!"

The rats, which had been approaching as if with one purpose, began racing in wild erratic patterns at the sound of the cry. Morton saw that the open manhole was now teeming with rats pressing back down, trying to escape, and the approaching swarm had turned away, like a brown wave rolling back down the beach.

Despite the suddenly receding attack, Morton's sense of fear continued to mount. The five kids huddled still closer together and grasped at one another for safety and comfort.

In a matter of moments the immense swarm of Two-Headed Rodents had entirely vanished. Silence closed in around them, and Morton felt everyone's grips loosen just as his own sense of fear subsided slightly. Then at the far end of the street a large lumbering shape approached. Morton braced himself for action, and Melissa tightened her fingers around the hilt of her sword.

The shape limped closer, and Morton realized that whatever was approaching was not a Snarf — at least, not fully. The figure appeared to be about seven feet tall, with immense rounded shoulders, like a giant hunchback. It was wearing an old, torn raincoat that was at least two sizes too small, and its hands were wrapped in bandages. Finally the creature came to a stop beneath the only streetlight in the area so that all could clearly see its face. Nobody spoke, though Morton heard several sharp intakes of breath. The face, despite its pallid silver shade, clearly belonged to none other than Brad Evans.

"Brad!" Robbie said, failing to mask a hint of hatred in his voice.

Brad raised his massive hand and brought a large green bottle to his lips. In the glint of the streetlight directly above,

Morton saw that the bottle had a yellow label with a picture of a black cat, and above that the words *Colby's CAT*.

And just like that, Morton realized exactly what had been happening in Dimvale. Suddenly the whole bizarre mystery of the back-page toys made perfect sense.

CHAPTER 17

THE TALE OF THE SAD WARGLE

The voice, which echoed in the now empty streets around them, was not at all what Morton had expected. He'd expected a deep, bellowing ferocity to match the intimidating form towering in their path, but Brad's voice was small and cracked, more like an injured animal than an angry one.

"I won't eat you if you promise to help me," he said.

Morton's fear drained away to be replaced by an unpleasant combination of guilt and pity. As cruel as Brad had been, even he did not deserve this horrific fate, and it was an unavoidable fact that they were at least partially to blame.

"We *are* trying to help you," James said. "We're trying to undo all the magic."

"But, but . . ." Brad started to pant heavily through his nose and tensed his bandaged fists. His whole body rippled and Morton could tell that much of what he was hiding beneath that oversize jacket was not human. "What do you mean 'trying'? You did this to me! You can make it go away! You have to make it go away!"

"It's not that simple," Morton said in a pleading voice. "We didn't intend to do magic. We got mixed up in something that happened between John King and Mr. Brown."

"Brown! I thought he might have something to do with it," Brad hissed. "But he's vanished."

"Actually, he's dead," Melissa said flatly.

Brad's monstrous green eyes grew wide. "Did you . . . ?"

"No!" Morton exclaimed. "It was . . . an accident."

The rhythm of Brad's breathing increased to an even more frantic pace and he turned to his left and right and began muttering, as if he were trying to digest what had just been revealed to him.

"Look, I need more Colby's Cat," he growled, holding up the green bottle that Morton now saw was only a quarter full. "Do you have any or not?"

"Colby's Cat?" James said, confusion clearly audible in his voice. "What are you talking about?"

Brad growled again. "You don't know? How can you not know? You're . . . you're a Snarf like me, aren't you?"

"I . . . I was, but I'm not now," James said, almost apologetically. "What is Colby's Cat?"

"Colby's Cure-All Tincture," Morton said. "It's a spicy drink you can buy from the back pages that's supposed to cure everything from acne to baldness. It was really just aniseed-flavored sugar water."

"So does it work now?" Melissa said.

At that Brad held his face up and pointed to the purple-tinged pupils of his large green eyes. "Does it look like it works?" he said angrily.

Melissa backed away. "I'm sorry," she said under her breath.

There was a long pause in which Morton imagined everyone was feeling as guilty and helpless as he was.

In the end it was James who spoke up.

"Look, what happened was an accident, and we promise we'll do everything we can to make you normal again, but you'll have to help us to help you."

Brad growled again and turned his demonic eyes on James. "Help? How? I don't know anything about magic."

"But you must know something," James said in a calming voice. "I mean, we know Nolan was mixing the potion to help turn you back into a human. Why didn't that work? And where is he now?"

Brad paced back and forth and started mumbling to himself again, as if he couldn't think without speaking aloud. "I might know something," he said, and then sniffed at the air. "But we can't talk here. The rats will come back soon. Follow me. I know a safe place." Then he turned and lumbered back down the middle of the street, hunched over and hobbling awkwardly like some strange two-legged camel.

At first nobody moved.

"Are we sure we can trust a Snarf?" Melissa whispered, leaning in close to James.

"He's not a Snarf," James said. "He's still part human."

"Part Brad," Robbie murmured. "Not much better."

James shot Robbie a disapproving look. "It doesn't matter. We have to help him."

"But what if he ate Nolan?" Robbie hissed under his breath.

Brad, who was several yards away, stopped suddenly and turned to face Robbie. "I didn't eat Nolan," he said.

Robbie turned abruptly, clearly surprised that Brad had heard him from so far away, but his face remained hard. "Then where is he?" he said.

Brad looked around at the dark streets again. "Like I said, we can't talk about it here; the rats will be back any minute." And he began hobbling along the street again.

"Robbie may have a point," Melissa said, whispering now to evade Brad's obviously heightened sense of hearing. "I mean, following a Snarf down a dark alley in the middle of the night is probably a teeny bit more dangerous than, say, playing with matches or skateboarding without a helmet."

"I know. But we don't have much choice," James said. "It's either follow Brad or face the rats."

James set off after Brad, and the others followed without further debate, although Robbie still seemed very unhappy about the idea. Less than three minutes later they arrived outside a semi-derelict row of houses on an abandoned street.

Robbie leaned over to Morton. "Of course," he whispered. "It's the old rehearsal space. I guess this is like his den, or nest, or whatever you call it."

"It's called a kraal," Morton said. "At least, in the story that's what it's called."

Brad approached one of the doors in the abandoned strip and glanced quickly up and down the street before fumbling with the lock and pushing it open. He then stooped low and squeezed his lumpy form through the opening. Morton peered in after him to see him descend a set of plywood stairs, which had old remnants of mismatched carpet stapled onto each tread.

"We're going down there?" Melissa said, standing just behind Morton.

James shrugged. "Why wouldn't we?"

"Because he's probably going to grind our bones to make his bread."

James gave Melissa a withering stare. "I think if he wanted to do that he would have done it already," he said, and pushed past her.

Melissa sighed and shook her head. "Well, I think we've moved on from skateboarding without a helmet to juggling with dynamite," she said, but followed James nonetheless.

The stairs smelled strongly of cats and mildew, but as Morton followed the others and wound his way around a set of narrow passages, a far more powerful odor of rotting meat took over. At last they arrived at a dingy room with holes in the plaster and ripped posters of local bands on the walls. A drum set was crammed into one corner, and a pile of torn blankets and what looked like chewed-up insulation filled the other.

"How long have you been hiding out down here?" James said, taking in the scene with a distraught look on his face.

"About a week," Brad said. "That's when it started to get really bad."

"But what about your parents?" Wendy asked. "Aren't they worried about you?"

Brad made a scoffing noise. "I told them I was going on tour with the band. Anyway, they wouldn't care even if I did turn into a Snarf, except they'd probably sell me to the circus."

"But you did turn into a Snarf, right?" Melissa said. "I mean, that must have been you we saw behind our house."

Brad nodded sullenly. "I've turned into a Snarf three times now. Nolan's been feeding me Colby's CAT — mixing it in with food. But it's not much of a cure. It wears off after a few days and then you need more and it starts to work less and less."

"So, Nolan does know about magic," Morton said, still a little confused.

"Not really. I mean, he's smart and everything. That's why I went to him. I thought, if anybody could figure out what to do, it'd be him, and he's a friend." Brad lifted his immense shoulders in a semblance of a shrug. "Well, closest thing I've got to a friend anyway. Funny thing was, I was sure he'd think I was playing some kind of trick on him, you know, to get him back for throwing me out of the band, but he believed me right away. He said he already suspected something like that was happening and he was pretty sure you were mixed up in it."

"Us?" Melissa said indignantly. "Why us?"

"Everybody knows all this weird stuff started happening when you moved to town," Brad said.

"You should have come to us sooner," James said.

Brad shook his head violently. "Why would I do that? I mean, all I know is, I got into a fight with you and the next thing that happens is I start turning into a monster."

A strange look came over James's face and he suddenly looked down at his feet. "Oh, yeah, of course," he said.

Brad shrugged again, surprisingly no longer looking angry. "Anyway, Nolan had a plan to help me. He found the story with the Snarf cure, and he started getting the ingredients together. But he couldn't find this parchment paper. We both knew it had to have something to do with John King because he wrote all those comics, so Nolan started looking into it and found out that King used to collect old books on witchcraft and all that spooky stuff, and he found out that some old guy who has a bookshop downtown bought all his books in an auction."

"Sydenham Crooks," Morton said.

"That's him," Brad said. "So we went to see him and asked if he had any of King's books, but he told us he'd never even heard of John King, so Nolan knew he was lying. So that night he went back and broke into the shop, and the next morning he came back with this really old book full of spells and magic and potions and all kinds of creepy stuff. It made me shiver just looking at it, but Nolan got really excited. He'd seen the ad for Colby's Cure-All Tincture in the back pages of *Scare Scape*, and even though he couldn't find the parchment paper, he said he'd found a different spell that might help, but he wanted to check up on it first and told me to hide the book and lie low while he did a bit more research. So that's what I did. For a little while.

"But the trouble was, I kept getting worse. Spines started growing on my back, and then I couldn't eat normal food at all. But what really made me panic was when I started belching out yellow smoke. That's when I . . . Well, I wasn't thinking straight and I started to think Nolan had forgotten about me. I mean, he seemed to have lots of time to write new songs for his band but no time to figure out how to do the spell."

Morton couldn't help noticing that Brad cast a resentful glance in Robbie's direction, but Robbie simply stared back defiantly.

"I started to get desperate," Brad went on. "I started thinking he was just stringing me along, just playing with me. So I thought, I'll just do the spell myself. That's when, well, I guess I didn't do it right."

Brad fell into a long silence, staring down at his bandaged hands to avoid eye contact. His face became so contorted and twisted that Morton was sure he was going to burst into sobs. But instead he keeled over and belched out an immense cloud of yellow smoke. The sulfurous smell made everyone cough and choke, and Brad took another swig from his little green bottle.

"I'm sorry," he said.

"It's okay," James said. "I know how you feel. Just try and stay calm and tell us what happened next."

"Nolan had found two bottles of the tincture, so I tried to do the spell myself," Brad said simply. "On Halloween night. And it did something. There was this weird blue flash, and I thought I'd got it right. But when Nolan found out what I'd done he got really angry. He said I'd done it wrong because the book said you had to draw a picture of the thing you wanted to make real on a piece of paper but I couldn't draw, so I ripped a picture of the Colby's CAT stuff out of the back of the comic and used that."

Morton thought again of the comic he'd found in Nolan's locker and how the entire double-sided page had been filled with all manner of tricks, trinkets, and creepy toys. Part of him wanted to scream at Brad for being so completely stupid, but then another part of him wondered just how he would have managed in a similar situation.

"You used the whole page, didn't you?" Morton said.

"Yeah," Brad said, in a pouting, guilty voice. "That's why Nolan was mad. He said all the toys on the page would be affected, and he started calling me names and stuff, which I didn't like. Anyway, we got into a big fight, and I just stormed off, and I got so angry I forgot all about the Colby's CAT.

"I guess that was the first time I turned into a Snarf. I don't really remember much of what happened. I can sort of remember eating a lot of rats. But somehow Nolan managed to put the Colby's stuff on some food and feed it to me, and I woke up down here feeling mostly normal again. But it's not a cure. We soon found out it doesn't last very long. And now I'm down to my last few drops."

Brad held up the bottle to show that his supply was indeed diminishing.

"You still haven't told us what's happened to Nolan," Robbie said. "I mean, if he found out about this other spell, the one that really reverses the magic, why didn't he just do it?"

"That's what he tried to do next," Brad said. "When we found out that Colby's wasn't going to work he started talking about the other spell. He called it a dousing spell, said it was a special kind of spell that could undo any magic. He said it would even undo all the stuff that I'd caused by doing the spell wrong."

"That sounds exactly like the spell we need," Melissa said, more than a hint of excitement in her voice.

"Yeah, but he never could find the special parchment paper. And when he couldn't find any more Colby's CAT he said things were desperate and that he'd have to risk going back to Sydenham Crooks's bookshop to find the paper. He said Crooks had all kinds of magic books and he was fairly sure he'd have some. So he left me with this bottle and went off to Crooks's shop alone."

Brad stopped talking, as if he'd finished his story.

"Then what happened?" James prompted.

"Nothing. I haven't seen him since. This morning I went looking for him, but I didn't even get within a block of his house. There were police everywhere."

"And you're sure you didn't eat him without realizing it?" Robbie said coldly.

Brad squinted angrily down at Robbie. For a moment, Morton wondered if he was going to lash out at him, but surprisingly he didn't. He just nodded and said, "Yeah, I'm sure."

"So, what did happen to Nolan?" James asked.

"I think Crooks has kidnapped him," Brad said.

"Why do you think that?" Wendy said.

"Because Crooks was hiding something. He started acting weird as soon as we asked him about King's books. You could tell he didn't want anybody to know he bought them. And Nolan seemed to think he was dangerous. I didn't think he was. I just thought he was creepy and weird and —"

Brad stopped talking abruptly and doubled over and

growled, as if in pain. A moment later another cloud of smoke erupted from him and he grabbed at his bottle and put it to his mouth yet again.

"You better go easy on that stuff," James said, daring to step closer to him.

Brad pulled himself back to a standing position. "Either way, I don't have long," he said. "So, now I've told you my story. Can you help me or not?"

"We can help each other," James said. "We need to get to Crooks's store and see what he's hiding in his secret room, but with the rats on the street, we can't get there alone. You can scare them off for us, right?"

Brad made a slow nodding motion. "We don't have much time though," he said. "I can only promise to help you while I'm still human. If I turn into a Snarf, then you're on your own."

CHAPTER 18

THE DRAWING ROOM

They had no more rat sightings on the journey to Crooks's bookshop, although Morton thought he heard distant scampering noises on several occasions.

When they arrived, the entire street was utterly dark. Neon signs and illuminated window displays were not allowed in Dimvale, which was one of the main reasons Dad had decided to move here. He had explained many times that streetlights and any other wasted light spilling up into the night sky ate away at the visible stars like a black fungus. Dad's description had always reminded Morton of the legendary Ink Blight from the Monster Tarot, which ate away at everything it touched. Coincidentally the Ink Blight was supposed to be caused by too much magic, and Dad had often joked that light pollution was caused by too much technology. But the stars were in no danger of fading away tonight. The Milky Way flared above them like a river of light, and Morton realized that this was another thing he loved about Dimvale. In the city, there were no stars.

"How do we plan to get in?" Robbie said, peering through the window.

"Stand back!" Brad said, raising his leg and aiming his oversize foot at the door, but Wendy stopped him with a sudden shout.

"Wait! It's already open."

Brad lowered his foot, and Morton saw that Wendy was right.

"That's weird," James said. "Why would the door be unlocked?"

"I don't think we have time to care," Morton said, and without pausing, he crept quietly into the store and led them past shadowy mounds of books to the green curtain.

"This is it," he said, raising his hand to push aside the curtain. As he did so, his hand brushed up against the painting, and instead of the cold, smooth plaster he'd felt the first time he'd touched it, he felt the fuzzy, soft warmth of velvet. Peering more closely he realized that this was not a painting at all, but a second, completely real curtain, and he looked up to see that the clock's hands were set to just after midnight. "It looks like somebody has left *all* the doors open," he said.

"What do you mean?" Melissa whispered, crowding in with the others behind him.

Rather than explain, Morton quickly whipped the second curtain to one side, and there, where once there had been nothing, lay a narrow passage with oak-paneled walls, illuminated by the orange glow of wall-mounted Victorian gas lamps. The passage sloped gently downward and went on for as far as the eye could see.

"I thought this curtain was supposed to be some kind of magical locked door," Melissa said. "Why is it open?"

"The clock's on three minutes past midnight," Morton

explained, "which means somebody has gone through here in the last three minutes."

"Maybe Nolan?" Robbie said.

"More likely Crooks," James put in. "Perhaps we should think about this before we go any farther."

"We don't have time," Brad growled. "And anyway, I'm not afraid of some stupid old man."

"You should be," Morton said. "He obviously knows a lot about magic."

Melissa, however, unsheathed her sword and stepped boldly through the curtain, pushing Morton aside. "I'm with Brad," she said, to Morton's surprise. "Trap or not, I'm ready to end this, and if Crooks is the one who's been spying on me with those creepy Bat Eyes, then let me at him."

Brad immediately followed Melissa through the curtain and the two of them marched off ahead.

Morton puffed his cheeks. "I suppose we don't have much choice," he said. "If we don't find The Book of Parchments, then we'll be eaten alive by Two-Headed Mutant Rodents before morning anyway."

"But what happens when the clock reaches five past?" Wendy asked. "Won't the curtain turn back into a solid wall and trap us inside?"

"Not if it works like the story in Scare Scape," Morton said. "The clock only locks the door from the outside. You can always get out from the inside."

"Well, that's some comfort, at least," Wendy said, and then she and the others followed Brad and Melissa through the curtain into the wood-paneled passage beyond.

As Morton trotted along, he wondered what they would find at the end of the hallway. Gas lamps lit the way, spaced at regular intervals, and a strip of paisley carpet ran along the floor. The space felt cozy and inviting, but musty, like a corridor in an old Victorian hotel. After a minute of walking though, Morton's impression started to change. He noticed the wood panels were beginning to look more aged, with peeling varnish and wet, moldy patches. The paisley carpet became threadbare. The farther they walked, the more extreme the decay became until very soon the carpet had worn away and the panels were literally crumbling to dust, revealing a featureless stone wall behind.

Eventually they were walking along a cold stone passage that smelled of damp earth and felt like it could easily be the entrance to a dungeon. A few minutes later, the stone tunnel branched into three directions and Melissa, who was still up front, paused.

"Now which way?" James said, moving up beside Melissa and shining his flashlight down each of the three passages. Brad began sniffing at the air. After a moment he pointed to the path directly in front. "That way," he said.

Morton looked into Brad's dark eyes and was about to ask him what he smelled but decided not to bother. A Snarf's sense of smell was second only to a Shark Hound's, and it was probably best just to trust it.

They all resumed walking, and less than two minutes later the passage opened up into an immense atrium, easily ten times bigger than Crooks's entire store.

Morton was amazed by the sight. Where the path behind had been carved out of dull gray rock, this entire chamber was finished in brightly polished red marble with magnificent columns, ornately designed floors, and a truly spectacular series of vaulted ceilings. The center of the room was furnished with a very large and elaborately carved table, standing upon the largest Persian rug Morton had ever seen. The table itself held a row of oil lamps that cast pools of light along its length, illuminating a jumble of vials and glass jars containing strange, unrecognizable things. But the sight that really made Morton's heart skip was the ring of large wooden bookshelves that framed the room like some Neolithic literary monument.

He almost sighed with relief. This surely, at last, was the lost library of King.

Everyone spilled out of the narrow hallway and into the cavernous room, which filled immediately with echoes of their footsteps.

Morton wandered toward the center of the room, noticing that off behind the bookshelves were several more arched openings with large shadowy alcoves beyond. Curiously, in the nearest alcove a tall cage, which reminded him of the cages that divers use when photographing sharks, stood incongruously right beside one of the stone pillars. He walked quietly over to it and, as he approached, caught a sudden glimpse of a lank figure curled up inside like a sleeping dog. The figure, roused by the sound of footsteps, jolted into a sitting position and looked around in confusion. Morton instantly recognized the dark, frightened face of Nolan Shaw.

"Nolan!" Morton screeched.

His cry alerted the others, who quickly came running over, and Brad hobbled right up to the cage and clutched his bandaged hands around the bars. "You're alive!" he said in a tone that made Morton think that Brad was more relieved than anyone.

Nolan blinked at the room around him as if to be sure he wasn't dreaming. "What are you all doing here?" he said groggily.

"When you didn't come back, I didn't know what to do," Brad said. "So I asked them to help. What happened to you?"

Nolan clambered to his feet and steadied himself on the bars, rubbing at a nasty graze on his forehead. "Crooks must have been expecting me," he said. "I waited until I saw him leave the store. Then I let myself in with this." He fumbled in his pocket and pulled out a small silver key with a skull at one end.

"The skeleton key," Morton exclaimed. "Of course! It opens any door."

"Yeah, not that it did me any good," Nolan said. "Somehow Crooks doubled back on me and was waiting inside. I don't know how he did it. I was sure I saw him leave."

"Wait a minute," Robbie said, stepping closer to Nolan. "Why are you still in that cage if you have a key that can open any lock?"

Nolan held up his palms, gesturing at the cage before him. "There is no lock," he said.

For the first time, Morton examined the cage closely and realized that not only did the cage not have a padlock, it didn't even have a door. The whole thing seemed to have been made from one continuous piece of iron.

"That's weird," he said. "How did Crooks even get you in there in the first place?"

"More important, why did he lock him up at all?" James said.

"I locked him up because he's a thief," came a croaky, high-pitched voice from behind them, "and no doubt I should do the same to you."

Everyone swirled around in shock to see the short stocky figure of Sydenham Crooks standing at the end of the narrow corridor. He was alone and unarmed, and Morton noticed that his face was a flushed ruddy red, not pale and gray as he remembered it. Despite this, there was still something about the curl of his lip that made him look confident and dangerous.

Without another word, he strutted over to the immense table, seated himself at the only chair, and opened a slender book that he'd had tucked under his arm.

"Since you will be spending quite a bit of time here, I should probably welcome you to my drawing room," he said, lifting a long pencil from the desk and holding it poised above the book as if he were about to write their names down.

"We weren't actually planning on staying," Melissa said, swinging her sword lightly in her hand.

Crooks gave Melissa a sour smile. "I doubt you were, but that's irrelevant. I can't let you leave now."

Brad strutted to the front of the group and growled angrily. "I'd like to see you stop us," he said.

Crooks locked eyes with Brad and sniffed dismissively. "Snarf is it? That's what you get for playing with things you don't understand."

Brad growled again and lumbered closer to the table, but

Crooks looked down and calmly scribbled something on the page before him.

Quite suddenly, from out of nowhere, a small section of bars appeared directly between Crooks and Brad, preventing Brad from getting any closer. Brad turned to look questioningly back at the others, but even as he did so, another small section of bars appeared behind him, then, before he had time to react, two more sections appeared on either side of him, followed by two more above and below. Brad was now completely contained in a cage almost identical to Nolan's, and it looked as though Crooks had conjured the cage simply by drawing something on the pages of the book. A sudden realization hit Morton.

"The Book of Parchments!" he exclaimed. "It makes whatever you draw real."

Crooks looked up at Morton and chuckled knowingly. "It does far more than that. This entire room exists in its pages, and you will soon learn that in here, the pen really is mightier than the sword." And as he said this, he quickly sketched something else. At the same instant a clan of Gristle Grunts appeared from nowhere and charged at Melissa, throwing her to the ground. She fell with a painful crack and her sword slipped out of her hands and slid across the glistening floor. Crooks then scribbled again in his book and a small Swag Sprite popped out of thin air, grabbed Melissa's sword, and then vanished again, taking the sword with it.

Brad grunted angrily and pulled at the bars of his cage, but they were completely solid, despite having been nonexistent a mere few seconds before.

The Gristle Grunts then backed away from Melissa, and she pulled herself to her feet, rubbing her arm painfully.

"Wait! We didn't come here to steal," James exclaimed. "We need help. We need to get rid of the rats and Brad's curse."

"And why should I help?" Crooks said in a dispassionate tone. "I had nothing to do with your misfortunes. You've brought those upon yourselves."

"But it was an accident," James pleaded. "It wasn't our fault."

"I know that!" Crooks snapped, jumping angrily to his feet. "I know exactly whose fault it was. It's the same everywhere he goes. Don't think I haven't watched him. Don't think I haven't seen his dark deeds, how mysterious things lurk in his shadow, how creatures emerge from the houses he inhabits, how innocent people die around him like moths in a killing jar. Believe me, I know whose fault it is. The man is a walking plague and you'll suffer at his hands just as I have."

"Who's he talking about?" Melissa whispered out of the corner of her mouth.

Morton could think of only one person. "He must be talking about King," he whispered back.

"King! Ha!" Crooks spat. "He was no king, although he was arrogant enough to give himself that name. He wasn't even a Smith when I found him. He was a nameless beggar, living under a bridge. I should have left him there. Left him to starve to death and spare the world the misery of his existence."

"But he was your brother," Morton said, feeling strangely defensive of the man he'd never even met. "Wasn't he?"

"In name only," Crooks replied, a bitter resentment in his voice. "But I don't share any of that black poison that ran through his veins."

"I take it you two didn't get along," Melissa said.

Crooks rankled at these words and appeared to be making a concerted effort to maintain his composure.

"It's impossible to 'get along' with a man with no soul," he said, looking back down at his book. "Now, if you'd all be so kind as to move to the alcove over there, please. This won't take a moment."

Melissa gaped at him in disbelief. "We're not just pieces of furniture, you know."

Crooks sighed crossly and began sketching again. Morton watched as something else emerged in thin air, just as the cage and the Grunts had done. The thing started out as a small white wormlike object, but as Crooks scratched rapidly across the page, Morton realized that this was just the tail of something much larger. Within seconds a spiny body, fearsome head, and finally a double row of rotating teeth appeared before them, and the immense Snarf, fully ten feet long, let out a piercing cry and lunged forward. The room filled with screams and Morton thought for a moment that those teeth would be the last thing he ever saw, but the beast stopped short, as if yanked back on some invisible leash.

"I thought you liked monsters?" Crooks said in a cruel voice, glaring at Morton. "How about this one?" And as his hand scratched across the page, a giant Toxic Vapor Worm appeared beside the Snarf. "Or these," Crooks said, and this time he produced a clutch of hungry-looking Ten-Eyed Salamanders, a Visible Fang, and two slavering Shark Hounds. The creatures all began to stomp, shuffle, and slither forward as if with one mind.

"I guess you're a fan of your brother's work after all," Melissa taunted.

"His work!" Crooks exclaimed, walking menacingly over to them, with complete disregard for the host of monsters standing right in the middle of his Persian rug. "Is that what they are to you? Monsters from a stupid children's comic? Ridiculous! You think King imagined these? King had no imagination. He invented nothing! These creatures all exist in other worlds, magical realms that King knew nothing about until my father showed them to him. They were in my father's books, the very same books that King stole. That's how selfish he was. He stole from the man who took him in and fed him. The very man who taught him to read!"

"That's certainly unfortunate," Wendy said in her politest voice, "but what does that have to do with us?"

At first, Crooks seemed to ignore the question, his eyes fixed on a distant point in the shadows, but finally he spoke again. "I spent my life tracking your beloved John King down, although he was always just John to me," he said. "We were only boys when we met. I found him living under a bridge by the river. He was starving, so I brought him food from home, and we became friends. At least, he pretended to be my friend. I learned later that he would say or do anything to get what he wanted. But we both liked to draw, and soon he got me to steal paper and pencils for him, as well as food, and we spent many happy hours sitting in parks, on street corners, wherever we could find a quiet place, just drawing the world as it passed by.

"But then one day my father caught me stealing and made me tell him why, so I took him to see John in his hovel under the bridge. That was a day I will regret all of my life. My father was a kind, compassionate man, and of course he couldn't bear to see a child suffer that way. He insisted on taking him in. Soon after, the boy with no name became John Crooks, my adopted brother."

The room became suddenly very still and Morton realized that everyone was listening with bated breath. Crooks was still gazing off into space, clearly possessed by some vivid image from his past.

"For a time that wasn't so bad," Crooks went on. "We played and drew and learned together, but as John got older he wasn't satisfied to have only my father's name and my father's roof over his head. He wanted more. He wanted my father's love. And that's when he started to play his games. He'd start doing extra chores around my father's bookstore to make me look bad. He pretended to be interested in the business and offered to help with the bookkeeping and stock taking and all those things that no honest child really gives a care about. At first I thought my father would see through it, that he would never fall for such obvious truck-ling, but King was clever.

"He wormed his way into my father's graces until one day my father made a terrible mistake, just as I had done when I first befriended John. He allowed him to see the truly rare books he hid away in his private study — books so powerful and dangerous that he wouldn't even let me, his real son, see them. Of course I knew of the books, and I knew that's how my father made his money. That was obvious even to a child. The rest of the store was just a front. The heart of the business lay in the truly rare books, and his serious customers would meet him by appointment after hours. But no matter how I begged, he wouldn't let me see inside his study. Only John was worthy of that apparently."

Suddenly Brad, who had been slumped over in his cage for the last few minutes, let out a shriek of pain, doubled over, and belched out an immense cloud of yellow smog. Crooks coughed and waved his hand fiercely in front of his face.

"We have to help him," James said in a pleading voice. "He doesn't have much time."

Crooks grabbed the book from the table and held it open over his left arm.

"Time?" he said, his gruff tone returning. "What does a child know of time? I am old, and I can tell you of time. One day, many years ago, your beloved John King broke into my father's study and stole everything. He took every last book and vanished from the face of the earth. The lost library of King is in truth the stolen library of Erasmus Crooks, my father, and I have spent an entire life working to reclaim it. So don't talk to me of time.

"At long last, after forty years of searching, I have found my birthright — the key to powers that my father intended for me to have, powers I would have had all along, if not for John. And then you come to try to steal them again! I have no intention of letting that happen, nor do I intend to let you leave with my secret. No, you will remain here."

"For how long?" Melissa said.

"Why, forever, of course."

"But . . . we're just kids." Melissa's tone was one of utter disbelief. "Surely you can't be that heartless."

Crooks turned suddenly, his cold eyes focused directly on Melissa's. "I don't think you've been listening, child!" he yelled, now almost crazed with anger. "A man who has had everything stolen from him can be nothing but heartless! I already told you King took everything from me. And I don't just mean the books. Yes, he took those, but he also took my heart, my soul, and any chance I may have had of true happiness on the very same day that he murdered my mother and father."

CHAPTER 19

THE EYES OF KING

Morton felt as though the marrow in his bones had been drained away. Could King really have been a murderer? Would he have killed in cold blood, just to gain access to a library of magical books?

"That's a very sad story," Melissa said, clearly not at all concerned with the details of King's life. "But I promise you we never knew John King, and after everything we've been through, I don't consider myself a fan, so if you would be so kind as to let us go, we promise —"

Melissa didn't get to finish. Crooks growled angrily and the ring of creatures tightened around them. "Don't patronize me! I'm not some crazy old man you can trick with nice words. You will never leave here, never! But unlike King, I'm no killer."

"So, you're going to leave us right here," Melissa said, turning up her nose in confusion, "until we're like eighty years old?"

"Not here, exactly," Crooks said, and then he looked down at his book and quickly sketched again.

Morton scanned the room wildly, expecting something else to materialize, but he saw nothing. Then, suddenly, there was a roar from Brad and he vanished completely from his cage. A moment later, Nolan too seemed to just drop out of existence.

"I don't think I like this," Melissa said, pressing closer. Then, without warning, the marble floor beneath their feet just ceased to exist.

Morton caught the briefest glimpse of what awaited him below — an intricate tangle of geometric lines, an immense, complex maze — and then he was falling.

The world around him spun and he toppled weightlessly through the air until, with a merciless slap, the ground rose up and knocked the wind right out of his stomach, and he lay on the floor completely unable to move or think. Far above he could see the ceiling of the cavernous library, and he saw Crooks's silhouette step to the edge of the hole in the floor and look down as he sketched. Morton realized that Crooks was not just filling in the gaps in the floor high above — he was also drawing a low ceiling on top of the maze. He was boxing them in.

Morton jumped to his feet, ignoring the pain in his back and legs. He saw at once that he was in a corridor exactly like the passage to Crooks's drawing room. It had a threadbare carpet running down the center and paneled walls with crude brass gas lamps on the walls. It seemed that Crooks had a limited imagination.

"Is anyone hurt?" Morton said, turning toward the others, but then froze and blinked in astonishment.

To his complete surprise he was utterly alone. He realized that though the others had been less than a dozen feet from him when they fell, they would now be in another part of the maze altogether. They would in fact still be just a few feet away from him but on the other side of the wall. . . .

His instinct was to run quickly up and down the passages closest to him, but he knew that the first rule of being lost in a maze was not to panic. He knew this because the first rule in every situation is not to panic, although this was not always an easy thing to avoid. He'd seen the size of the labyrinth from above before he fell, and he knew it was truly enormous. Every hour he spent trying to escape was an hour the Two-Headed Mutant Rodents would be eating their way through Dimvale.

Suddenly a distant sound interrupted Morton's thoughts. It was a faint, fluttering sound, like the flapping of a coat in the wind.

Morton peered along the passage and at first could see nothing, but then, in the distance, a tiny speck of shadow appeared that grew rapidly in size until Morton recognized the dark leathery shape swooping toward him. It was a Bat Eye.

A moment later the Bat Eye was upon Morton and it flew right up to him and began flapping above his head like a giant annoying insect. Morton's worry shifted to anger at the thought of Crooks watching him through the creature, and he started jumping up and down and swatting at it.

"Get out of here! Go! Go away, you horrible thing!" he yelled, but the Bat Eye maintained a safe height, waiting until Morton grew tired before swooping again.

"Leave me alone!" Morton shouted, feeling his anger slowly fading to despair. "Haven't you seen enough?"

But the Bat Eye clearly had no intention of moving off, and in fact was joined by two more of the creatures. They all dove at his head but stopped short of actually touching him. Morton thought this was very strange behavior. Why would Crooks want to use Bat Eyes to annoy him? Surely a clutch of Electric Killer Eels or a swarm of Dragon Flies would be better suited to the task.

Morton's despair faded for a moment and a curious suspicion bubbled up inside him. He noticed that between each swoop the Bat Eyes were fluttering off to the end of the passage, almost as if they were trying to lead him. . . .

Realization flashed into Morton's brain with such intensity that his entire body felt suddenly hot. It wasn't Crooks who was watching him, nor had it ever been Crooks following them around with Bat Eyes. It was King!

Suddenly it all seemed so obvious. Of course, if King could perform magic, which it seemed he could, then he could conjure Bat Eyes, and if he could conjure Bat Eyes, then he wouldn't have to be blind. He could have used Bat Eyes to be his own eyes. Hadn't Mrs. Smedley even said that there were always bats around his house? That would explain how he had been able to see well enough to write his diary, and it explained how he had been able to outwit Brown when Brown tried to kill him in his attic. It also explained why the Bat Eyes had visited Morton the night he'd discovered the box of King's photographs. Obviously that wasn't an accident. King had *wanted* him to find that box.

Why or how King could be using Bat Eyes from beyond the grave was not so clear, but Morton knew he'd done it before, with the Zombie Twins.

The Bat Eyes swooped at Morton again, and this time he followed them along the corridor. As he had suspected, now that he was following them, they stopped swooping altogether and simply continued flying through the maze. Morton's heart began racing with excitement as the Bat Eyes picked up speed with each turn until very soon he had to run merely to keep up.

Finally, after about ten minutes of running, he rounded a sharp ninety-degree corner and collided at full speed with a tall, bony figure. The figure shrieked in surprise and then, before Morton even realized who it was, it threw its arms around him and squeezed him so tightly that he thought his ribs were going to crack.

"Morton, thank heavens," Melissa said. "We thought we'd never find you."

Melissa released Morton from the tight hug, and he noticed she had a white wool twine tied around her waist.

"Wendy's scarf," Melissa explained. "We decided to split up to find you, but Wendy made sure we wouldn't lose one another. She wanted to use my silk sweater too, but I told her —" Melissa stopped short and looked up in horror at the Bat Eyes, which were now fluttering patiently overhead.

"It's not what you think," Morton said. "They led me to you."

At that moment James, Robbie, Wendy, and Nolan came around the corner followed by a lumbering Brad, who looked far less human than the last time Morton had seen him.

Everyone rushed over to Morton and made various expressions of relief and happiness to have found him, but the Bat

Eyes seemed to grow impatient and began swooping down at their heads and flying off down the hall in a repeated pattern as they had done before.

"What's going on?" James said, swatting at them.

"I can't explain it," Morton said, "but I think they're trying to help."

"What if it's another trap?" Nolan said, ducking his head nervously.

"We're already in a trap," Robbie said. "How much worse can it get?"

"Well, a lot, actually," Melissa said. "But I don't think we have many other options, and Brad's looking pretty hungry, so I think we should go."

Everyone else seemed to agree with this, and Morton led the way, once again following the Bat Eyes, which now flew with such clear direction that they looked to Morton more like small black eagles than bats.

This time the journey seemed to go on forever and Morton felt as if they were going in circles, but finally, just when he thought they'd have to stop for a rest, something began to change. The wooden panels started to fall away in decay until only the bare stone beneath was visible, and then, up ahead, the passage forked into three.

"I think this is the intersection we passed on the way down," Morton said.

"So where are they leading us now?" Melissa said.

A few seconds later Melissa's question was answered when the tireless Bat Eyes finally stopped their headlong flight and began to flutter in tight circles right in front of the now familiar green velvet curtain.

Morton felt a wave of relief wash over his body and looked up at his saviors, but they were already fluttering away, vanishing back into the darkness from whence they came. Morton watched them go with a growing sense of wonder. He had no idea how he had done it, but he knew that somehow John King had once again come to their rescue from beyond the grave.

CHAPTER 20
THE FIERY FINALE

Morton crept quietly up to the green velvet curtain and inched it ever so slightly to one side to see the squat figure of Crooks pacing nervously up and down, muttering under his breath and wringing his hands. A moment later Morton saw what was troubling him. The street beyond the window was heaving and writhing with a solid mass of dark, bristly fur. Two-Headed Mutant Rodents were everywhere, scraping at the glass and nibbling around the door frame. Crooks paced a moment longer and then darted over to the small desk behind the cash register, where The Book of Parchments lay open. He picked up a pencil but paused over the blank pages, then started muttering again as if unsure what to do.

Morton let the curtain drop and put his finger to his lips. "He's in there," he said in the softest whisper he could manage.

"Never mind Crooks. Where's the book?" Brad said, louder than Morton would have liked.

Morton put his finger to his lips again and looked back at Brad. His whole body was starting to change now, and he was twitching and shivering as if every inch of him was in pain.

"He has it," Morton replied. "But I think we need to make some kind of a plan."

"We just need the book!" Brad roared, fumbling inside his raincoat to retrieve the bottle of tonic. When the bottle appeared, Morton saw with dismay that it was now completely empty. Brad nonetheless put it to his cracked silvery lips and sucked at it like a man dying of thirst in the desert. It did him no good. He dropped the bottle to the carpeted floor and curled over, making a sound of anguish. Smoke poured out of his mouth like polluting smog from a factory chimney. An immense yellow cloud filled the passage, blocking all visibility, and when the fog cleared moments later Brad was barely recognizable. His face had swollen to almost twice its size, and lumps were bubbling up on his chin like hard purple mushrooms. His eyes were now almost as big as his fists, and his shoulders had swelled into small mountains of lumpy gristle. Everybody took several steps back as he drew himself to his full, intimidating height.

"Out of time!" he growled, his voice now barely comprehensible, and he yanked the curtain aside and shot across the room toward Crooks like a stampeding elephant.

Crooks looked up just in time to see the large lumpy creature hurtling toward him and managed to dive out of the way. Brad collided with the small desk, which collapsed completely under his weight, spilling pencils, papers, and The Book of Parchments to the floor. Crooks, who had stumbled onto his back, saw the book amid the rubble and managed to swipe it up quickly. Brad then rolled clumsily back to his feet and once more shot toward Crooks with a ferocity unlike anything Morton had ever before seen.

Crooks, however, had just long enough to snatch a pencil from his lapel pocket and scribble randomly on the open page before him. The pencil lines materialized like a web of steel in the air and Brad collided with the mesh and became instantly tangled, crashing to the floor with a loud thud. But Crooks didn't stop there. He scribbled feverishly in his book until Brad was so completely enmeshed that almost nothing of his body could be seen.

"Stop!" Wendy shrieked. "You'll suffocate him!" But Crooks didn't seem the least concerned with this.

"Out!" he commanded, clambering to his feet. "Out into the open where I can see you, or I will do worse than suffocate him."

Everyone complied with his instructions and shuffled out from behind the curtain to stand beside the now immobile form of Brad.

"You idiots!" Crooks shrieked, like a teacher reprimanding naughty children. "You're even more stupid than I thought. You conjured a plague of rats? Why?"

"We didn't conjure them," Melissa said. "They just started breeding. We thought you knew that."

"I knew nothing of the sort," Crooks said. "These things are out of control. They'll destroy the whole town."

Morton stared at Crooks curiously. "How can you not have known that?" he said.

Crooks glanced at him but didn't seem to understand the question.

"You don't actually know much about magic at all, do you?" he added.

"More than you!" Crooks spat childishly.

"Yes, but not more than John King," Morton said.

"What does that matter? He's dead, and now I have reclaimed my father's library. Soon I will learn far more than he ever knew."

Crooks's response confirmed what Morton was already beginning to suspect about him, but he had no time to dwell on that right now. Right now he had to come up with a way to get that book from Crooks's hands before Crooks had time to dispose of them in a more permanent manner. Melissa was obviously thinking the same thing, because she nudged Morton with her elbow and pushed something into his hand. Morton looked down to see the empty Colby's CAT bottle and noticed that Melissa was glaring over toward the window.

Morton looked over and could see nothing but a step-ladder, some books, and, beyond that, a heaving ocean of fur roiling down the street outside. He looked questioningly back at her and she gave him a small nod and then stepped forward so that she was standing directly between him and Crooks.

"Are you sure King is dead?" she said in a conversational tone that was more suited to a Sunday afternoon tea party than the bizarre scene they were currently inhabiting.

Crooks appeared surprised by both the question and Melissa's seeming lack of fear.

"Of course I am. He drowned in his own well. Everyone knows that."

"Well, everyone's heard that," Melissa said, "but can you be sure it's true?"

Crooks's whole body tensed and he glanced quickly around him like a hunted man. "He would never have parted with his books while he lived," he said.

Melissa pouted her lips and swayed her head from side to side, at the same time elbowing Morton in the ribs. Morton looked again at the bottle with no clue what Melissa intended for him to do.

"But it sure would *throw* you off if he was alive," Melissa went on, overly exaggerating the word *throw*. "I mean it would *shatter* your whole world, wouldn't it, if that turned out to be the case?"

Now Morton thought he understood what Melissa intended, and even though it was perhaps the craziest idea Melissa had had to date, he couldn't think of a better one, so, while Crooks was still nervously pondering Melissa's questions, Morton gripped the heavy glass bottle as firmly as he could in his small hand and hurled it with all his might at the cracked pane at the front of the store. The bottle shot straight through the glass, causing it to splinter into a dozen jagged fragments, which toppled out into the street with a loud clatter.

Suddenly a fetid stench filled the air, and the squealing, scampering sound of ten thousand Two-Headed Mutant Rodents burst in upon their ears. Crooks let out a scream of surprise and turned to face the gaping hole as the swarm of ravenous creatures leaped over the windowsill and spilled across the floor in an unstoppable wave of fur and teeth.

"Are you insane?" he shrieked, but Melissa was already on the move and she leaped clear across the room and kicked

The Book of Parchments free of Crooks's hands, sending it spiraling into the air. Morton watched it flip around like a many-winged bird and raced over and caught it just before it fell directly in the path of the ever hungry swarm of rats.

In the next instant they were surrounded. Morton felt the now familiar sensation of needle-sharp claws grasping at his legs at the same time that he saw rats leap up at Melissa and Crooks.

Crooks shrieked again and stumbled backward, away from the inexhaustible rush of Two-Headed Rodents, and then turned on his heels and bolted down the alcove. The instant he had pulled the curtain closed behind him, it turned to the solid wall Morton had seen on his first visit, but he didn't have time to be amazed by the sight. The Rodents were now attacking everyone, leaping onto their legs and climbing up their bodies. Morton began kicking and swatting to get them off, but he knew there were too many.

"Quick! Behind the curtain!" Wendy yelled, and she clambered up onto a bookshelf and turned the hands of the clock back to midnight. The solid painting turned again to a soft hanging drape, and both Wendy and Melissa bounded through. James followed and held the curtain open, beckoning to the others.

"Come on, it will close soon."

"But what about Brad?" Morton called, looking at the motionless mass of wire mesh.

"Leave him!" Robbie shouted, tugging at his elbow. "He's not worth it!" But Morton didn't move.

Robbie tugged again, but this time Morton pulled his arm away, feeling suddenly very angry. "Look, don't you get it?"

he yelled. "None of this is Brad's fault. It was me who found the gargoyle. Me who broke the first finger. Me who gave James the comic."

"But you didn't mean to do those things," Robbie said, his face stony.

"Yeah, well, did it ever occur to you that maybe Brad didn't mean to be mean?"

"How can you not mean to be mean?" Robbie shouted in a skeptical tone.

"You heard what he said about his parents selling him to a circus. Try to imagine what that would feel like for just one minute."

Morton saw a flicker of understanding in Robbie's eyes, and his friend made the slightest of nods, but neither of them had time to discuss it further. Rats were still swarming in through the broken window, covering every available inch of space, and several more leaped up at Morton and Robbie, despite their efforts to kick them away.

Suddenly James and Nolan appeared beside them. "Grab hold," James said, pointing to Brad's tightly bound beefy legs, and Morton and Robbie each grabbed an ankle while Nolan and James grasped firmly on to the wire around his chest.

"Heave!" James shouted, and all four of them leaned back and put their full weight into moving Brad's inert mass.

To Morton's immense relief, Brad's body began to slide across the floor, and they were able to drag him quickly along the narrow alcove and through the curtain. As soon as they were on the other side, Morton yanked the inside curtain closed. A few Two-Headed Rodents crawled under the curtain after them, but only a few, and Morton realized with relief that the clock must once again have reached five past twelve, sealing the wall behind them.

James, Nolan, and Robbie set to kicking and squashing the rats that had passed through. The Rodents dispersed quickly, running off down the passage, screeching in panic as they went.

"Melissa's right," James said as the last of them vanished out of sight. "Monsters are cowards."

Morton didn't think they were cowards exactly, but now was not the time to discuss it. Somewhere beneath the tightly bound mesh Brad let out a painful wail.

"We've got to get him free," Nolan said. "He'll suffocate."

Morton turned hopefully to The Book of Parchments. The book itself didn't look at all special, but when he put his hands on the pages inside, he knew that this was no ordinary paper. It was cool to the touch and seemed almost to tingle under his fingertips. He flipped quickly through the book and saw that many of its pages were still blank and unused, but some had illustrations of rooms and curious objects. He wasn't surprised to find one page with a very large and intricate maze, and another with a floor plan for a large room that had exactly the same layout as the library. The drawings were, for the most part, all very carefully rendered, with clear straight lines and fine inked-in details, but when Morton found a rough scribble of lines he knew he'd found what Crooks had drawn to bind Brad.

Brad made another pained wailing sound.

"If I had an eraser," Morton said, "I think I could set him loose."

Nolan produced a short stub of pencil from his pocket, the top of which had a lightly chewed pink eraser, and handed it to Morton. "This should work," he said.

"Thanks," Morton said, and he immediately began rubbing at the nest of lines that Crooks had scrawled onto the page. The paper was so smooth and strong that the drawing wiped clean away without leaving even the slightest smudge, and as Morton had suspected, the tightly bound strands of wire vanished with the lines on the page. Brad, however, was barely conscious, and Nolan rushed to his side.

"We're losing him," he said. "We're going to have to do the dousing spell now."

"Now?" Morton said. "How can we do it now? Don't we need bats' blood and a whole bunch of other stuff?"

To Morton's surprise Nolan pulled a stainless steel flask and a small brown paper bag from his jacket pocket. "I have everything here. All I need is a page from that book and —"

Before Nolan could finish, a high-pitched scream reverberated from somewhere behind them and the four boys all turned to stare down the illuminated passage.

"Melissa and Wendy!" James exclaimed. "Where are they?"

Morton suddenly realized that he hadn't seen them at all since they passed through the curtain.

"They must be down there with Crooks!" Robbie said.

Morton jumped to his feet and was about to run in the direction of the scream when James grabbed his shoulder and stopped him.

"Morton, think!" he shouted. "It's obviously a trap."

Morton turned back to face James. Of course he was right.

"I know, but we have The Book of Parchments now, right?"

"So?" James said. "He's got a whole library of books on magic down there. Who knows what else he has tucked up his sleeve."

"I'm not so sure about that," Morton said. "I'm starting to think he doesn't know much about magic."

Nolan, James, and Robbie all looked at Morton as if he was completely out of his mind.

"I know it sounds crazy, but I think we can outwit him. With this book we can conjure a Snarf of our own, or a troop of Gristle Grunts, or a swarm of Smother Fish," Morton explained.

James didn't appear convinced, but just then there was another echoing shout from below, followed by the sounds of a scuffle.

Morton turned toward the sound. "We don't have a choice," he said. "We have to go."

"You're right," James said, and he turned to Robbie and Nolan. "You two stay with Brad. If we're not back in ten minutes, then whatever you do, don't come looking for us."

Nolan and Robbie nodded grimly as Morton and James took off down the shallow descent of the passage, running all the way.

When they arrived at the opening to the library, they paused in the shadows and peered cautiously ahead. The room was completely silent and appeared empty, although several bookcases were overturned, with King's precious books spilled on the marble floor.

"Definitely looks like a trap," James whispered, creeping ahead to get a better look. "What do you propose?"

Morton flipped The Book of Parchments open to the page with the detailed inked floor plan of the library. "Anything I draw on this page," he explained, "will appear in the room, so all we have to do is get Crooks to come out into the open and then I can draw a cage around him, just like he did to Brad and Nolan."

"Oh, now I see. You want me to be the bait," James said, sounding not too happy.

"No need to bait the trap," came Crooks's voice from somewhere in the shadows, and a moment later he walked out from one of the alcoves and stood calmly in the bright light of the oil lamps.

"Where are the girls?" James demanded in a voice that was part rage and part fear.

Crooks pointed at the book in Morton's hands. "First give me that," he said.

Morton placed the pencil on the paper. "First you let the girls go," he said. "And don't try any tricks. I can draw too."

"You still think you have a choice, don't you?" Crooks said, eyeing the book and smiling in a way that made Morton feel uneasy. "Although I don't suppose there's any harm in you seeing them." And before he'd even finished speaking, Morton spotted something moving in the shadowy alcoves. He made out the silhouettes of Wendy and Melissa immediately, but they were each in the grip of two other people, and Morton couldn't even begin to imagine who these strangers were, but a moment later the figures moved into the light. James yelped in surprise.

The two men were both Sydenham Crooks, except their skin was a little grayer and the color of their clothing was a little more muted. Crooks had obviously drawn replicas of himself, and only now did Morton realize he'd encountered one of these illustrated clones of Crooks before. That must have been how Crooks had surprised him the first time he'd entered the store.

"They always say if you want anything done, then you have to do it yourself," the real Crooks said, still wearing the same unsettling smile.

"Morton, look out!" Melissa shouted, just in time to make Morton aware of another gray-skinned clone creeping up behind him.

Morton darted over to the large table in the center of the room and lay the book open in the light of the lamp. Quickly he began to scrawl rough cages around each of the Crooks clones, managing to trap three of them with ease. But there were more of them than he could keep track of, and suddenly one of them grabbed him by the shoulders and tried to drag him away. Morton clung on to the edge of the table and managed to drive an elbow into his attacker's stomach, causing it to fall back momentarily, but the battle was far from won. Morton could see now that there were dozens, possibly as many as fifty zombielike copies of Crooks drawn on the page, all with brown tweed suits and tiny red bow ties. . . .

Suddenly James let out a cry, and Morton looked over to see four clones overwhelming him, dragging him to the ground. A fifth was reaching for the open book beneath Morton's hand.

In a moment of sheer desperation, Morton could think of only one thing to do. He tore the top page right out of The Book of Parchments and stuffed it down into the glass chimney of one of the oil lamps glowing serenely on the table. Instantly the illustrated replica at his elbow jumped back and let out a scream of anguish as veins of fiery light ignited over his whole body, until he simply exploded in a burst of orange fire. At the same time all the other illustrated Crookses stopped in their tracks and started vanishing in puffs of flame.

James and the girls were free, but in the next instant Morton realized his mistake. Quite suddenly the entire room burst into flame as tiny rivulets of golden fire shot through the walls all around them.

"You fool!" the real Crooks screamed, and he leaped across the room and grabbed at the now torn remains of The Book of Parchments. Morton grasped at the book too and tried to snatch it away, but Crooks gripped it tightly with his clawed hands, and as the two of them tugged it, Morton heard a loud ripping noise and Crooks stumbled backward with the book clutched greedily to his chest.

By now the rivulets of fire were traveling at lightning speed and already they had spread across the entire room, leaving large black ashen voids in their wake. Crooks, still stumbling, backed up against a dark crevasse in the floor and teetered on the edge. He let out another cry of terror, and Morton watched in horror as he grasped at empty air, spinning his arms like a giant wrinkled bird in an attempt to prevent his fall.

Morton raced over to grab Crooks but it was as if the world had slowed down, and with each step he took, Crooks's frantic body tilted more steeply toward the black void behind him.

There was nothing Morton or anyone else could do. By the time he'd skidded to the edge of the smoking gash, Crooks was already a pinpoint of color in the swirling darkness below.

Morton lingered for the briefest of moments, but the sound of roaring flame was intense now, and suddenly Melissa and Wendy were beside him.

"No time!" Melissa said, and she yanked him to his feet and flung him in the direction of the exit. Morton saw that more charred gashes were opening up beneath them, and the three of them leaped over the remaining solid patches of floor as if playing some fatal game of hopscotch until they arrived at the opening to the passage. Unfortunately it looked as though they were already too late. The entrance was now nothing but a ring of blue flame billowing out hot air like the mouth of a small volcano. James was standing a few feet from it, shielding his face from the intense heat.

"It's no good," James said. "We'll be roasted alive."

Morton turned back to look around, but the view behind was even worse. The charred black voids were spreading over the entire room.

"What are we going to do?" Wendy shrieked as flames shot out of the cracks in the floor.

"We're going to have to run for it," Morton yelled, pointing at the fiery tunnel ahead.

"That's impossible," James said.

"We'll fall into the abyss with Crooks if we don't try," Morton shouted back, but even as he spoke, something came crashing toward them from the heart of the fiery tunnel. There was a sudden cry and a loud inhuman screech and then from out of the fire burst an immense creature wearing a smoldering jacket.

"Brad!" Morton exclaimed.

Brad grabbed Wendy and Melissa and tucked them under his arms, and Robbie, who was riding on his back and covered in soot, yelled out to the others, "Quick, climb on."

Nobody hesitated. Morton and James leaped onto Brad's immense back and hung tightly around his neck, and before they even had time to speak, Brad turned around and bolted again directly through the heart of the fire.

Morton closed his eyes tight. The heat dashed against his skin like hot sand and his clothes started to feel like somebody was ironing them while they were still on his body. He was sure that his head was about to spontaneously combust. But then, just when he thought he couldn't take any more, they burst out of the suffocating heat and he dared to open his eyes. The passage ahead was still intact, although he could feel the fire racing up behind them.

Fortunately Brad did not slow down. With the green curtain visible up ahead, he redoubled his pace and Morton felt as though he were sitting on the back of a steam train going at full speed.

In just a few more immense strides, Brad arrived at the curtain, threw it back, and bounded into the store, practically crashing into the wall at the far end. The rats, which were now several feet deep, screeched hungrily, but Brad let out a much more terrifying cry and Morton felt the icy chill of fear paralyze his whole body.

The rats scattered as a wave of terror spread out around them, and at last Brad released Melissa and Wendy, and Morton and the others climbed gingerly to the floor. Nolan rushed up to them.

"Do you have the book?" he screeched above the clamor of rats and the ever-increasing roar of flames. But Morton didn't have the energy to respond. He simply turned and watched as the flames raced up the corridor, washing away what was left of Crooks's illustrated world in a fiery rain. Morton braced himself for the explosion of heat, but as the fire leaped up at the curtain, something unexpected happened. Instead of the flames breaking through to feed on the shelves of dry dusty books, they stopped, as if trapped behind a window, and then suddenly, the flames were gone and nothing but a solid black wall remained.

Morton let his body go limp and he flopped back onto a pile of books, utterly exhausted.

"The book?" Nolan repeated. "We need the book to reverse the magic!"

Melissa appeared beside Nolan and stared down at Morton. "Where is it?" she asked, only barely able to mask the tremor in her voice.

Morton closed his eyes and saw again the horrifying image of The Book of Parchments toppling into the ashen void right along with Crooks, and he lay there, feeling lifeless and defeated. How could he tell them that the book was gone, that all their efforts had been in vain?

He opened his eyes and stared back at Melissa and Nolan and was about to shake his head and explain that the book, that all of King's books, were gone forever. But he realized that he was clutching an object so tightly in his fist that his fingernails were digging into his palms, and only then did he remember the tearing sound that he had heard as he struggled to wrench the book from Crooks's iron grip.

He sat up and opened his fist to discover a single torn and crumpled sheet of pearlescent paper resting on his palm.

"The last sheet," Morton said. "I thought it had all been lost."

"One sheet is enough!" Nolan exclaimed with a grin.

Brad made a strange gurgling sound, which somehow managed to sound happy and demonic at the same time.

Nolan then leaped into action, first asking Brad if he would step outside and scare away any approaching rats so that they could work unhindered. Brad didn't seem to understand, and he merely stood there panting and wheezing, but Melissa seemed to get through to him. While she coaxed him into sitting on a milk crate just outside the storefront, Nolan pulled the flask of bat's blood and the other ingredients from his pocket. "Everything's here," he said. "All that's left is to draw a picture of all the things we want to douse."

"That's a lot of drawing," Robbie said. "We need a Two-Headed Mutant Rodent, a Snarf, and presumably all of the back-pages toys."

"I'll do it," Morton said. "I'm pretty sure I can remember them all."

Nolan handed Morton a pencil and left him to draw, while he began preparing the other ingredients and rummaging around the store for some kind of container. Morton grabbed a large hardcover book and smoothed out the torn piece of parchment.

It took him about ten minutes to draw everything, and when he was finished he barely had any room left on the paper. "Is there anything else we want to get rid of?" he asked. "Because I'm pretty sure we'll never find any more of this paper, so this really is our last chance to undo all the magic."

"How about Inspector Sharpe?" Melissa said. "It would be nice to get her off our backs."

Morton looked up at her, not quite sure whether she was serious. Wendy cleared her throat and put her hand on Morton's shoulder. "I think she's joking," she said.

"So, we're sure that's everything?" James said.

Everyone nodded silently, and Nolan took the piece of paper from Morton and pushed it to the bottom of an old coffee mug. He then poured the dark red liquid from the flask and crumpled up some of the dried ingredients, which Morton couldn't remember off the top of his head but looked to be leaves and some kind of powder.

Instantly the paper seemed to melt like wax in a fire and the dark liquid began to glow with a pulsating purple light.

Everyone held their breaths, and Morton listened and watched for some magical implosion or flash, but a moment later the glowing liquid faded to a lifeless gray and nothing seemed to happen at all. In fact, everything went so utterly quiet that for one fleeting moment Morton wondered if the spell had made the entire world vanish.

After another few seconds of absolute stillness, Morton

could stand the tension no longer and he dashed out into the silent street.

What he saw almost made him weep with joy. Never in his life had he imagined that the sight of Brad's pink pimply face could have made him so happy, but there he was, covered in soot, sitting in confused silence like a lost puppy, and Morton practically wanted to run up and hug him.

Brad looked back at Morton, then, realizing that something had changed, he quickly tore the bandages from his hands and stared at them as if they were the most beautiful sight he had ever seen. In the next moment tears were falling from his face and gathering in his sooty palms like small crystals, and his body began to heave in silent sobbing motions.

Morton did hug him then, because he didn't know what else to do.

CHAPTER 21

THE FAMILY TREE

The others poured out of the store and began peering into the silent blackness around them. Brad quickly wiped his eyes and jumped to his feet and tried to look stern, but somehow the expression didn't seem to fit comfortably on his face any longer.

"Brad's back to normal," Morton said, feeling tears of relief welling up in his own eyes. "I think it worked."

"Do you feel normal?" James said.

Brad took several seconds to clear his throat before he at last managed to respond. "Yeah, I do," he said. "I feel . . . I feel great." And then after a long pause he added, "Thank you."

Nolan meanwhile ran into the middle of the road and stood, straining his eyes and ears in the darkness. "I don't hear any rats," he said.

"I don't hear anything at all," Melissa said. "Could they have just vanished into thin air like that?"

"Probably," Morton said.

"But how can we be sure it worked?" Melissa persisted. "What's to say the rats won't just show up again tomorrow night?"

"It definitely worked," Robbie added, and Morton saw that he was wearing the X-ray Specs. "Here, try these."

Robbie handed the Specs over and Morton put them on. Instead of the eerily illuminated skeletons he'd seen when he last tried them, he now saw nothing but a dim blur of shadowy forms moving around him. He took them off and nodded to the others. "Robbie's right," he said. "The magic is gone."

"Well, that was easy," Melissa said, sighing with relief. "No cats to shoo away, no books to hide, no gargoyles to get rid of, no loose ends at all."

"I don't think that's quite true," James said. "I mean, our school looks like a herd of elephants were playing soccer in the hallways, and Nolan's parents are going to want to know where he's been for the last couple of days."

"Oh, that won't be a problem," Nolan said. "I'll just tell them I fell and hit my head and woke up in an alley. That's almost true anyway."

"What about you, Brad?" James said. "Surely your parents don't really believe you've been on tour in the middle of the school year."

Brad shrugged. "Like I said, they don't exactly notice what I'm doing. So long as Inspector Sharpe doesn't come asking questions again, they'll leave me alone."

"And leaving you alone is good?" Wendy asked, sounding confused.

"As good as it gets," Brad said, and something about the tone in his voice made it clear that he didn't want to discuss it any further.

Nolan turned away from the group and looked back

toward the main street. "I think we should get going," he said.

"I agree," Melissa said. "This night has gone on quite long enough." And with that they all trooped off together along the street.

"Listen, I wanted to say I was sorry," Nolan said as they marched tiredly along.

"Sorry? What for?" Melissa asked.

"Well, if I'd trusted you sooner, things might not have gotten so messed up. I thought it was you guys who were responsible, but I was wrong. Turns out you're pretty awesome."

"That's us," Melissa said. "The awesome foursome, except, you know, there's five of us."

Nolan made a nervous laugh, and soon they arrived at his street and he bid everyone good night.

The others continued to trudge through the night until Brad and Robbie also turned off to head home, leaving James, Morton, Melissa, and Wendy to walk the last few blocks alone.

When Morton finally clambered into bed, he felt like he had climbed into heaven. He had never before imagined that a soft, warm mattress and the smell of freshly laundered sheets could feel so soothing and wonderful, and he tried to lie awake to savor the wonderfulness for as long as he could but inevitably he slid into a deep blissful sleep and dreamed of nothing at all.

He awoke to the smell of freshly baked bread and thought he was still dreaming, but when he ventured downstairs he saw two crusty loaves on the table, which James and Melissa were already chomping through eagerly. Dad was reading the newspaper and sipping his tea with his feet up.

"Good news about those rats," he said, folding the paper forward and glancing over the top at Morton and the others. "The poisonous gas was a big success. They fired off the canisters at midnight and it seems it did the trick. There's not a two-headed rat to be seen in Dimvale this morning."

"Oh, good," Melissa said. "So we won't need a babysitter breathing down our necks anymore, then."

Dad smiled sadly at Melissa. "I'm sorry she was such an annoyance to you," he said. "She did try very hard to make you happy."

"Oh! I didn't mean it like that," Melissa said, her face going the color of the cherry jam on the table. "I just mean . . . Well, I'm too old to need a babysitter. We agreed to that, right?"

"We did," Dad said. "And in any case, I couldn't impose on Mrs. Smedley any more than I already have. She has a job of her own and an aging mother to tend to."

"So, no more fresh-baked bread or scones for breakfast," Morton sighed.

"Well, I don't know about that," Dad said. "In fact, Mrs. Smedley has lent me one of her recipe books and it's given me some great new ideas."

All three children groaned out loud.

"What's wrong?" Dad said. "Did I say something funny?"

"No," Melissa said, getting up from the table. "Just remember you can't use bath salts instead of baking soda."

"Ah, yes. That was a bit of a blunder," Dad said. "Although I still don't quite understand why that didn't work. Chemically they're almost identical."

James, Morton, and Melissa left for school a few minutes

later, and Morton was surprised to see Jake's yellow car parked at the end of the driveway.

"Oh no," Melissa said with a sigh. "There's a loose end I'd forgotten about."

James and Morton exchanged glances. "But we thought you liked Jake," Morton said.

"I do," Melissa said. "I like Swiss cheese too, but it doesn't mean I want it to follow me around all day."

"I've never seen you kissing Swiss cheese though," James said teasingly.

Melissa shot him an indignant stare. "How did you . . . ?"

"We weren't spying," Morton put in quickly. "We just accidentally saw . . ."

Melissa's cheeks glowed vividly for the second time that morning. "I . . . I had to," she stammered. "It was for a good cause."

"It's okay," James said. "This is our home now. You're allowed to make new friends, put down some roots."

"Well, he's not my type," Melissa said flatly.

"So what's your type?" James asked casually.

"More sort of . . . Well, um, I . . ." Melissa growled in frustration. "I don't know, but it's not that," she said, and she pointed to the eager face of Jake waiting beside the back door of his car just as Wendy approached from across the street looking a little more disheveled than usual.

The four of them arrived at Jake's car at almost exactly the same moment.

"Morning," Jake said, and the others all returned the greeting.

"I feel like I could sleep for a week," Wendy said. "My dad had to shake me to get me up this morning."

"It's a good thing the tennis courts are closed then," James said. "Tuesday's our usual night."

"Actually, I've been looking into squash," Wendy said, her face lighting up. "We could check that out at the sports club — oh, unless Melissa . . ."

"Jake's teaching me to drive," Melissa said, "so you guys can go do whatever you want."

"Squash it is, then," Wendy said. "Might as well start living normal lives right away."

"Start living normal lives?" Jake echoed, with a confused look on his face. "Has something bad happened?"

"Oh, I'm just kidding around," Wendy said, realizing her mistake. "Blame Melissa. Her dramatic ways are rubbing off on me." And with that the three of them jumped into the car and drove off, leaving Morton and James to walk to school.

"So, do you think it really is over this time?" Morton asked.

"I don't see why it shouldn't be," James said. "I mean we've definitely got rid of the last of our wishes, and I'm pretty sure we won't be hearing from Crooks again any time soon, so yes, I really think it is."

Morton nodded thoughtfully, but he couldn't help feeling that there was something they still hadn't figured out. James could obviously read this from his face.

"You don't think it's over, do you?" he said.

"Well, there's still King's enemy," Morton replied. "I mean, the one he wrote about in his diary."

James pressed his lips together thoughtfully. "You don't think it was Crooks?"

"No. Crooks didn't know nearly enough about magic. And if you think about it, King would surely have mentioned if the enemy he was writing about was his own adopted brother."

"You're probably right," James said. "But you know what I think? I think now that The Book of Parchments and all the other books are gone, we'll never hear of magic again."

Morton smiled. He hoped that James was right, that whatever strange and magical things had happened in the past, would now stay in the past, but no matter how hard he tried, he could never be quite as optimistic as James.

When they arrived at school, Morton wasn't at all surprised to find several police cars parked along the sidewalk. He was, however, surprised to find Julie waiting outside the school yard entrance with her back against the wall for the second day in a row, popping gum and looking unusually thoughtful.

Morton got that churning butterfly feeling in his stomach that he always seemed to get around Julie, and he braced himself for the worst, but Julie actually smiled at them as they approached.

"Hi, James. Hi, Morton," she said in a friendly tone that Morton hadn't heard before.

"Hi," James replied. "What's up?"

Julie shrugged and pointed at a group of police officers and teachers. Morton turned to look where she was pointing and saw the familiar hard face of Inspector Sharpe, talking with Principal Finch and a few other teachers. All of the teachers looked pale and confused, especially Finch, who was continuously rubbing the bridge of his nose. No doubt Sharpe was asking them if they remembered anything strange about yesterday, and they were all realizing they didn't remember anything at all.

"Weird thing happened last night," Julie said. "Apparently some kids must have stayed behind and vandalized the school."

"That is weird," Morton said, frowning in a way that he hoped made him look surprised.

"Yeah, I don't get it," Julie went on. "I mean, why would anyone want to vandalize a school? And the weirdest part is, they left a bunch of cheap toys behind in one of the closets."

"Kids just being kids, I guess," Morton said.

Julie nodded and shrugged. "Yeah, I suppose. Well, catch you later," she said, and turned to walk off.

As soon as she'd gone, Robbie approached from the opposite side of the school yard.

"I presume you've already seen Sharpe," he said, pointing over his shoulder with his thumb.

"Yeah, but there's no way she could pin anything on us," James said, "so I'm not worried."

Morton had to agree that they'd done a pretty good job of hiding any magical activities, but he wondered again how much Sharpe really knew.

"Come, on, cheer up," James said, nudging Morton on the shoulder. "We did it. Look around, everything's back to normal."

Morton looked around and had to face the fact that aside from the huddle of police officers, everything did look normal. Kids were running and playing and kicking balls and trading cards and laughing as if they didn't have a care in the world.

"You're right," he said. "It's just, I'd almost forgotten what normal feels like and it's going to take me a while to get used to it."

For the rest of the day, Morton's mood got brighter and brighter. The Mesmer Disk had worked perfectly and nobody seemed to have the slightest memory of anything to do with back-pages toys or Derek's ghastly club, and Derek himself had reverted to being an eccentric loner.

All the other kids seemed to be completely back to normal too, and Willow made good on her promise not to tell anyone what had really transpired. In fact, she seemed to relish the idea of sharing a secret with Morton. Every time she passed him in the hall she tapped the side of her nose and nodded knowingly.

"Well, that looks about as normal as anything I've ever seen," Robbie said as he and Morton watched the kids playing soccer at afternoon recess. "But, uh, there is still one thing I've been wanting to tell you."

"Oh?" Morton said, noting an odd, embarrassed look on Robbie's face.

"Well, it's about all that stuff Julie was saying." Robbie paused for a moment, seemingly at a loss for words. "Well, it wasn't true, I mean, I do want to hang out with you, and you are my best friend, but, uh, I guess I might have said some things to her that made her think what she told you was true. I mean, it wasn't anything much, just, uh, we were just joking around on Halloween and I guess I just kind of wanted her to think I was cool or . . . I don't know. I don't know why I did that. I'm sorry."

"It's okay," Morton said, feeling a strange sense of relief at Robbie's words. "I think I already figured that out for myself. She was doing the *thing* on you, right?"

For a moment, Robbie looked surprised by this suggestion, but then his face changed to one of annoyed recognition. "You know what, you're absolutely right!"

Morton made a grim smile. "And you don't really think she looks like an albino turtle, do you?"

"I guess not," Robbie confessed with a heavy forlorn sigh. "She looks more like, I dunno, one of those marble statues you see in museums."

"A marble statue with a cool voice," Morton added.

This time the two of them sighed in unison and sat for a moment in silent reverie, until at last Robbie spoke up again.

"Anyway, I'm done with all that," he said. "I'm quitting the band."

Morton almost leaped up joyously at these words, but managed to make himself frown and looked earnestly at Robbie. "Oh, that's a shame," he said. "Why is that?"

"Well, last night when Brad and I were walking home we got to talking and I realized that Brad really wants to be in the band more than anything. It's all he has, and the truth is, I wasn't that into it. So we just asked Nolan this morning if he'd take him back, and he agreed. So that's that. Brad's the new singer in Shatter Box. I hope you're not too disappointed. I mean, I know you were really looking forward to that first concert."

"It is a shame," Morton said. "But I guess we all have to make sacrifices, right? And I think Brad needs something to help him get back on his feet, so it was very generous of you."

Robbie shrugged. "I never thought I could forgive him for what he put me through, but you know, he was telling me some stories about his dad, and it turns out we have a lot in common. Although, I think I'm a lot luckier than he is because I've got something I don't think he'll ever have."

"What's that?" Morton asked.

"Really great friends who pretend to like punk bands, even when they don't," Robbie said with a wry smile.

Morton felt a wave of guilt and relief wash over him. "Sorry," he said. "It's just not my thing."

Robbie laughed and punched him on the shoulder. "It's okay. I don't mind that my best friend just happens to be the world's worst liar."

Morton grinned broadly. He was very happy that the truth was out at last, and he was also very happy that the bell rang at that very moment so he didn't have to discuss his feelings about the band or Julie any longer.

Later that day the sun came out and warmed up the cold November air, making it feel just for a few hours like a late-summer afternoon. James headed straight from school to squash practice with Wendy, and Morton and Robbie walked home together talking about comics and old tin robots and all the kinds of random pointless things that kids are supposed to talk about.

They parted company at the end of the driveway as usual and Morton sauntered down the path to find Dad crouched at the bottom of the yard, off beyond the old well, wearing his boots and gardening gloves.

"I thought I'd find you here," Morton said.

"Oh, yes, I'm taking advantage of the last of the warm weather to get the garden back into shape, now that those infernal rats are gone."

"What's that you're planting?" Morton asked, noticing that Dad was packing fresh soil around a small sapling. "They're not bulbs."

"No, actually, this is something special," Dad said. "I didn't want to make a big ceremony about it, but I was going to show you later. It's a chestnut tree."

Morton felt his eyes moisten immediately. He'd never seen a chestnut tree before, but he knew at once why Dad was planting it. Mum had always said that one day they'd have a big house with lots of land and they'd grow all their own fruit and vegetables and plant a chestnut tree at the bottom of the yard. For reasons Morton never discovered, Mum had loved chestnut trees above all others. She even had a poem that she'd say to them every night when she tucked them into bed.

> *I love you big as the moon,*
> *Wide as the sea,*
> *Tall as the oldest chestnut tree.*

"It's for Mum, isn't it?" Morton said.

Dad smiled and put his arm around Morton. "Yes. She'd never forgive me if I didn't plant it. She loved trees, and she always said I had a lot in common with them."

"Huh?" Morton said. "Why would she say that?"

"Well, she insisted that trees loved stars too, you see, which I suppose is true."

"It is?"

"Yes, well, they prefer the one star closest to us, which just happens to be the sun, but it's definitely a star. Their whole reason for existence is to absorb as much starlight as possible, and she said I was the same. I just wanted to absorb as much starlight as I could. You know, she never complained about me working nights, but I always feel guilty about it."

"You do?" Morton said, wondering why Dad was choosing to bring this up now.

Dad looked at Morton with a soft smile. "Yes, of course I do. In fact, since you're here, I did want to talk to you about that." Dad cleared his throat and his tone became a little more serious. "I've been thinking. What with all the hoopla that's been happening around here, I think maybe it's time for me to throw in the towel. Give up working nights."

"But how could you still be an astronomer and not work at night?"

Dad puffed his cheeks. "Well, I don't have to be a practicing astronomer. I could get a teaching job, or even do something completely different. I'm not a bad gardener — maybe I could set up a landscaping business, and then I'd be home every night, just like a normal parent."

Morton wanted to fling his arms around Dad and tell him that was the best idea he'd ever had. He wanted to say that having him home every night, to tuck him into bed and read him stories and just to know that he was there if Morton woke up for whatever reason would make him the happiest kid in the world. He also wanted to tell him that even Melissa would secretly love it and that he should hand in his notice right away.

But he didn't.

"You're a stargazer, Dad," he said. "Looking at things that are billions of miles away is what you love to do. If you couldn't look through a telescope, for you, that would be like being blind. You'd never be really happy again, and nobody wants that. Not me, not James, not Melissa, and most of all, not Mum."

Dad looked utterly surprised by Morton's response. He opened his mouth to speak but was clearly at a loss for words. Finally he just pulled Morton into a big hug. "You know," he said, "you're growing up into a fine young man. Your mother would be bursting with pride right now."

At last, Dad let Morton go and got back to his feet. "Come on," he said. "Go grab that shovel over there and you can help me put this in."

Morton reached for the shovel leaning against the wheelbarrow and began helping Dad sprinkle soft earth over the roots of the small tree. As he did so he gazed around at the yard. At the lawn, where they'd first discovered the gargoyle. At the potting table, where they'd read King's diary. At the well, where King had met his untimely end. And at the small basement door, where they'd crept out in the night to confront a full-grown Snarf. And as he looked around, he had a sudden profound realization that for better or for worse, Dimvale was where he belonged, and this old mysterious house with its peeling paint, crooked porches, and secret attics was now his home, and it would be for the rest of his days.

ACKNOWLEDGMENTS

For those authors who insist that writing is not a solitary affair, I would like to politely disagree. For the most part it is entirely a solitary and grueling event that requires the discipline of a Zen monk. For that reason, I must apologize to all the people I have ignored, forgotten, and generally taken advantage of during the writing of this book. You know who you are, and I'm really sorry. Let's get together soon!

In addition, there are of course the people who contributed directly to the manuscript, whose names should appear here. They include my agent, Rosemary Stimola, and her editorial assistant, Allison Remcheck — both brilliant and insightful as always. Thanks to Heather Young, for once again being my mirror, mirror, on the wall and letting me know which are the worst pages of them all. To Willa, the best daughter in the world, for being my first reader and giving the inside scoop on my target audience. To Margot, for awesome edits, and all the inexpressible sacrifices that only a true partner can endure. To Dave Cullen, for taking up the quill of John King, and to the other Sam (Bosma), who conjures amazing images from his equally amazing brain. And last, but the very opposite of least, is Nick Eliopulos, my incredible editor at Scholastic. Nick has labored through many drafts, cajoled, coaxed, and most importantly cared for every word of this manuscript. Thank you, Nick! Seriously.

ABOUT THE AUTHOR

Sam Fisher was born in England, and decided at the age of five that he wanted to be a writer. He now lives in Canada, where he teaches screenwriting, invents gizmos, and builds things out of wood. He wrote *Scare Scape* for his three fantastic children.